BOOK NEWS

Sign up for exclusive updates and offers at
news.jljarvis.com

GET THE AUDIOBOOK

jljarvis.com/cottage

THE COTTAGE AT PEREGRINE COVE

THE COTTAGE AT PEREGRINE COVE

A SWEET SECOND CHANCE ROMANCE

J.L. JARVIS

J.L. JARVIS

BOOKBINDER PRESS

ISBN (ebook) 978-1-942767-83-1
ISBN (paperback) 978-1-942767-84-8

Published by Bookbinder Press
bookbinderpress.com

CHAPTER 1

The road into Peregrine Cove twisted through weather-beaten pines and rocky outcrops, and the scent of salt air thickened with each mile Tess Bradford drove. Peregrine Cove. The hand-painted sign with a carved falcon mid-flight loomed ahead. Its weathered welcome sent an ache through her chest. Sharp and familiar, it took her back to a late August day. As a young girl in the back seat, she'd stared back at that sign while her parents' voices turned bitter and the town faded from view.

As Tess slowed her silver Honda to the village speed limit, her pulse quickened. She was home, or what had been home, during those fleeting summers when Aunt Morna's cottage offered refuge from the storms and bitter silences that filled her own house.

She cracked the window, and sea air rushed in, carrying echoes of teenage laughter, hers and Noah's, as they raced to the harbor at dawn. Below, fishing boats bobbed in the water, their masts casting shadows in the afternoon sun. The *Mary Eleanor* was still there, its blue paint bright and defiant. Did Mr. Pierce still take it out sailing, or had Noah taken it over?

Noah. Her throat tightened. This wasn't about him, she reminded herself. It was about Aunt Morna, the cottage, and the inheritance—a blessing or a burden, depending on tomorrow's meeting with Mr. Hargrove.

A week earlier, Tess had slipped into town for the funeral, hiding behind sunglasses and a black hat, avoiding everyone until Noah found her graveside.

"Tess," he'd said, his voice rough.

She'd managed a nod, murmured, "Noah," and uttered a few perfunctory words before fleeing to Boston to grieve.

Now she was back. She guided the car up the winding driveway until the cottage emerged with its silvery cedar shingles, white trim faded to bone, and wild roses climbing the trellis. She shut off the engine and sat gripping the wheel.

Early June in coastal Maine usually brought gentle warmth, but today's ocean breeze carried a chill. Tess reached for her cardigan and stepped out. The steady pounding of a hammer on wood broke the silence. As she rounded the car, she froze.

Noah Pierce straightened from the porch's corner, broad-shouldered and solid where he'd once been all teenage angles and endless energy. His sleeves were rolled to his elbows, revealing tanned forearms and a faded scar near his wrist that she didn't recognize. Stubble darkened his jaw, but his sea-glass green eyes were unchanged, except for a guarded manner in place of the open warmth she'd once taken for granted.

A carpenter's pencil sat behind his ear as he wiped the sweat from his brow with the back of his hand and then turned. With a flinch of surprise, he said, "Tess." He recovered and gave a curt nod.

Her heart pounded. She'd braced for this town and this house, but not him. "The lawyer called me back," she said, gesturing toward the house. "What's going on?"

He turned to the railing and probed a rotted section. "I've been fixing some things that need fixing," he added. "Since Morna got sick." His tone was flat, but the words stung with their implication: I was here, and you weren't.

Tess nodded. Aunt Morna's cancer had struck fast, with only six months from diagnosis to death two weeks ago. Noah had been around helping out with odd jobs. She'd seen him at the funeral, of course. "Thanks," she said. "For that."

He grunted, a sound that could have meant anything, and turned back to the porch. The dismissal stung. He kneeled and pried at another warped board with a crowbar. The wood splintered under his steady pressure. Three sharp strikes drove a nail home. "The northeast corner's shot. There's moisture under the flashing. The joists are mostly done, and the railing's next," he said with a sideways glance.

Porch repairs. That's what they were reduced to, as if their last moment here hadn't been under a summer moon with her suitcases packed, his eyes pleading, her silence deafening. She stepped closer, the third step creaking underfoot. Her fingers brushed the railing, tracing the faint T+N they'd carved at sixteen. She glanced up in time to see his jaw tighten as she pulled her hand back.

A breeze flung chestnut strands across her face. She tucked them back and met Noah's eyes over the vast, silent chasm between them. Tess took a step forward. In the growing dark, it was almost as though they were seventeen again, before everything had gone wrong.

"Once the estate's settled," she forced the words out, "I'll have to sell. My life is in Boston, so ..."

He paused, hammer hovering. "Morna wanted it kept in the family." His voice roughened with grief, or maybe a sense of betrayal. "She had hopes for this place."

"I know, but—"

"We'll see what Mr. Hargrove has to say." Noah slid the hammer into his tool belt.

Tess frowned. "What's that supposed to mean?"

"It means just that. We'll see." He peered at her and added, "I got a call, too. I'll be there. Apparently, Morna left something to me."

While Tess wondered what that could be, Noah gathered his tools and stood. "Watch that third step. It's rotting. Back railing, too. I'll tackle it tomorrow." He grabbed his toolbox and brushed past her without a glance. "Lock up when you're in." His boots crunched down the drive as he faded into the dusk.

Tess stood alone, the porch groaning beneath her. Why hadn't she visited Aunt Morna more? Guilt gnawed at her as she thought of the years lost to Boston and the excuses that followed. She fumbled to retrieve the key from under the flowerpot. The lock stuck until she gave the handle a sharp upward yank. Inside, the door creaked shut, and darkness swallowed her.

She flipped the light switch. Nothing. With her phone's flashlight, she found a lantern on the hall table along with a note in Noah's scrawl.

Fuses are in the kitchen drawer. -N.

Even now, he couldn't stop looking out for her. She pressed her fingers to her eyes, fighting tears.

Her shoes scuffed against the worn floorboards as she moved through the hall to the kitchen and set down the lantern. Its glow caught a slim journal on the counter. Aunt Morna's, with its familiar cover stamped with faded herbs. Tess hesitated, then opened it. Pages of neat script listed plants—lavender, thyme, basil— plans for an herb garden her aunt never lived to plant. The last entry, dated months ago, was written in her aunt's shaky hand: *Tess loved the lavender. Noah says he'll help.*

Seized by heartache, Tess sank into a chair, journal in hand. A sprig of dried lavender fell onto her lap and released its faint scent. Suddenly, she was sixteen again, kneeling in the dirt of the herb garden in full bloom.

Aunt Morna adjusted her wide-brimmed hat as she handed Tess a lavender cutting. *'Smell that, girl. It's hope in purple.'*

Noah sprawled nearby and teased, "She'll turn it into perfume and sell it in Boston."

Her aunt laughed, rich and warm, and Tess grinned. The sun was hot on her shoulders as Noah's arm brushed hers, and they dug stakes together. That was just before her mother yanked her away to boarding school, before the letters stopped, and Aunt Morna faded to phone calls and guilt.

Tears blurred the page. Why hadn't she fought to stay? To come back? Aunt Morna had waited and tended her garden and cottage while hoping that Tess would return. And Noah had been here, all the while keeping it alive when she hadn't.

She set the journal down and rose. The living room smelled of dust and the sea. Her gaze settled on Aunt Morna's armchair, green velvet worn thin at the arms with a faint stain where Tess had spilled cider at twelve. She sank into it, springs groaning, and let her head tip back. How many nights had her aunt sat here, waiting for a call Tess never made? She'd meant to visit two years ago at Christmas, then last summer, but deadlines always won out over the endless pitches and proofs, not to mention the eternal chase for a promotion. Now Aunt Morna was gone, and this house was her last word.

The lantern flickered. "I'm here now," Tess whispered to the house, to her aunt, and to the girl she'd lost. "I know it's too late, but I'm home."

Her phone buzzed, cutting through the quiet. "Tess Bradford," she answered in a voice steadier than she felt.

"Tess! The Parker numbers are in," Daniel crackled from Boston. "Sixty-eight percent engagement spike. They're thrilled."

A faint smile tugged at her lips. "Good news."

"We're pitching you for the Brenner project as the East Coast team leader. How soon can you wrap up whatever's keeping you?"

Tess glanced at the lantern, the lavender, and the journal. "I need a few days. Complications."

"This is career-making, Tess. Don't let it slip past you."

"I won't," she said, ending the call.

Boston pulled. There, she was on the brink of a promotion, security, and the life she'd worked for. All she had to do was go home.

She looked out the window where the harbor lights glittered on the water. She'd forgotten how alive this place seemed with its raw and unpolished beauty. It was nothing like Boston's sleek lines and hardscapes. A memory flickered. At fifteen, she and Noah snuck out to the dock with cider swiped from the pantry. They'd tripped over nets, laughing as his shoulder bumped hers, and they sat dangling their legs over the edge of the dock. The cider was sweet, and the stars were so bright overhead that, with Noah at her side, Tess felt invincible.

He'd grinned. "We could do this forever," and Tess had believed him.

Then, the following summer, her mother's voice had cut through the air, sharp as a gull's cry. "Pack. We're done here."

The memory faded, leaving her cold.

A sudden breeze rustled through the open window, fluttering the curtains Aunt Morna had sewn decades ago. The lantern cast a warm glow across the kitchen's worn surfaces. In the dim light, she noticed something she'd missed earlier. On the windowsill was a small potted plant, barely sprouting, with Noah's handwriting on a sticky note: "Last of Morna's lavender. I thought you might want it."

Her throat tightened at the gesture, a poignant reminder of Noah's character. Despite his anger over her desire to sell the cottage, he still honored Aunt Morna's wishes.

Tess touched one of the tiny leaves, surprised by the

strange swell of emotion it stirred. She hadn't planned on taking anything back to Boston except closure. Her condo's sleek, minimalist décor had no place for cottage relics. Yet something about this fragile plant, suspended between its past and uncertain future, seemed uncomfortably familiar.

Tess climbed the stairs to the familiar creaking of boards underfoot. Her old room waited with its sagging twin bed and the quilt patched where she'd singed it with a candle at thirteen while sneaking a ghost story past bedtime. She dropped her bag. Across the hall, Aunt Morna's door hung ajar. Tess paused, then stepped inside. The room still smelled of her aunt, lavender and liniment. A faint whiff of sickness still clung to the walls. Slipped into the frame of the dresser mirror was a photo: Tess at ten, gap-toothed and clutching a fish beside Noah, who grinned with a net slung over his shoulder. She traced the frame, guilt twisting deeper. She'd let this slip for a life that now appeared as thin as the dust on these boards. A breeze stirred the curtains, faded blue and cross-stitched along the hem. Tess lingered, feeling the house seem to breathe around her and sigh for an era that was lost.

The familiar symphony of creaking wood and whistling drafts that had lulled her to sleep every summer night of her childhood played on. Tomorrow would bring lawyers and decisions, but the practical path lay before her. She would settle the estate, list the property, and return to her real life.

So why did the word "home" still get caught in her throat?

Tess moved to the window and pressed her hand against the cool glass. Boston was home now and had been for years. The cottage was just a chapter to close, a responsibility to fulfill.

Yet, as her old room stirred memories she'd kept locked away, Tess couldn't shake the feeling that returning to Peregrine Cove had opened something inside her she wasn't quite prepared to face.

CHAPTER 2

Tess woke to sunlight pouring through gauzy curtains and the faint cry of gulls beyond the cottage walls. For a moment, she blinked at the unfamiliar ceiling, disoriented, until her memory snapped into place. Peregrine Cove. Aunt Morna's cottage. And Noah. She could almost hear her aunt's voice drifting up the stairs, calling her down for pancakes. But the house was silent now.

Her phone glowed 7:32 a.m. on the nightstand, hours until her meeting with Walter Hargrove, Aunt Morna's lawyer. That left plenty of time to shower, dress, and mentally prepare for what should be a straightforward process. Her aunt used to talk about Tess one day living here, so when the lawyer asked to meet, she wasn't surprised. There would be papers to sign. The next step wouldn't be easy. As much as she wanted to keep it, she couldn't live here full time, which its current condition demanded. Even if she had the time to oversee the scale of work needed, she didn't have the means to maintain a second home. Aunt

Morna had left her a money pit. No, keeping the cottage was out of the question.

Tess's sleep had been fitful, plagued by images of Noah's guarded eyes and the feel of his calloused fingers. She shook it off and padded downstairs to the kitchen.

The coffee maker hummed as she fumbled with the grounds. A chipped mug caught her eye—Aunt Morna's, painted with a clumsy falcon Tess had made at eight. She gripped it, flooded by a memory.

A summer morning, at thirteen, Tess sat at the table while Aunt Morna flipped pancakes at the stove. Noah's eyes twinkled as he snuck extra blueberries onto Tess's plate.

"You'll spoil her," Aunt Morna had teased, pretending to swat his hand with a spatula. Tess could almost see Morna's twinkling eyes and hear her bright laugh.

Tess had grinned, his knee brushing hers under the table, a secret warmth blooming. Now, the mug trembled in her hands, coffee sloshing. She set it down, her eyes fixed on the chair where her aunt had sat, the memory of Noah's laugh echoing in the stillness.

The coffee gurgled to a stop, filling the space with its sharp scent. Tess poured a mug and cradled it as she wandered into the living room. She needed its clarity today. The lawyer was expecting her at noon to discuss the estate. She'd figure out what to do with the cottage for now and be back in Boston by the weekend. Clean, simple.

The toolbox Noah had handed her sat on the oak table, its battered metal glinting in the morning light. She set her mug beside it and ran her fingers over the table's scars. Memories tugged at her—Noah sneaking her extra blueberries under Aunt Morna's mock-stern gaze. Their laughter echoed off these walls. She sighed and pushed the past aside. Sentiment wouldn't help her today.

Her gaze drifted to the bookcase, its shelves sagging under a jumble of paperbacks and knickknacks. A photo album, its leather spine cracked with age, caught her eye. She pulled it free and sank onto the couch. The first page stopped her cold: a Polaroid of her with a four-teen-year-old Noah. They both grinned as they stood on the dock with their arms slung around each other's shoulders. Her hair was a wild tangle from swimming, and his freckles were stark against his sunburned nose. Her aunt had snapped it, teasing, "You two are thicker than thieves."

Tess turned the pages slowly, each photo a punch to the gut. She and Noah raced down the beach, sand flying. Noah held up a crab while she shrieked with delight. The summer they were sixteen, they sprawled on the porch with popsicles. His knee brushed hers as they looked up at the stars and argued about constellations. She lingered on that one, her chest tightening. That was the summer their friendship changed into something unspoken but electric. She remembered the night she'd almost kissed him until her mother's voice sliced through the dark.

She snapped the album shut, her coffee cooling untouched. Enough of the past. It was time to face the day and look forward.

～

WITH HER MIND STILL REELING, Tess grabbed her keys and headed to town. The drive to town took ten minutes. Peregrine Cove's main street unfolded in muted gray, with its shuttered shops, a café, and the lawyer's office wedged in between. Tess parked her Honda and mounted the steps to the office. Her breath puffed as she pushed through the door. A receptionist waved her to a back room. She opened the door and froze. Noah sat across from Hargrove. He'd swapped his flannel for a clean shirt, and his expression showed mild confusion.

"Tess." Hargrove rose from his chair. "Good. You're both here."

She glanced at Noah. As an awkward silence stretched out between them, Noah shifted in his seat.

Hargrove, a wiry man with gray hair, gestured to the chairs. "Have a seat. We'll go through it." Tess took a seat beside Noah. Her unease grew. Hargrove opened a folder and slid a paper across the desk. "Morna left a trust. She named you, Tess, as the primary heir to the cottage. But there's a condition." He handed each of them a copy and read the key section aloud.

"To my niece, Teresa Bradford, I leave my cottage at Peregrine Cove to be held in trust for one year. Teresa must reside there as her primary residence during this period. Should she fail, ownership passes to the trustee, Noah Pierce, who has maintained the property."

Trustee, Noah Pierce. She stared at the words. Her hands gripped the paper until it crinkled. A year? Her life uprooted from Boston. Noah as trustee. She looked up at Hargrove. "I have to live there for a full year, or it's his?"

"Correct." Hargrove nodded. "Starting when you took possession, which looks like yesterday."

Noah's chair scraped the floor as he leaned forward. "Trustee? I didn't sign up for this."

"I advised her against it, but she thought it would be better this way," Hargrove replied. "She said you'd do the right thing."

Tess glanced at Noah. "Couldn't he just decline and leave the cottage to me?"

Hargrove shook his head. "She didn't name a successor trustee, so the estate would go to probate, and the court would choose another trustee."

Frustration roiled within her. "How long would that take?"

Hargrove waved a hand toward the document. "Longer than this."

Tess shot a stormy look at Noah. "I'm sorry, but I have a hard time believing she didn't hint at this. I mean, you've been fixing that cottage for months."

"For her!" Tess had never seen such fire in his eyes. "I fixed it for her because she needed help. I don't want your cottage."

"My cottage?" She laughed with a bitter twist. "It's only mine if I uproot my life. Otherwise, it's yours. How nice for you."

"Nice?" His tone hardened to match hers. "I don't need this place. I've got my own life here."

"Then why did she do this?" Tess snapped and stepped closer.

Hargrove cleared his throat. "Morna believed in you both. She told me she wanted Tess back in the Cove."

"Back?" Tess's voice climbed. "By coercion?"

"Your leaving was hard on her."

"Well, it wasn't exactly easy for me. My parents shipped me off to boarding school. It's not like I had a choice."

Hargrove raised a hand. "In any event, the trust stands. Tess, you stay a year, and it's yours. Leave, and Noah gets it."

"Understood. Excuse me. I think we're done here." Tess grabbed the will and stormed out. Noah's steps followed close behind.

Tess burst into the lot, the trust crumpled in her fist. Noah's boots thudded behind her. She spun around as the wind tossed her hair. "So you're fine with just waiting me out?"

He stopped a foot away, clenching his jaw. "Morna did this, not me."

"Why?" she pressed, crossing her arms against the sudden chill. "Why us?"

He raked a hand through his hair and looked out at the harbor. "Maybe she hoped you would stay."

Tess laughed. "Quit my job and upend my life while you play backup heir? It's not like you're even family."

Noah's gaze snapped to hers. "You really think I planned this? Tess, I know I'm not family, but I buried her, too. I've been holding this place together for Morna while you were—"

"Gone?" she cut in, daring him. "Go ahead. Say it. I was gone, and you were here being your old saintly self."

"Yeah, you were gone, and I was here—not being a saint. In case you forgot, it's what neighbors do."

The words cut deeper than she'd anticipated. "That's not fair."

He shrugged. "Hey, we all make our choices."

"I didn't choose to leave," she shouted, her voice cracking. "I was seventeen. My parents shipped me off."

"Tess, it's been fifteen years." His tone softened despite the tension vibrating between them. "Look, Tess, I'm not the enemy." He stepped closer.

As she looked into his eyes, a stab of aching emotions threatened to rise to the surface. If she didn't leave now, everything would spill out—all the pain going back to her youth and everything she had buried inside.

She climbed into her Honda and slammed the door. The will landed on the passenger seat. She drove back to the cottage, her grip tight on the wheel. Her mind churned with anger, pain, and disbelief. A year here or lose it to Noah. Aunt Morna had gambled on Tess's reaction and Noah's dependable nature.

Tess pulled into the driveway and sat, engine idling. Her phone buzzed in her purse. She fished it out and saw her boss's name on the screen.

"Tess Bradford," she answered, deliberately steadying her voice.

"Tess! The Parker campaign numbers are in." Daniel's voice crackled with energy. "Your strategy increased their social engagement by sixty-eight percent! The client is thrilled."

Despite everything, Tess smiled. "That's fantastic."

"We're putting you forward for the Brenner account. It would mean managing the whole East Coast team. I know the timing's not ideal with your aunt's passing, but how soon can you be back?"

Tess stared at the cottage through the windshield, with its peeling paint, sagging gutters, and all the memories it held. "I'm not sure yet. There are ... complications with the estate."

A pause. "Tess, this is a career-making opportunity. Don't let it slip away."

"I know. I just need a few days to work some things out."

After ending the call, Tess sat motionless. The Brenner account. The promotion she'd been working toward for two years. All she had to do was drive back to Boston and leave the cottage—leave Noah—behind.

She needed some air and perspective. Lucy's Café flashed in her mind. A coffee in a quiet corner and Lucy's calming advice might steady her.

She drove back to town and parked outside the café, where its faded sign swung in the breeze. Inside, the scent of cinnamon and roasted beans filled the air. A woman with dark hair tied in a bun, Lucy Dunn, Aunt Morna's old friend, stood behind the counter. She looked up and smiled with recognition.

"Tess Bradford." Lucy wiped her hands on an apron. "Heard you were back. Coffee?"

"Please." Tess slid onto a stool. "Black."

Lucy poured a mug and set it down. "Rough morning?"

Tess huffed a laugh. "You could say that. I just left Hargrove's. Aunt Morna's will's a mess."

Lucy raised an eyebrow. "The trust?"

Tess froze mid-sip. "You knew?"

"Morna told me last fall." Lucy leaned on the

counter. "She always said you belonged here. Noah was her backup. I had my doubts, but there was no talking her out of it."

Tess set the mug down hard. "She blindsided us."

Lucy nodded with a knowing look. "If it helps, she did it out of love. She always thought you belonged here." She looked down and added, "With Noah."

"We're not teenagers anymore." Tess's voice rose. "We've grown up. And apart. We barely spoke at the funeral. And at the law office? That wasn't pretty."

"It hurt him, your leaving." Lucy shrugged. "And Morna saw that." She added softly, "It hurt Morna, too."

Tess stared into her coffee. "I didn't leave by choice. My parents sent me away."

Lucy softened. "Morna knew that. She never blamed you. Maybe this is her way of fixing it by giving you a reason to stay and giving both of you a reason to work it out."

Lucy wiped the counter, her movements slowing. "You know, Noah came in here every Sunday morning to get Morna her favorite blueberry muffin, even when she was too sick to leave the house. The last time he was here, I caught him looking at that old photo of you two behind the register." Lucy gestured toward a corkboard covered with faded snapshots. "He'd never admit it, but there's still something there. That man has built walls higher than the lighthouse, but they're not as solid as he thinks."

Tess turned to look at the photo of Noah and her at sixteen, heads tilted together, caught mid-laugh on the pier. A pang of bittersweet nostalgia shot through her.

"I've got a life in Boston—a job, an apartment. I can't just leave everything for a year."

"Can't you?" Lucy asked.

Tess traced the mug's rim. There was a time when her heart had been here—with Aunt Morna, with Noah, in those summers of laughter and unspoken promises. The T+N carving on the porch rail flickered in her mind. "Maybe, but it's not that simple."

A few locals at a nearby table glanced over and whispered.

Lucy followed her gaze. "Your return's got people talking."

"Great," Tess muttered. "Just what I need."

Lucy grinned. "Welcome back to small-town life."

Tess raised an eyebrow and reached for her purse, but Lucy touched her hand to stop her.

"Coffee's on me today."

Tess managed a small smile. "Thanks." She sipped and let the warmth settle her nerves. Lucy's words echoed in her mind. Morna thought she belonged here, together with Noah. She saw Noah pushing her on the swing that hung from the ash tree as his laughter mingled with hers. What a change from the Noah she'd just left. She'd come here expecting to inherit the cottage and sell it. But since coming back—coming home—all the memories it held had taken hold of her heart. Now, the thought of letting go seemed like too much to bear. Her mind and her heart were clouded with conflicting emotions until she didn't know what to do.

The café's hum faded as she stared out the window toward the harbor. Morna had bet on a memory of two teenagers in love, but she'd overlooked the reality of two adults with years of hurt between them.

Tess's phone buzzed again—a reminder about tomorrow's conference call. Boston was calling her back, promising security, advancement, the life she'd built brick by careful brick.

But as the gulls wheeled above the harbor, something unraveled inside her. Maybe it wasn't just about the cottage. Maybe it wasn't even about Noah.

Maybe it was about the lonely girl who once sat every night writing letters she knew she wouldn't send while her heart broke in a drafty dorm room.

The cottage keys weighed down her pocket. One year. She lifted her coffee and made a silent toast. "Well played, Aunt Morna," she whispered. "Now what?"

Outside, storm clouds gathered over the water, and somewhere across town, Noah Pierce was no doubt making plans of his own.

CHAPTER 3

Tess gripped the steering wheel of her Honda as she pulled back into the cottage driveway. Crumpled beside her on the passenger seat lay the will. Its words burned into her mind. Live here for a year, or it's Noah's. The lawyer's office had been a battlefield, with Hargrove's calm reading, Noah's denial, and their argument spilling into the parking lot. Lucy's words at the café hadn't helped—Aunt Morna wanted them together. Now, the afternoon sun slanted through the pines, and her chest ached with a sense of betrayal. Her aunt had orchestrated all this, with the cottage as a trap—a trap shared with Noah.

She shut off the engine and surveyed the cottage. Its faded clapboards and shutters hid the bars of her new prison. But Noah's battered pickup parked beside it, the tailgate down, tools scattered, was not. After the law office, she'd expected him to take a day off to recover. She sure needed one.

A fresh thud rang out. Noah kneeled on the porch, hammer in hand, driving a nail into a warped board with the same steady focus she'd seen yesterday. Something snapped inside her. Noah shouldn't get to stay here like nothing had changed—not while her world was tilting off its axis.

She shoved the car door open and grabbed the will. Her boots hit the ground hard as she marched up the steps. "Noah!"

He paused mid-swing and looked up. Sweat glistened on his brow despite the chill, and his gray-green eyes narrowed with a flicker of wariness. "Back already?" He set the hammer down with a deliberate thud on the boards.

She thrust the will at him. "We need to talk about this."

He stood and wiped his hands on his jeans. His flannel stretched tight across his shoulders as he straightened. "We talked at Hargrove's," he said. His voice was quiet, but an edge crept in. "What's left to say?"

"Plenty," she said and stepped closer. She held the will between them like a shield. "There's no way you didn't know about the trust. Look at yourself—fixing this place like it's already yours. Aunt Morna told you."

He lowered his eyes to the trust, then met her gaze squarely. "I told you. I didn't know. When she got sick, she asked me to look after the cottage. And I said yes. That's it."

"Liar." Tess's voice trembled with accusation. "You expect me to believe she set you up as trustee and never said a word?"

"Yes," he said calmly.

She jabbed a finger at his chest. "You're just waiting for me to bolt so you can take it."

Before she could touch him, he clasped her wrist and lowered her hand. "The only thing I'm waiting for is for you to calm down."

Tess yanked her wrist back and snapped, "Well, I'm sorry, but this all seems a little convenient."

He tossed his head back with a dry, bitter laugh. "Convenient? For her, yes. But I didn't ask for this. She needed help, and I was here."

The implication didn't escape her. "Oh, and I wasn't?"

A knowing look was his only answer.

Tess flinched and felt heat flood her face. Her voice rose with a mix of rage and hurt. "I didn't leave by choice, Noah. My parents shipped me off to boarding school with no warning. I was seventeen, stuck in a dorm with no phone. You think I wanted that?"

Noah heaved a deep breath. "I think it doesn't excuse fifteen years."

"I was seventeen and stuck with no way out."

"And I was eighteen." He lowered his voice. "And left wondering why my best friend disappeared."

Too devastated to speak, all she could do was shake her head. The anger that had propelled her up the steps began to dissolve, replaced by a hollow ache fifteen years in the making.

She pictured him at eighteen, and her tone softened. "You were my best friend, too." She swallowed hard before adding, "I thought you were more."

His eyes searched hers, the storm in them easing. He didn't speak for a moment, seeming to weigh his words.

"I thought so too." His voice was rough-edged, but quieter now. "That night on the swing, I almost kissed you. Then, the next day, you were gone. No goodbye. Nothing."

Tess wrapped her arms around herself and fought the ache in her chest. "I wanted to say goodbye. That morning, I screamed at my mom. I threw a lamp and broke it, but she dragged me to the car, anyway." Silence fell between them, weighed down by all the lost years. The harbor wind rustled the pines, and a gull cried overhead.

Tess peered at the document in her hand, now creased from her grip. "Lucy said Aunt Morna wanted me back at the cottage with you connected to it. Why would she think that after all these years?"

Noah rubbed his jaw and frowned at the floor. "I don't know. But she never mentioned a trust. She just asked me to keep the place standing. It mattered to her."

Tears stung her eyes. "It mattered to me, too. But I couldn't come back. I'd been so happy here, but then my parents turned it into something to argue about. Something happened with my mother and Aunt Morna. The thought of coming back brought it all to the surface. After a while, it was easier to avoid it."

"And me?" His brow furrowed.

"You moved on. We grew up." Tess hesitated, memories surfacing of her mother's tight-lipped fury whenever Noah's name came up. She would cut Tess off mid-sentence, eyes flashing with an old, unresolved anger.

She couldn't bear Noah's pained look, so she went on. "We argued—my mother and I. She said you'd hold me back—that I needed to focus on college and my future. I can still hear her saying, 'Small towns breed small minds.'"

Noah's face hardened, but he didn't look surprised, leading Tess to wonder what her mother might have said to Noah.

"I didn't have a choice," she continued. "So, I got on with my life, and I put the Cove behind me." Tess swallowed hard. "I'm sorry I wasn't here for her—or you."

In silence, Noah gazed at the harbor with that closed off look he used to get. Tess shifted her weight and heaved a deep sigh, her eyes fixed on the trust. "I don't know what to do."

"You don't have to decide today. Hargrove said a year from yesterday, right?"

"Yeah."

"Then take your time. It's your cottage. I'm not pushing you out."

She studied him. He looked as drained as she was. "Okay."

He turned back to his work, picked up his hammer, and drove a nail with a firm strike.

Tess stepped inside and let the door swing shut. The living room wrapped around her with its faint lavender scent. She sank onto the couch. Her anger had burned out, leaving a tangle of regret. Noah's words echoed. *'I waited, Tess.'* She saw him at the mailbox and herself in that dorm, pen in hand.

Outside, the hammer thudded its steady pulse. Tess crossed to the window and watched him work. His flannel stretched across his back as he bent to his task. She could hear Lucy's voice. *'Morna thought you belonged together.'*

Together. Fifteen years had carved a gulf between them, yet here they were, bound by this place and her aunt's last wish. Noah's presence, his grief, and his stubborn hammer strikes tugged at her in ways she couldn't ignore.

She pressed her palm against the cool glass. Boston waited for her—deadlines, meetings, a promotion—all the trappings of the life she'd built to prove her mother wrong. To prove she could succeed on her own terms. But standing in this cottage, with its creaking floorboards and faded curtains, she felt the first real sense of belonging she'd had in years.

The porch boards groaned as Noah shifted his weight. He paused, his gaze drifting toward the window where she stood. For a moment, their eyes met through the glass. She didn't move away. Neither did he.

One year in Peregrine Cove. One year of mornings with gulls crying overhead and evenings with whispering tides. One year of passing Noah on the street, in the café, at the dock—carrying this newfound knowledge between them like a fragile, dangerous thing.

She turned from the window, her decision still unformed but shifting like sand beneath the tide. On the mantel, Aunt Morna's antique clock ticked away the seconds, counting down a year that hadn't even begun.

CHAPTER 4

Tess woke to a gray dawn, the soft patter of raindrops against the window pulling her from restless dreams. Outside, the harbor was choppy, whitecaps visible even from her bedroom window as dark clouds gathered on the horizon. She checked her phone. It had been two days since she'd arrived in Peregrine Cove, two days since her life had been upended by Aunt Morna's final surprise.

Yesterday's tense truce with Noah had left her unsettled, opening old wounds she'd thought were long healed. And now she faced an impossible choice—stay in Peregrine Cove for a whole year or lose the cottage to him.

The deadline ticked in her mind: one year. A lifetime away yet approaching with unstoppable certainty.

She got up and hauled her suitcase to the dresser. Unpacking was a form of surrender—jeans in a drawer, sweater on a hook, toothbrush by the sink where rust stained the porcelain.

Her laptop sat on the bedside table, with emails

from her Boston marketing firm awaiting responses, client meetings that needed rescheduling, and a handful of projects she'd now have to juggle. A life carefully constructed over fifteen years now hung in the balance against this unexpected twist.

Tess typed a brief message to Daniel, her boss and mentor at the firm. *The situation with my aunt's estate is more involved than expected. I might need to work remotely for a while. Is that possible?*

She hit send before she could second-guess herself, then stared at the screen, surprised by her own message. Was she actually considering staying? Even temporarily?

The cottage creaked around her in a familiar symphony of settling wood and aging joints, forming a counterpoint to the building storm outside. Tess threw off the quilt and padded to the window. The bay was steel gray, and the typically blue water now mirrored the turbulent sky. The weather was moving in fast, according to the local forecast on her phone—the first significant storm of the season.

Her phone buzzed with Daniel's reply.

Of course. We'll make it work. Call me when you can to discuss the details.

Just like that, a door opened that Tess hadn't expected. She could stay without sacrificing her career, at least short term. Whether she wanted to was another question.

After a quick shower, she dressed in jeans and a thick sweater, the cottage's old heating system struggling against the dropping temperature. Coffee in hand, she wandered through the rooms, seeing them with fresh eyes—not just as the backdrop of childhood summers, but as an adult appreciating Morna's care for the home despite limited funds.

The craftsmanship in the crown molding, the hand-turned balusters on the staircase, and the original heart pine floors, worn smooth by generations of footsteps, lent the home timeless charm. This place wasn't just valuable for its waterfront location or square footage; it was a testament to an era when homes were built to last centuries, not decades.

No wonder Noah had spent so much time maintaining it. The thought of him came unbidden, along with the memory of his hands methodically measuring, sanding, and replacing what was broken without disrupting the whole. He understood what made this place special, just as she did.

Restless, Tess pulled on her rain jacket, grasped Aunt Morna's journal, and stepped onto the back porch. The wind caught her hair, whipping it across her face as she viewed the backyard. Beyond the small lawn lay Aunt Morna's pride and joy—the herb garden that had supplied her kitchen and her numerous homemade recipes for as long as Tess could remember.

She expected to find it overgrown or withered. Instead, neat rows of herbs filled the rectangular beds bordered by weathered stones. Rosemary, thyme, sage, and Aunt Morna's beloved lavender all stood in orderly succession, clearly tended to despite the cottage's three months of emptiness since her aunt's hospitalization.

Curiosity pulled Tess across the wet grass. The small garden shed by the herb beds was padlocked, but she remembered the key's hiding place—a loose stone in the path, beneath which Morna had always kept a spare. It was still there, a bit rusted but functional.

The shed door creaked open, releasing the earthy smell of potting soil, dried herbs, and old wood. Gardening tools hung on the wall, each in its designated spot. Packets of seeds were arranged alphabetically in a wooden box, and terracotta pots lay nearby, stacked by size. Everything was organized, just as Aunt Morna had always kept it.

A truck rumbled up the drive. Tess peered out at Noah's beat-up Ford with its tailgate scarred from years of hauls. He climbed out, toolbox swinging, with his flannel shirt stretching across his shoulders as he headed for the porch. Her pulse jumped. She hadn't braced for him today. He kneeled by the railing, hammer thudding.

Tess turned away and thumbed through the garden journal that documented plantings, harvests, and the rhythm of the garden seasons. She ran her fingers over the familiar handwriting that filled its pages.

The last entry was dated November 15, mere weeks before Aunt Morna's hospitalization.

Planning for spring already. This winter will pass. Lavender needs dividing. The lemon thyme is spreading too aggressively near the sage. For new plantings: purple basil (3 plants), heirloom tomatoes (by the south fence), and alpine strawberries (in the terra-cotta pots). I must remember to order those climbing rose starts I saw in the catalog, the ones with ...

The entry seemed to trail off mid-thought, as if Aunt Morna had been interrupted and never returned to finish it. A lump formed in Tess's throat. Her aunt had been planning for a spring she wouldn't live to see.

A movement outside the shed window caught her eye. Through the rain-speckled glass, she could see the herb garden more clearly. There, marking neat rows in the freshly turned soil, stood small wooden stakes with seed packets attached, protected from the elements by clear plastic covers. Purple basil. Heirloom tomatoes. Alpine strawberries. Every plant Aunt Morna had listed in her final garden plan was ready for planting when the weather warmed.

The sound of the shed door opening made her turn. Noah stood in the doorway, rain darkening his shoulders, surprise evident on his face.

"Tess." He glanced at the journal in her hands. "I was coming to check on the shed roof before the storm hits full force."

"You planted her garden," Tess said softly, the realization washing over her. "Everything she wanted this season."

Noah shifted uncomfortably. "Just keeping things going." He gestured toward the journal. "She asked me back in January when I visited her at the hospital. She was worried she wouldn't be back home in time for planting."

"But you're still—" Tess began, then stopped, more moved than she cared to admit.

"It's no big deal." Noah's shrug belied the care evident in every prepared row and every protected seed packet. "The lavender's her favorite. I couldn't let it die out just because ..." He trailed off, unable or unwilling to finish the thought.

Tess swallowed hard, studying Noah's face. The man who'd been her childhood friend, then an enemy, now stood before her as something else entirely—someone who had shared her grief, who had continued to honor Aunt Morna in quiet ways while Tess had been absent. Someone who had cared enough to see to every detail of her aunt's final garden wishes.

Her eyes stung, and she blinked against unexpected tears. "She would have loved this." Tess closed the journal with careful hands. "That you remembered everything, even the strawberries in the terracotta pots."

Noah's gaze met hers, vulnerability flickering across his features before he looked away. "She talked about those strawberries and how we used to eat them straight from the plants as kids."

The fact that he remembered made her chest tighten. For fifteen years, she'd imagined Noah as someone who'd taken her place in Aunt Morna's life. But looking at the careful preparations he'd made, Tess realized he hadn't replaced her at all. He'd simply loved Aunt Morna, too, in his own way.

Something shifted in Tess's perception. The antagonism she'd felt toward Noah as a potential rival for the cottage softened, replaced by conflicting affection and apprehension.

The wind picked up, rattling the shed's windows. "That storm's moving in faster than expected," Noah said, seeming eager to change the subject. "We should head back to the cottage."

Tess returned the journal to its place on the workbench. As they stepped outside, she took one last look at the prepared garden. It wasn't just soil and stakes, but a final promise being kept.

Inside the cottage, she was hanging up her jacket when Noah joined her.

"I need to secure the rest of the porch shutters and check the boat," he said without preamble, water beading on his shoulders and in his hair.

"The boat?" Tess echoed, still processing what she'd seen in the garden. "Aunt Morna's?"

"It's still at the marina." He ran a hand through his damp hair. "The harbormaster called—they're expecting sixty-mile-per-hour gusts by noon." He glanced at her, then away. "I can handle it, but I thought you should know I'll be working outside."

"I'll help," Tess said, surprising herself as much as him.

Noah's eyebrows rose. "You don't have to."

"It's my aunt's cottage. My aunt's boat." She reached for her jacket again. "Besides, it'll go faster with the two of us."

For a moment, she thought he might refuse, but then he nodded. "We should hurry. The weather's turning fast."

They secured the cottage first, Noah closing storm shutters over the most vulnerable windows while Tess gathered anything that might blow away from the porch and yard. They moved with surprising efficiency, anticipating each other's movements despite the years apart. The muscle memory of summers spent preparing the cottage for storms was still intact.

When the last shutter was latched, Noah turned toward his truck. "Now for the marina."

The drive down to the harbor was tense with the effort of navigating increasingly poor visibility. Rain lashed the windshield while the wipers struggled to keep up. In the passenger seat, the familiar landmarks of Peregrine Cove transformed into ghostly outlines through sheets of rain. She gripped the door handle as Noah navigated a deep puddle, the truck hydroplaning before regaining traction.

"I can't believe she kept that old boat. I thought she'd have sold it years ago," Tess said, needing to break the tense silence.

"She sailed until last summer." Noah fixed his eyes on the road. His knuckles whitened on the steering wheel as a gust buffeted the truck. "I took her out whenever the weather was good."

The image of Aunt Morna—who must have been seventy-five last summer—out sailing with Noah brought a lump to Tess's throat. Another aspect of her aunt's life she'd missed entirely.

The marina came into view, with its boats rocking violently in their slips while waves crashed against the breakwater. Noah parked as close as possible, but they still had to sprint through the driving rain to reach the harbormaster's office.

Inside, controlled chaos reigned. Boat owners rushed in and out, soaking wet and calling to each other over the howl of the wind. The harbormaster, a weathered man in his sixties whom Tess vaguely remembered from childhood, nodded in recognition when he saw them.

"Pierce. Bradford." He handed Noah a clipboard. "Morna's boat is in slip twenty-three. Double-check the lines—we've already had two snaps on the north dock."

Noah scrawled his signature and passed the clipboard back. "We'll take care of it, Frank." He turned to Tess. "Ready?"

She nodded, bracing herself as Noah pushed the door open against the wind.

Noah led the way along the heaving docks, one hand steadying Tess when a strong gust nearly knocked her off balance. The familiar sensation of his grip on her elbow sent an unexpected warmth through her despite the cold rain.

"There," he shouted over the wind, pointing to a sleek sailboat about thirty feet long. There it was. The *Mary Eleanor*.

They worked together to secure the boat, checking lines, adding fenders, and ensuring everything that could move was tied down. Tess fell into a familiar rhythm with Noah, anticipating what he needed before he asked, just as they had done as teenagers, helping Aunt Morna prepare for summer squalls.

"The bow line needs reinforcing," Noah called, tossing her a length of heavy rope. "Remember the—"

"Bowline knot, I know," Tess shouted back, her fingers already working through the familiar pattern. "Through the rabbit hole, around the tree, back through the hole again."

The mnemonic device he'd taught her fifteen years ago came back. Muscle memory took over as she tied the knot that had once taken her hours to master. Noah's surprised smile when she held up the finished work sent a flutter through her chest that had nothing to do with the raging storm.

A violent gust rocked the dock, sending spray over both of them. Tess lost her footing on the slick wood, pitching sideways toward the churning water. Noah's arm shot out, catching her around the waist and pulling her against his chest. For a moment, they stood locked together, his warmth a stark contrast to the cold rain.

Their eyes met, and something passed between them—a memory of what they used to be.

"Still clumsy as ever, Bradford." There was no edge

to his words, just the ghost of the teasing boy he'd once been.

"Still showing off, Pierce," she countered, the familiar rhythm of their old banter rising to her lips unbidden.

His laugh, brief but genuine, caught on the wind. He didn't let go of her waist. "I'm glad you're here." His voice was so quiet she had to lean in to hear him over the storm. "It would've been harder to do this alone."

Tess held his gaze, water streaming down both their faces. "Good thing I stayed, then."

For one fleeting moment, time collapsed, and they were teenagers, soaking wet and laughing in a summer storm as the world narrowed to just the two of them.

Then reality forced them back to the present, and Noah stepped back. His hands fell away from her waist. "We should get back to the cottage. This is only going to get worse."

The drive back was even more harrowing as runoff streamed over the road, bringing with it debris from fallen tree branches. By the time they reached the cottage, both were drenched despite their rain gear.

"The power might go out," Noah said as they stomped onto the porch, shaking off water. "There's a generator in the shed with a full tank of gas, just in case. I checked last week."

"Of course you did," Tess murmured, but without the resentment that might have colored the words two days ago. She pushed her sodden hair away from her face. "You think of everything."

"Not everything." Noah's eyes lingered on her face for a moment. He looked away, rubbing the back of his neck. "Just the practical stuff."

Inside, she handed him a towel from the downstairs bathroom. Their fingers brushed, and that same electric awareness passed between them.

"You should get into dry clothes." Noah rubbed his hair with the towel. "I need to check on Mrs. Henderson next door. Her son's out of town, and she gets nervous during storms."

Tess nodded, suddenly aware of how her wet clothes clung to her skin and just as aware of Noah averting his gaze. "Thank you. For the boat and the shutters."

"Part of the job." He shrugged, but it didn't quite convey the casualness he was aiming for.

"Is that what this is to you? A job?" The question slipped out before she could reconsider it.

Noah's expression turned serious. He took a step closer, close enough that she could see the raindrops still clinging to his eyelashes. "You know it's not."

The weight of everything unsaid hung between them—fifteen years of absence, the almost-kiss on the porch swing, yesterday's revelations, and the trust that bound them together whether they wanted it or not.

Noah broke the tension. "I'll come back to check on you after the storm passes. If you need anything before then, call me." He scribbled his number on a notepad by the phone, a strangely intimate gesture in an age of digital contacts.

After he left, Tess stood in the foyer, water puddling around her feet as she listened to the weather raging outside. She changed into dry clothes, made tea, and sat in Aunt Morna's rocking chair, watching raindrops race down the windows not covered by shutters.

Her phone sat on the side table with Daniel's message still open.

Of course. We'll make it work.

A path back to Boston remained open. She could walk away, sell her interest in the cottage to Noah, and return to the life she'd built.

But then she thought of Noah in the garden shed, fulfilling Aunt Morna's final wishes, or Noah on the docks with his sure, steady grip as he caught her from falling, and Noah saying, 'you know it's not' when she asked if this was just a job to him.

She would need to return to Boston to meet with some clients. Her team was expecting her back. Her apartment would need attention. Her whole life waited there, predictable and secure.

Yet the thought of leaving now, with so much unresolved, made her chest tighten. A few days ago, she couldn't wait to leave. Now, she needed more time to understand what she'd found here and what she'd left behind fifteen years ago.

Before she could overthink it, Tess picked up her phone and typed two messages.

The first was to Daniel: *I'll need to extend my remote work for a week—maybe two. I'll call tomorrow with the details.*

Then to Noah: *I'm staying, but just for a week, maybe two, while I decide about the rest of the year later.*

She hit send, then set the phone aside, surprised by the sense of relief that washed over her. It wasn't a full commitment to the entire year, but it was a beginning. It would give her a chance to explore what might have been or what might still be.

Through a gap in the storm shutters, she watched

Noah's truck turn into Mrs. Henderson's driveway. His phone must have chimed with her message because he paused before getting out and pulled his phone from his pocket. Even at this distance, she could see his posture change as he read her words, though his expression was unreadable.

For a long moment, he sat in his truck, looking toward Aunt Morna's cottage—toward her. Then he slipped the phone back into his pocket and continued with his task, his movements sure and steady despite the storm's fury.

Thunder rolled across the bay, vibrating through the old cottage. Tess wrapped her hands around her mug and allowed its warmth to seep into her fingers. Through the window, she could just make out the edge of the herb garden, the lavender bowing but not breaking under the onslaught of wind and rain.

Like the garden, something long dormant inside her had begun to stir, coaxed to life by unexpected care, by the discovery that even in absence, some connections remain. Not quite trust, not yet forgiveness, but perhaps the beginning of understanding.

She would stay for a week. Test the waters. Like the lavender in Aunt Morna's garden, maybe roots, once established, never truly died—they just waited for the right season to bloom again.

CHAPTER 5

The morning after the storm dawned clear and brilliant, as if the tumultuous weather had scrubbed the world clean. Tess stood on the porch, coffee mug cradled in her hands and viewed the aftermath. Branches and debris littered the yard, and a large pine had fallen across the road about a hundred yards down, but the cottage itself had weathered the storm intact.

Much like she had.

Her decision to stay—even just for a week or two—felt both terrifying and strangely right. Her phone buzzed in her pocket. The screen displayed an unfamiliar local number.

"Hello?"

"Tess? It's Lucy Dunn. From the café?" The voice was warm. "I'm calling everyone in town. We're organizing cleanup crews after the storm. Thought you might want to join in. It's a great way to reintroduce yourself to Peregrine Cove."

Tess hesitated. She had planned to spend the day

setting up her remote office in Aunt Morna's sunroom, making the cottage livable for her extended stay.

"We're meeting at the town green in an hour," Lucy continued. "Bring anything you've got—chainsaw, rake, shovel—the works. And wear some work gloves and boots. It's a muddy mess out there. Noah's coordinating the marina team—they got hit pretty hard."

At the mention of Noah, that now-familiar flutter stirred in her chest. She hadn't seen or heard from him since sending that impulsive text yesterday. Had he been pleased? Disappointed? His lack of response left her unsettled.

"I'll be there," she found herself saying.

An hour later, Tess parked near the town green, surprised by the number of vehicles already gathered. At least thirty people milled about, organizing into teams and distributing equipment. She recognized some faces from childhood summers—older now, but still familiar.

Lucy spotted her from across the green and waved her over to a folding table laden with thermoses and pastry boxes.

"You came!" Lucy gave Tess a quick one-armed hug.

"It seemed like the neighborly thing to do," Tess said, accepting a pair of work gloves from a stack on the table.

Lucy's knowing smile suggested she heard the unspoken motivation. "Most of the heavy lifting is happening down at the marina and the north shore road. Fallen trees, dock damage. The team here in town is handling debris cleanup and checking on elderly residents."

"Where do you need me?"

"Actually ..." Lucy's expression turned shrewd. "They could use another set of hands at the marina. Noah's team is shorthanded with the Petersons out of town."

"Subtle," Tess murmured.

Lucy's laugh was unrepentant. "Morna would've wanted me to meddle a little."

Tess couldn't help but smile. "Fine. The marina it is."

"Take these." Lucy handed her a box of pastries and a large thermos. "The crew down there missed breakfast. Tell Noah it's on the house."

As Tess turned to leave, an older man with a weathered face and a harbormaster's cap approached. He studied her with narrowed eyes.

"So, you're Morna's niece." His tone sounded more like an accusation than a greeting.

Tess smiled and extended her hand. "Yes, Tess Bradford."

"Finally decided to show up."

Tess felt her cheeks warm.

"Hank Morrell. I've known your aunt for forty years and saw her nearly every day—more than some family can say."

He emphasized the word "family," with unmistakable judgment.

"Hank," Lucy warned, but the man continued.

"Three months in the hospital and not one visit from her relatives. She had to hear about you from Noah, bringing her updates on the phone like it was some kind of consolation prize."

The words hit Tess like a physical blow. She'd

known about Aunt Morna's hospitalization for barely a week before her death—the result of her aunt's stubborn insistence that no one "bother" her with news of the illness. She'd been planning to visit the following weekend.

"I didn't know she was ill until—"

"Save it," Hank interrupted. "Just don't expect everyone to welcome you with open arms just because you've got Bradford blood. Some of us remember who was actually there for Morna." With that, he turned and walked away, joining a group heading toward the north road.

Lucy squeezed Tess's arm. "Don't mind Hank. He and Morna were close. He's taking it hard."

"It's fine," Tess said, but it wasn't. The man's words had voiced her own deepest guilt—that she should have somehow known and been there. She could have done more than make an occasional phone call in her aunt's final years.

"Go on to the marina," Lucy urged gently. "Noah could use the help, and the fresh air will do you good."

The marina parking lot was a hive of activity when Tess arrived. Boats had been tossed around like toys, some piled against each other, others tilted at precarious angles in their slips. The walkways were strewn with debris, and one of the smaller docks had completely detached and was now floating aimlessly in the harbor.

She spotted Noah in an instant. He stood on what remained of the main dock, gesturing as he spoke to a group of fishermen. Even from a distance, she could see the natural authority in his stance, the way the others listened intently to his instructions. This was a side of

Noah she'd never known—the leader, the one people turned to in a crisis.

He looked up as she approached, surprise flashing across his features before he schooled them into neutral politeness.

"Lucy sent reinforcements," Tess called, holding up the pastry box and thermos. "And breakfast."

A murmur of appreciation rose from the gathered workers. Noah said something to the group, who dispersed to their tasks, then made his way toward her, navigating the treacherous footing of the damaged dock with practiced ease.

"I didn't expect to see you here," he said when he reached her.

"Lucy called and said you were shorthanded." Tess handed him the provisions. "So put me to work."

Noah studied her for a moment, as if assessing her sincerity. "We're securing the loose vessels first, then clearing the debris from the main dock. It's not glamorous work."

"I'm not a glamorous person, so I'll manage just fine." The quip was a glimpse of the easy banter they'd once shared.

A half-smile touched his lips. "Fair enough. We can use you on debris detail with Gus and Maya." He nodded toward a young couple sorting through piles of broken wood and fiberglass at the dock's edge.

Tess nodded, then hesitated. "I just ran into Hank Morrell. He seems to think I abandoned Aunt Morna." The words tumbled out before she could stop them.

Noah's expression softened. "Hank's grieving. He doesn't know the whole story."

"Which is?"

"That Morna specifically asked me not to tell you about her illness until she was ready. She didn't want you having to drop everything to rush back here." He ran a hand through his hair. "I argued with her about it, but she was adamant. You know how she could be. I'll set Hank straight."

The knot in Tess's chest loosened. "Why wouldn't she want me to know?"

"She said you'd worked too hard building your career to jeopardize it." Noah's eyes held hers. "She was proud of you, Tess."

Tears pricked Tess's eyes. The thought of Aunt Morna protecting her career even from a hospital bed was both comforting and devastating. "Thank you for telling me that."

Noah nodded once, then gestured toward the debris pile. "Now, about that glamorous work."

For the next several hours, Tess worked alongside the townspeople, many of whom introduced themselves as friends of Aunt Morna's. They shared stories as they worked—how her aunt had organized the annual harbor cleanup, her famous lavender shortbread at the summer festival, and how she always sailed around the harbor on her birthday.

With each anecdote, the connection deepened not just to her aunt but to this town that had loved her. These weren't just Aunt Morna's neighbors; they were her community, her chosen family. They had welcomed Tess without hesitation, as if her blood tie to Aunt Morna made her one of them by default.

Well, most of them had welcomed her. Hank's words still stung, a reminder that her absence had been noted, her lack of visits tallied by those who'd been present day after day.

By midday, the worst of the damage had been dealt with. The floating dock was secured, the boats were righted and checked for damage, and most of the debris was now cleared from the walkways. Tess sat on an overturned crate, massaging her sore shoulders as the workers began to disperse for lunch.

"You're going to feel that tomorrow." Noah approached with two bottles of water. He handed one to her and sat on a neighboring crate.

"I'm already feeling it today," Tess admitted, accepting the water gratefully. She took a long drink, acutely aware of his proximity. They sat in companionable silence for a moment, watching the harbor's choppy waters begin to settle as the post-storm winds diminished.

"I got your text," Noah said. "About staying."

Tess nodded, unsure how to respond. "It's just ... a trial period."

"Any particular reason for the change of heart?" His tone was neutral, but Tess sensed the weight behind the question.

She considered deflecting, making a joke about the trust conditions or her boss's flexibility. But something about the moment—the shared work and the genuine connection she'd felt with the townspeople who'd loved Aunt Morna—demanded honesty.

"I'm not sure yet. Maybe I just need to understand why my being here mattered so much to her."

Noah nodded slowly, his eyes on the horizon. "I think she'd be pleased."

"Even though it means you might not get the

cottage?" The question slipped out before she could reconsider it.

"Tess." He turned to face her. "I never wanted your inheritance. I just promised Morna I'd make sure the cottage was cared for, one way or another."

The sincerity in his voice was unmistakable. Tess regretted allowing her knee-jerk suspicions to cast him as an adversary.

"I'm sorry," she murmured. "For assuming the worst."

Noah shrugged, but his expression softened. "It's a complicated situation. Neither of us asked for it."

"No, we didn't." Tess studied his profile, the strong line of his jaw, the slight crinkles at the corners of his eyes that hadn't been there fifteen years ago. "But here we are."

"Here we are," he echoed.

The dockmaster's whistle broke the moment, signaling it was time to get back to work. Noah stood and offered Tess a hand up, which she accepted after a brief hesitation. His palm was warm against hers, callused from years of manual labor but gentle in its grip.

"I should check on the progress with the north dock." Noah released her hand a fraction of a second slower than necessary.

"And I should probably head back to the cottage to set up my workspace." Tess brushed sawdust from her jeans. "I'm starting remote work tomorrow."

"I'll leave you to it, then." With a nod, Noah headed toward the north dock, leaving Tess with an unexpected awareness that something was changing between them.

Back at the cottage, Tess began the process of

moving in. She unpacked her suitcase into drawers that still held sachets of Aunt Morna's lavender, arranged her toiletries on the bathroom shelves, and set up her laptop in the sunroom that would serve as her office.

As she worked, she found herself opening cabinets and closets she'd bypassed during her first days, exploring the cottage with new eyes. In the kitchen, she discovered Aunt Morna's recipe box, filled with hand-written cards yellowed with age. She sat at the kitchen table, sifting through them, smiling at her aunt's meticu-lous handwriting and occasional commentary: "Too sweet—reduce sugar next time" or "Perfect with fresh thyme."

One recipe caught her eye—Aunt Morna's famous herb bread. But what made her pause wasn't the recipe itself, but the notes scrawled in a different handwriting at the bottom of the card: "Added rosemary, 1 tbsp. Better with honey instead of sugar."

The writing was unmistakably Noah's, his strong, angular script a contrast to Aunt Morna's elegant cursive. Tess stared at it, trying to picture Noah and Aunt Morna in this kitchen, baking together, making notes, tasting, and adjusting. It seemed so domestic—a side of their relationship she'd never imagined.

A knock at the door pulled her from her thoughts.

Noah stood on the porch, a toolbox in one hand. "I thought you might want help securing that loose shut-ter. The one on the west side was rattling pretty badly during the storm."

"I didn't even notice," Tess admitted as she let him in.

Noah set the toolbox down and then noticed the recipe card in her hand. His expression shifted, vulnerability flashing across his features. "My mother's favorite. We used to bake it together, the three of us. After she died, Morna insisted we keep the tradition to remember her."

The revelation stunned Tess. She knew Noah's mother had died when he was in high school—a car accident the summer before their almost-kiss—but she'd never known about this connection to Aunt Morna.

"I didn't realize you two were so close."

Noah's laugh held no humor. "Where did you think I was all those years you weren't visiting? Morna was the closest thing to a mother I had left." He took the recipe card from her, running his thumb over his own handwriting. "We made this the day before she went into the hospital. She couldn't stand long enough to knead the dough, but she supervised every step."

The image was almost too painful to contemplate— Aunt Morna, already ill, insisting on maintaining a tradition that connected the three of them across time and loss.

"I'm sorry." Tess meant it in more ways than she could express. "I should have been here more."

Noah looked up with softening eyes. "She understood your life was in Boston. She never held it against you." He replaced the recipe card in the box. "Besides, you're here now. That's what matters."

The simple acceptance in his words moved her more than any absolution could have. Tess blinked back tears.

"Now, about that shutter." Noah cleared his throat and reached for his toolbox. "It won't take long to fix. I can show you how, in case it happens again."

"I'd like that." Tess was grateful for the change of subject.

They spent the next hour working side by side. Noah demonstrated how to check for loose hinges, tighten screws, and apply weather-resistant oil to prevent rusting. His hands moved with practiced efficiency, but he slowed his movements when showing her the techniques, careful to make sure she understood.

"You're a good teacher," Tess said as they finished the second shutter.

"I coach Little League in the spring." Noah offered a modest shrug. "You learn to break things down into steps."

Another piece of his life she'd known nothing about. "Do you like it? Coaching?"

"Oh, yeah. It's the best part of my week," he admitted, his expression warming. "There's nothing like watching a kid connect with the ball for the first time. There's that moment when they realize they can do something they thought was impossible."

Tess could almost see Noah on a dusty baseball diamond, patient and encouraging, celebrating small victories with unbridled enthusiasm. The image made her smile.

"What?" Noah asked, catching her expression.

"Nothing. Just trying to picture you with a whistle and a clipboard."

"Just a cap, no whistle. And I'm very intimidating in my coaching stance." He demonstrated, crossing his arms and adopting a serious expression that broke into a grin when Tess laughed.

"Terrifying," she agreed.

They finished the repairs and found themselves on

the porch with the afternoon stretching before them. The air had warmed as the sun did its best to erase the memory of yesterday's storm.

"Have you eaten?" Noah asked. "Since breakfast, I mean."

Tess realized she hadn't. "No, actually."

"Me neither. I packed lunch. There's plenty for two if you're interested." He gestured toward his truck. "Don't get your hopes up. It's just sandwiches."

The invitation, while casual, was fraught with significance. It was only a shared meal, but it would be on the porch where they'd once nearly crossed a line neither had been ready for.

"I'd like that." Tess was surprised to find that she meant it.

Noah retrieved the lunch from his truck, and they settled on the porch steps, the wooden planks warm beneath them. He handed her a wrapped sandwich and an apple, then opened a thermos of coffee, pouring some into the cap for her before drinking from the thermos.

"Just like old times." He smiled. "Remember that summer when we used to sneak snacks out here while Morna was napping?"

Tess did remember. They'd been fifteen, hungry every hour of the day, constantly raiding the kitchen. "You always took the blame when she caught us with food on the porch."

"Because you were a terrible liar." Noah laughed. "Your face would turn red the moment she looked at you."

"It did not!" Tess protested, but she knew it was true.

"Please. You were transparent. Still are." Noah took a bite of his sandwich, eyeing her over the bread. "I bet you still can't bluff at poker."

"I've improved," Tess protested, though in truth, she was still hopeless at any game requiring deception.

They ate in comfortable silence for a while, the sound of waves and gulls overhead the only soundtrack they needed. Tess couldn't remember the last time she'd had lunch outdoors, much less sitting on the porch steps like a teenager.

"This is nice," she said.

Noah nodded, his expression thoughtful. "It is."

After lunch, Noah packed up the remaining food and stood to leave. "I should get going. I promised Mrs. Henderson I'd check her roof for storm damage."

"Always the handyman." Her tone held more admiration than teasing.

"Just doing what needs doing." Noah shrugged, but she could tell he was pleased by her approval. "I'll see you around, Tess."

When he'd driven out of view, Tess returned to the cottage, motivated to continue unpacking and make this space her own, at least while she was here.

The cottage sunroom functioned perfectly as her home office. Tess spent the rest of the afternoon arranging her laptop, portable monitor, and reference materials on the antique desk that had once been Aunt Morna's bill-paying station. The room faced east, capturing morning light while avoiding the direct afternoon glare that would have made computer work difficult.

She'd just finished a video call with Daniel, establishing her remote work protocol, when a knock sounded at the front door. The porch was empty when she answered, but a cardboard box sat on the welcome mat containing a package of cleaning supplies, basic groceries, and a collection of Aunt Morna's house keys, all labeled, of course.

A note was tucked inside:

I had to run to the store, and I thought these might help. The storm knocked out the well pump at the Henderson place. I'll be working there till late. -N

It was such a simple gesture, yet it spoke volumes. Noah had anticipated needs she hadn't even recognized yet, just as he'd apparently been doing for Aunt Morna all these years, supporting her from the periphery.

Tess brought the box inside, touched by Noah's thoughtfulness. She spent the evening organizing the cottage for her extended stay, moving clothes into drawers instead of living out of her suitcase, arranging her toiletries in the bathroom cabinet, and finding places for the books and personal items she'd brought from Boston.

With each object she placed and each space she claimed, the cottage became less like a shrine to Aunt Morna and more like a home. While not entirely hers, it was no longer a museum of memories she was afraid to disturb.

As darkness fell, Tess was drawn to the porch. The night air carried the scent of sea salt and pine, with the distant rhythm of waves against the shore forming a steady accompaniment to the occasional call of a night bird. She settled into the porch swing—the same one where she and Noah had almost kissed fifteen years ago —and nudged it with one foot, setting it in motion.

Her phone sat on her lap, open to her conversation

with Noah. She began typing, then deleted, then typed again as she searched for the right words. *Thanks for the supplies and the keys. I've set up my office and start work tomorrow.*

She hit send before she could overthink it, then set the phone aside, focusing instead on the stars emerging above the bay. The swing's gentle creaking soothed her, a familiar sound from childhood summers that somehow made this new arrangement feel manageable.

Her phone chimed with Noah's reply: *Good. The well pump's fixed. Mrs. H says thanks for the cookies you brought over this morning.*

Tess smiled. They were just store-bought, but she'd dropped them off after learning about the pump issue. It was the sort of thing Aunt Morna used to do, a small gesture of community she wouldn't have thought of a week ago.

Another message followed: *If you need anything, I'm just past the pine grove. Same house. The door's yellow now, not blue.*

The same house, of course. While she'd been building a life in Boston, he had been deepening his roots here.

Yellow suits you better than blue, she texted back, surprised by the ease with which the teasing comment came. *Less brooding.*

Three dots appeared as he typed, disappeared, and then appeared again. At last: *Some of us have evolved past our brooding teenage phase. The jury's still out on you, Bradford.*

A laugh escaped her, genuine and unexpected. This was how they used to be long before romantic feelings had complicated everything. Perhaps that was the best place to start rebuilding.

She replied. *Evolved? Oh, you mean aged.*

Noah: *Ouch. My wounded dignity.*

Tess grinned at the phone like a teenager. *Your dignity will survive. It's had practice.*

Noah: *True. It lived through that Chowder Festival when you made me wear the red lobster hat.*

The memory surfaced. Noah at sixteen towered over most of the other volunteers but sported a ridiculous foam lobster hat because she'd dared him. He wore it the entire day, even after the football team showed up and teased him mercilessly. Seeing him take it with his usual good nature made her heart swell with affection.

That hat was a privilege, she typed. *Some might even say distinguished.*

Noah: *Distinguished isn't the word I kept hearing. Ridiculous, asinine, pathetic—but distinguished? Not really.*

Tess: *Well, I thought you looked perfectly ...*

He sent a raised eyebrow emoji. *Don't finish that thought.*

She smiled and typed, *Cute.*

Noah: *That's the look I was going for: cute lobster.*

A comfortable silence settled. Tess watched the stars and wondered if Noah was doing the same, perhaps from his own porch just beyond the pine grove. Close enough to visit, far enough to maintain independence. A metaphor for where they found themselves now.

Her phone chimed once more: *Goodnight, Tess. Welcome home.*

'Welcome home.' Not welcome back but home. As

if he recognized what she was only beginning to admit to herself—that the cottage, this town, had always held a piece of her heart, no matter how far she'd run or how firmly she'd convinced herself she belonged elsewhere.

"Goodnight, Noah," she said and then set down her phone.

The porch swing creaked as she pushed off again, letting the familiar motion rock her gently. A week. Who was she kidding? She needed more time than that. More time for what? To figure out something I never expected? To wonder if this could be home? After fifteen years away, she was stunned by how quickly she could feel at home again. Or maybe it was a simple mixture of grief and nostalgia. And Noah. But that mixture was tangling itself in her life, a life she'd spent fifteen years building. Now she had to decide if what she had left with Noah was worth exploring or better left in the past.

CHAPTER 6

The streets of Peregrine Cove hadn't changed in fifteen years. Faded awnings covered the storefronts. The same brass bell jangled when Tess pushed open the hardware store door, and the same weathered faces turned to study her as if she were curious flotsam washed ashore in a storm.

"Tess Bradford," Martin Grayson said from behind the counter.

Tess smiled, fingers rising to brush a strand of hair behind her ear, a gesture her mother had tried to break her of since childhood. "Hello, Mr. Grayson. It's good to see you."

"Morna always said you'd be back someday."

She never said that to me, Tess thought, but kept her smile fixed. "I need some supplies for the cottage. Noah Pierce is helping with the renovations, but there are a few things I wanted to pick up myself."

She could feel the ripple of interest that passed through the three other customers browsing the narrow aisles. Noah's name, linked with hers, would be all over town by lunchtime.

"Noah's got a good head on his shoulders." Martin reached for a notepad. "What's on your list?"

Before Tess could answer, the back curtain parted, and a tall figure stepped through carrying a box of inventory. Rob Pierce, Noah's father, stopped mid-stride when he saw her, his face shifting from pleasant to stone.

"Rob, look who's back in town," Martin said, oblivious to the sudden chill.

Rob set the box down with deliberate care. "Tess." His voice was flat. "Heard you were in town. Staying long?"

"A week or so." Tess tried to match his neutrality, but she felt like a teenager once again caught in an adult standoff she didn't understand.

Rob's mouth tightened. "My son's got a business to run, you know. He can't just drop everything for pet projects." He waved a hand vaguely.

"I'll pay him for his time." Tess's spine stiffened.

"Yeah, figures." Rob's eyes, the same startling blue as Noah's but colder, assessed her. "Your mother always did believe money fixed everything."

Martin cleared his throat. "That list, Tess?"

Grateful for the interruption, Tess handed over the paper she'd prepared. While Martin gathered her items, Rob's presence loomed like a shadow at her back, moving between shelves, helping other customers, but always circling back to where she stood.

"Boston must keep you busy," he said, sliding a box of nails onto a shelf near her.

"It does." Tess ran her fingers over a display of drawer pulls, wondering which would best suit Aunt Morna's old kitchen cabinets. "But some things are worth making time for."

"Like cottages? But not the people who live there." His sharp-edged words lingered.

Tess turned to face him. "Morna was important to me. This is about honoring her wishes."

"Funny way to honor someone. Disappear for fifteen years until there's property to claim."

The injustice of it stung. "I wrote or called every month, and I visited when—"

"When it suited you," Rob finished. "Just like your mother, leaving debris in her wake." His gaze hardened. "My son included."

Speechless, Tess clutched her purse tightly.

Rob gave her a smile that didn't reach his eyes. "Peregrine Cove has a long memory, Tess. So do Pierce men."

"Your order's ready," Martin called, breaking the moment. "And don't forget, Tess. The festival committee meeting's at four in the town hall. Morna always handled the lighthouse display, so tradition says it's yours now."

Tess blinked. "I didn't realize—"

"Morna would like that." Martin's eyes twinkled. "It's just for a week. The Spring Chowder Festival is next weekend."

The request left her floundering. Boston deadlines loomed, the cottage repairs were barely started, and now this—an unexpected obligation to a town that seemed to be watching her through narrowed eyes, measuring her against both her aunt's legacy and her mother's desertion.

Rob's quiet chuckle held no warmth. "Welcome home, Tess."

≈

THE BELL on Lucy's Café door jingled as Tess pushed it open, seeking refuge from the whispers that had followed her down Main Street after leaving the hardware store. The morning rush had ended, leaving only two older men playing chess by the window and Lucy herself wiping down the counter.

"There she is," Lucy called, her smile genuine among a sea of suspicious faces. "Have a seat. You look like you could use some coffee."

Tess slid onto a stool, dropping her hardware store purchases at her feet. "Is it that obvious?"

"Small town, big eyes." Lucy poured coffee without asking and pushed it across the counter. "Rob Pierce giving you trouble?"

Tess's head snapped up. "How did you—"

"I saw you heading into the hardware store earlier. And everyone knows Rob's working there now during the off-season, when the fishing's slow. I think Martin keeps him on out of friendship."

Tess wrapped her hands around the warm mug. "He made it clear I wasn't welcome. He said something about my mother leaving 'debris in her wake.'"

Lucy straightened, something cautious crossing her expression. "Rob and your mother have ... history."

"History?"

Lucy glanced toward the chess players, then back to

Tess. "Before you were born. Before she met your father."

Tess nearly choked on her coffee. "My mother and Rob Pierce? Noah's father?"

"They were the talk of the town one summer. Inseparable. Rob was already making a name for himself as one of the harbor's most reliable fishermen. Elizabeth was ... well, Elizabeth was beautiful and knew it." Lucy's voice held no judgment, just matter-of-fact observation. "Everyone thought they'd get married."

"What happened?"

"At the end of that summer, your mother met a flat-lander with old family money. Two weeks later, she ended things with Rob, and by Christmas, she was engaged to your father." Lucy shrugged. "Rob was devastated. He threw himself into work and didn't date for years. When he finally married Noah's mother, people wondered if he'd ever really gotten over Elizabeth."

The revelation turned everything sideways. Noah's father wasn't just some small-town grump. He was a man Tess's mother had deeply wounded.

"And now here I am," Tess said slowly, "looking just like her, spending time with his son."

"Life has a sense of humor," Lucy agreed. "But you're not your mother, Tess. And Noah isn't Rob."

Tess sipped her coffee, thoughts swirling. "He said my mom always thought money fixed everything."

"She wanted a bigger life and security. You can't fault her for that." Lucy's eyes were kind but direct. "But she did burn some bridges, and Rob was the most spectacular fire."

"And he thinks I'll do the same to Noah." The realization landed with uncomfortable clarity.

Lucy tilted her head. "Will you?"

Tess opened her mouth to deny it, then closed it again. Hadn't that been her plan? Renovate, sell, leave? Just like her mother, she'd move on to something bigger somewhere else.

Instead of answering, Tess said, "The festival committee is meeting at four. Apparently, I've inherited Aunt Morna's lighthouse duties."

Lucy smiled, allowing the deflection. "With Noah."

Tess took a moment to recover. "Is there anything you don't know?"

"Occupational hazard." Lucy refilled Tess's mug. "Just remember, you get to write your own story, not relive anyone else's."

The chess players signaled for refills, so Lucy moved away, leaving Tess with uncomfortable questions and the lingering image of her mother and Rob Pierce, both young and in love. Fifteen years later, the shadow of their broken romance still lingered over Peregrine Cove.

THE TOWN HALL was stuffy with afternoon heat and the perfume of elderly committee members who'd been running the Spring Chowder Festival since Tess was in pigtails. She slipped into a back seat, hoping to keep a low profile until she learned what was expected of her.

No such luck.

"Tess Bradford!" Gladys Harper's voice cut through

the pre-meeting chatter. "Come right up here, dear. We've saved Morna's seat for you."

Every head turned. Heat climbed up her neck as Tess made her way to the front, where a chair waited between Gladys and, of course, Noah Pierce, who eyed her approach with an expression hovering between amusement and sympathy.

"Fancy meeting you here," he murmured as she took her seat.

"Apparently, I inherited this," she whispered back. "Although nobody thought to mention it until an hour ago."

His mouth twitched. "The Cove is full of surprises."

Gladys brought the meeting to order. "The Spring Chowder Festival has been our town's pride for ninety-seven years. This year will be no exception." She beamed at the assembled members. "Now, as we all know, Morna's lighthouse display has always been the centerpiece." She patted Tess's hand. "And now, her niece will carry on the tradition."

That caught Tess off guard. "I'm not sure what that entails, exactly—"

"Noah will show you." Gladys waved her hand. "He's helped Morna with the mechanics of it for years."

Tess glanced at Noah, who raised an eyebrow. "Mechanics?"

"I've tweaked it a little," he explained. "Rotating light, foghorn, the works. Morna stored it in the boathouse."

Great. Not that she would have minded working with Noah, but since seeing his father, the whole thing seemed awkward.

The meeting droned on, assigning booths and activities with the precision of a military campaign. Tess stared at Noah's hands as he jotted down notes. The same strong, capable hands that had once held hers on midnight beach walks now moved with the confidence of a man who knew his worth.

" ...so that's settled," Gladys concluded. "Noah and Tess on the lighthouse, just as Morna would have wanted."

The meeting dispersed into clusters of chattering volunteers. Noah turned to her, notebook closed. "Want to see what we're in for? The boathouse isn't far."

Tess thought of her laptop waiting at the cottage, emails unanswered, the Boston life temporarily on hold. "Lead the way."

They walked in silence, past curious glances and whispered comments. The Cove observed them like a collective entity, storing notes for later discussion over dinner tables and morning coffee.

"Sorry about the ambush," Noah said as they left the town center behind. "I should've warned you about the festival duties."

"It's fine," Tess admitted.

"So, what is it? You're obviously in a mood."

She almost denied it, but Noah always could read her. "Your father made it clear that not everyone's thrilled about my return."

Noah's stride faltered. "When did you see my dad?"

"This morning at the hardware store. He said some things about my mother. And me."

Noah sighed, running a hand through his hair.

"That's one thing about my father. He can hold a grudge."

Tess stopped walking. "So, you know about my mother and your father? Because I didn't until this morning."

Noah stared at her. "Not much. Just that they were friends. Well, that's his version, but it doesn't take a rocket scientist to figure out it was more." He shook his head. "Then she dumped him for your father. You really didn't know?"

"No."

With a shrug, he resumed walking. "It's ancient history. Dad shouldn't have taken it out on you."

Tess hurried to catch up. "No argument there."

They reached the boathouse, a weathered structure at the shoreline. Noah unlocked the padlock with a key from his pocket.

"You have a key to my boathouse?"

He gave her a look. "I've been maintaining this lighthouse model for five years, so yes. Morna trusted me with it."

The boathouse interior was surprisingly orderly. Tools hung on pegboards, coils of rope were neatly arranged, and dominating the back wall stood a magnificent five-foot model of the Peregrine Cove Lighthouse, a perfect replica, down to the weather-beaten red and white stripes and the glass-enclosed tower.

"Oh, wow," Tess breathed, moving closer.

Noah's face softened with pride. He flipped a switch, and the lighthouse beam began to rotate, casting small circles of light around the dim boathouse. A moment later, a mournful foghorn sounded.

Tess was stunned. "I don't remember it being so animatronic!"

Noah chuckled. "I just added a rotating light. But people like it—especially kids."

Tess ran her fingers over the miniature keeper's cottage attached to the lighthouse base. "I remember this from when I was little. I played with it like a doll-house. My Barbies saved a few shipwrecks."

Noah stood beside her, close enough that she could feel his warmth. "She told me about that."

Something in his voice made her look up. Their eyes met, and for a moment, she glimpsed the boy she'd known in the man beside her—earnest, kind, with that spark of admiration that had once made her feel like the most important person in his world.

"We need to refresh the paint," he said, breaking the spell. "And check the wiring before the festival. It shouldn't take more than a couple of days."

"No problem," Tess said, surprising herself. Boston suddenly seemed far away, pulled away by the soft lighthouse beam and its unexpected memories.

Noah reached for a paintbrush on a nearby shelf, his arm brushing against hers. The contact, brief as it was, sent a familiar shiver through her. "Red and white." He handed her the brush. "Traditional."

"Some traditions are worth keeping," Tess replied as she accepted the brush.

His smile, quick and genuine, caught her off guard. "Let's get started then."

Tess kneeled beside the model that had somehow become her inheritance—one more thread binding her to a place she thought she'd outgrown.

~

HOURS LATER, Noah checked the electrical components while Tess detailed the miniature windows and doors.

"You're still good at the detail work." Noah studied her steady hand as she traced the outline of a window frame.

"Marketing strategy requires precision," Tess replied with a grin. "Although it's usually digital campaigns, not nautical models."

"Right. The big-city career." There was no judgment in his tone, just curiosity. "Do you like it? Boston?"

Tess paused, brush hovering. The automatic "I love it" seemed hollow. "It's ...busy. There's always a lot going on. Never boring."

"Unlike here."

"I didn't say that."

Noah shrugged, adjusting a wire. "You didn't have to. You left fast enough that last summer."

The old wound surfaced in his voice, though he tried to hide it. Tess set down her brush.

"I told you. That wasn't about Peregrine Cove. Or you." The admission cost her, exposing a vulnerability she hadn't planned to reveal. "My mother packed me off to boarding school. Then college. The internship in Boston. It was ... expected of me."

"And now?" Noah fixed his eyes on her. "What's expected of Tess Bradford now?"

The question disarmed her. What was expected? Success, certainly. Advancement. The right connections, the right address. The trajectory her mother had mapped since pulling her from Peregrine Cove after that last golden summer.

"I'm still figuring that out," she admitted.

Noah nodded, something like understanding passing between them. "Just so you know," he said, returning to the wiring, "I stayed here by choice, not default. The Cove gets in your blood."

Tess was struck by a strange mix of surprise and envy at his certainty, his rootedness. Before she could respond, her phone buzzed. Her boss's name flashed on the screen.

"I should take this." She stepped outside.

THROUGH THE BOATHOUSE WINDOW, Noah watched her pace along the shoreline as the call continued. Even from a distance, he could see the shift in her—shoulders squaring, voice taking on the crisp efficiency he'd heard that first day at the cottage. Boston Tess, the marketing strategist, not the woman who'd just been painting lighthouse windows with unconscious joy.

When she returned, her expression had hardened into something more familiar, the polished professional. "I need to head back. They moved up a deadline."

Noah nodded, wiping his hands on a rag. "The festival's Saturday. We'll need another session or two to finish."

"Tomorrow?" Tess suggested, gathering her things. "Afternoon?"

"I'll be here." He watched her prepare to leave, then asked, "Is everything okay? With work?"

Tess hesitated, then offered a smile that didn't quite

reach her eyes. "Just work being work. Nothing I can't handle."

As she walked away, Noah switched off the light-house beam, plunging the boathouse into shadow. Through the window, he could see her figure growing smaller along the path, caught between two worlds, the one she'd left and the one still calling her back.

CHAPTER 7

Peregrine Cove transformed itself for the annual Chowder Festival, with garlands of wildflowers and strings of lights brightening storefronts. The morning air buzzed with excitement as vendors set up booths along the harbor front, filling the air with the smell of frying dough and fresh seafood mingled with salt air. White tents housing the competing chowder stations lined the boardwalk as chefs stirred enormous pots of their secret recipes.

Tess stood back, admiring the finished lighthouse display in its place of honor at the festival entrance. In their three days of working together, she and Noah had progressed from careful small talk to the easy, familiar rhythm of their old friendship. If more complex feelings simmered beneath the surface, Tess ignored them.

"Not bad for a city girl." Noah appeared beside her with two cups of coffee.

Tess accepted the cup as their fingers brushed in the exchange. "I just followed Aunt Morna's design."

"She'd be proud." Noah's voice was soft, without artifice.

For a moment, a sudden tightness in her throat kept her from speaking.

"We should test the foghorn one more time." Tess reached for a practical task to ground herself.

Noah's eyes, too observant by half, caught her emotion. He nodded, allowing her the escape. "Yeah, let's make sure everything works before the crowd descends."

Together, they crouched behind the display, shoulders brushing as Noah checked connections and Tess held a small flashlight. The physical closeness was both natural and electrifying.

"Hand me that wire cap?" Noah asked, his palm outstretched.

Tess placed it in his hand, trying to ignore how warm his skin was against her fingertips. "Is it supposed to be this complex? It's just a light and a horn."

Noah smiled, the corners of his eyes crinkling in a way that reminded her of late-night beach fires and whispered promises. "Morna's specs. It had to be authentic. Real lighthouse, real mechanisms. Just smaller."

"She never did anything halfway."

"Neither did you." Noah connected the final wire. "I remember that about you."

Tess looked up, surprised. They'd maintained an unspoken agreement to keep conversation firmly in the present, cautiously stepping around their shared past.

"Some things change." Tess tried to deflect.

"And some don't." His gaze held hers for a beat longer than necessary before he flipped the switch.

The lighthouse beam swept across their faces, illuminating the shadows between them. The foghorn sounded, drawing appreciative cheers from early festivalgoers. Noah stood and offered Tess his hand. After a moment's hesitation, she took it and allowed him to pull her to her feet. The casual strength in his hands, calloused and certain, caught her off guard. He held on a fraction longer than necessary, and Tess felt heat climb up her neck.

"Someone wants your attention." Noah nodded toward Gladys Harper as she scurried over to the lighthouse.

"Best lighthouse display in ten years of the Peregrine Cove Chowder Festival!" Gladys announced, pinning a blue ribbon to the base. "And just look at how that beam catches the water. Magnificent! It's the proper festival centerpiece your aunt always wanted."

The crowd that had gathered applauded politely. Tess, uncomfortable with the attention, tried to step back, but Noah's hand found the small of her back and kept her in place.

"Take the compliment," he murmured near her ear. "You earned it."

The warmth of his breath against her skin made her hyperaware of every point of contact between them—his hand on her back, their arms almost touching, the subtle lean of his body toward hers that felt both protective and possessive.

"It was a team effort," she told Gladys, finding her voice.

"The way it should be," the older woman replied with a knowing smile that made Tess wonder what gossip had been circulating about her and Noah.

As the crowd dispersed toward other attractions, several townspeople approached, offering tentative welcomes. Unlike the cool reception at the hardware store, there was genuine warmth in their greetings, as if the lighthouse display had somehow validated her presence and confirmed that she wasn't a complete outsider.

"Mrs. Callahan," Tess recognized the bakery owner, who used to slip her an extra cookie. "It's been a long time."

"Too long." The woman squeezed her hand. "It's so good to see you."

More followed—the postmaster, Tess's former English teacher, and the couple who ran the bookstore. Each greeting chipped away at the invisible barrier Tess had sensed since her return. Noah stayed beside her and occasionally supplied a name she'd forgotten.

"They're warming to you," he said after the initial rush subsided.

Music started up near the harbor gazebo as fiddles, guitars, and a local band set up for the evening festivities.

Noah said, "Want to check out the rest of the festival before the dancing starts?"

Tess hesitated. The sensible choice would be to thank him for his help and retreat to the cottage, to the laptop and the Boston clients awaiting her attention. Instead, she found herself nodding.

"Lead the way, Pierce."

They wandered through the Chowder Festival as twilight descended and sampled competing chowders. Second-guessing the judges' decision, Noah voted for Mr. Flannery's traditional recipe, while Tess preferred a surprising twist with roasted corn and bacon from the new chef at the harbor restaurant. They lingered over fried clams and blueberry tarts, then stopped to admire a maritime craft display and watch the children's games. Noah seemed to know everyone as he exchanged greetings and introduced Tess with a casual, "You remember Tess Bradford," that somehow bridged the fifteen-year gap.

What surprised her most was how easily they fell into old patterns, growing more natural together with each passing hour. The Noah beside her was both familiar and new, the boy she'd known overlaid with a man shaped by years she'd missed out on.

"Still have a sweet tooth?" he asked, nodding toward a candy apple stand.

Tess laughed. "You remember?"

"How could I forget? You used to hide Aunt Morna's caramels in your pocket during summer picnics." His smile was teasing. "You thought you were so slick."

"She always knew."

"Of course she did." Noah purchased two candy apples, handing one to Tess. "She didn't miss much."

Their fingers brushed in the exchange, and Tess was struck by how many times they'd touched today— small, seemingly incidental contacts that left her skin tingling. She bit into the apple to hide her reaction, the sweet crunch grounding her.

"She had to have known this cottage situation wouldn't be easy for me."

Noah thought for a moment. "Morna wanted you to find your place, whether that's here or in Boston."

"And what does Noah Pierce think?"

His eyes met hers, startlingly direct. "I think you belong wherever you feel most alive."

The simplicity of it caught her off guard. There was no pressure, no judgment, just a truth offered without expectation.

As darkness fell, the festival lights came on, strings of bulbs crisscrossing overhead, casting a golden glow over the harbor front. Their lighthouse beam swept back and forth over the water.

As the band shifted to a slower tune, couples gravitated toward the makeshift dance floor near the gazebo. Noah watched them for a moment and then turned to Tess.

"Dance with me?" he asked, setting aside his half-eaten apple.

Fifteen years ago, at their high school dance, he'd asked the same question with teenage nervousness. But now, the invitation came with the quiet confidence of a man who knew what he wanted.

"People will talk," Tess said, even as she moved toward him.

"They're already talking." Noah placed his hand on her waist.

The first touch was electric, his hand warm through the thin fabric of her dress, her palm against the solid wall of his shoulder. They stood frozen for a heartbeat, absorbing the shock of contact before muscle memory took over, and they began to sway.

"It's been a while," Tess murmured, hyper-aware of the inches between their bodies.

"Like riding a bike." Noah's voice was low and intimate. "Some things you don't forget."

The music wrapped around them as Noah's hand

splayed wider on her back, drawing her closer. Tess could smell him now—salt air, soap, and him—a scent she'd never quite forgotten.

"You've gotten better at this." Tess fought to keep her voice steady as they moved together. "No bruised toes. Yet."

His laugh rumbled through his chest, so close to hers. "I've had some practice."

"With whom?" The question slipped out before she could stop it.

Noah's eyes caught hers with a flicker of amusement and warmth. "Jealous, Bradford?"

"Curious," she corrected, feeling the heat rise to her cheeks.

"Festival dances. Community events." His thumb traced a small circle against her back, sending shivers along her spine. "Nothing serious."

The implication hung between them. Unlike us.

The song changed to one with a slower tempo. Around them, other couples drew closer. Noah's hand tightened on her waist, a question in the pressure. Tess answered by closing the space between them.

Their bodies aligned—his chest against hers, her head fitting perfectly beneath his chin as if the years apart had been nothing but a momentary separation. Noah's breath hitched, the only sign that he felt the same magnetic pull she did.

"This feels …" Tess began, unable to find words adequate for the sensation of rightness and danger twined together.

"I know," Noah murmured into her hair.

Her hand slid to his neck while his arm wrapped more fully around her waist. The festival, the watching eyes, and the complications that waited all receded. There was only the music and the heat between them.

"Tess." Noah's voice was quiet and rough. "When you leave—"

"Not now," she interrupted, not wanting reality to intrude. "Just ... dance with me."

He nodded and pulled her impossibly closer. Tess closed her eyes and gave in to the sensation. The current that had always run between them may have been dormant for years, but it had never been extinguished.

The song was coming to a close when Noah tensed. Tess opened her eyes to find Rob Pierce standing at the edge of the dance floor, watching them with an expression that turned her blood cold.

Noah saw him, too. "Dad—"

Rob's voice cut across the remaining music. "I need a word, son." His eyes flicked to Tess, then away with unmistakable disapproval. "About the boat. Engine trouble."

The spell shattered. Noah's arms loosened, though he didn't step away entirely. "Can't it wait?"

"I'm afraid not." Rob's tone left no room for argument. His pointed glance at Tess was a warning Tess felt in her bones.

"Go on." She stepped back from Noah's embrace. "It's okay."

Noah hesitated, looking torn. "I'll be right back."

"Take your time. I should head back to the cottage, anyway. Early start tomorrow." The excuse sounded hollow even to her.

"Tess—"

"It's fine, Noah. Really." She managed a smile. "Thank you for today. For everything."

Before he could respond, she turned away, moving through the crowd with practiced ease, intent on making a graceful exit. Behind her, she heard Rob's voice, too low to make out the words but urgent enough to know they weren't just talking about boat engines.

The festival lights blurred as she walked faster, away from the music, away from the dance that had meant too much. Her body still hummed with the memory of Noah's touch and the way they'd fit together. Dangerous thoughts for a woman planning to leave.

From the harbor edge, Tess looked back. The light-house model's beam swept steadily across the water, a rhythm unchanged by the turbulence beneath her ribs. Their creation stood strong and beautiful, a testament to what they could build together. If only it weren't temporary, like everything else in Peregrine Cove.

Noah found her halfway up the beach path that led to Aunt Morna's cottage.

"Tess, wait." His longer strides closed the distance between them. "We can't just leave things like this."

She turned, arms crossed protectively over her chest. "I think your father's the one who did that. Let me guess. There's no boat trouble, just me."

Noah raked a hand through his hair and admitted, "He's concerned I'll repeat past mistakes."

"And I'm the mistake?" The question was direct, unavoidable.

"In his eyes? Yes." Noah stepped closer, his features shadowed in the moonlight. "In mine? Never."

"Your father's a hard man to ignore."

"He means well. He's just ... He thinks you'll leave again, leaving me here." His eyes searched hers. "Maybe he's right."

"I never meant to hurt you." The thought opened a wound. "Back then, I didn't have a choice."

"But now we do." Noah sighed. "Dad's cautious, with good reason. But he doesn't get to decide this for me."

"Decide what?"

Noah's gaze was steady, unflinching. "How I feel about you. Then or now."

The words demanded a response. They were at a precipice, and Tess was terrified she would fall. "I have to leave sooner or later," she said, clinging to practicality like a lifeline.

"I know." Noah nodded, accepting what she couldn't bring herself to confirm. "But right now, you're here."

He stepped closer, moonlight catching the angles of his face. "With me."

Her heart hammered against her ribs as he reached for her hand, his touch achingly gentle, as he slipped his hand around hers.

"Walk me home?" she asked, her voice barely above a whisper.

Noah's smile was slow, a hint of the boy she'd once loved mixing with the man who now stood before her.

They walked in silence, hands joined, the only sound the rhythm of waves and their matched footsteps on the path. No words seemed adequate for the current flowing between them, too strong to deny yet too complicated to embrace.

At the cottage door, Tess turned to face him, their

hands still linked. "Thank you for today. The lighthouse was perfect."

"We make a good team." Noah's voice was soft as his thumb traced circles on her palm.

"We always did."

The admission lingered in the cool night air. Noah's gaze dropped to her lips, a question in his eyes that made her pulse skip. For one breathless moment, Tess thought he might kiss her. She wanted him to, with an intensity that frightened her.

Instead, he lifted their joined hands and pressed his lips to her knuckles in a gesture that was old-fashioned and unexpectedly intimate.

"Goodnight, Tess." He released her hand slowly, fingers trailing against hers. "Sweet dreams."

As he walked away, Tess stood frozen on the porch, her skin burning where his lips had touched. The night's festival sounds wrapped around her and drifted across the cove on the breeze, along with the steady sweep of the lighthouse beam.

Inside, her laptop waited with Boston emails and deadlines, the Harrington campaign pitch due Monday, and three client calls scheduled before noon. They were reminders of a life she could not keep ignoring, a life she had built with such careful precision.

Outside, Noah's retreating figure walked a path she'd abandoned. With no warning, it beckoned again. Life here would be messy and less certain, and yet it promised a future more vivid and real than the filtered Instagram version she'd constructed in Boston.

CHAPTER 8

Tess stood back from the window frame, brush in hand, satisfaction warming her chest as she examined her work. The old casement gleamed with fresh white paint. She'd never considered herself particularly handy, but after three days of painting the exterior trim on the cottage, she'd discovered a quiet pride in these tangible accomplishments.

"Not bad for a marketing executive," she murmured to herself, dipping her brush back into the paint can.

"You missed a spot."

She turned to find Noah leaning against the doorframe with his arms crossed over his chest and the hint of a smile playing at the corners of his mouth. The late July sun slanted through the windows and cast a glow on his profile, an unexpected reminder of summers long past.

"Where?" She turned back to the window, squinting.

"I'm kidding." He pushed off from the doorway and crossed to her side. "It's perfect."

The compliment filled Tess with a ridiculous flush of pleasure. "I'm ready to go pro."

"I'd hire you." Noah's voice was endearingly warm.

"Thanks." She capped the paint and set down her brush. "But I've still got a day gig."

"Which is what, exactly?" Noah asked, genuinely curious. "I know you're in marketing, but what does that actually mean?"

Tess almost leaned against the freshly painted windowsill but caught herself. "I help companies tell their stories. Figure out what makes them special, then translate that into something that resonates with people."

"Like ... advertising?"

"Sometimes. But it's more about creating desire for things people don't know they need yet." She smiled. "Making the ordinary seem extraordinary."

Noah looked thoughtful. "So that's what you did with Boston? Made it seem extraordinary to justify staying away?"

The question hit with unexpected force, like stepping on a loose board she hadn't seen coming. It wasn't accusatory. That would have been easier to deflect. Instead, there was a genuine curiosity that demanded honesty.

"I—" She started, then stopped, caught between defensiveness and a truth she hadn't completely examined. "Maybe. Or maybe I was just trying to outrun my mother's expectations."

"You mean nagging?" The thought held more truth than she cared to admit. Noah's expression softened. "Sorry. That was harsh."

Tess shook her head to dismiss it. He was no

harsher than her mother, who used to call him that annoying boy down the street.

"Come on," he said after a moment. "We've been at this all day. Let's get some air."

They walked in comfortable silence along the harbor path as the late afternoon sun warmed the weathered planks underfoot. Fishing boats bobbed in their slips, their day's work complete, while gulls wheeled overhead in lazy circles.

Tess said, "What made you stay in the Cove?"

Noah's stride didn't falter, but she sensed a change in his mood. "You mean instead of leaving like everyone expected?"

"I just ... I remember you talking about architecture programs, maybe Boston or New York."

He smiled faintly. "Dreams change. Or maybe they just get more realistic." He gestured toward the harbor. "I found I liked fishing with my father, but I loved working with my hands. I started apprenticing with my grandfather in his wood shop after school. By the time he passed away, I had enough skill to take over his clients. Turns out there's always work for someone who can build things properly."

"You're good at it." Tess thought of the craftsmanship she'd seen in his repairs around the cottage.

"I like building things that last," he admitted. "Things that still mean something years later." Unlike relationships. The implication was unspoken, but clear.

They reached Lucy's Café just as the dinner crowd was beginning to gather. Lucy waved them to a corner table, bringing coffee without being asked.

"You two making progress on that cottage?" she asked, setting down thick white mugs.

"Getting there," Tess replied. "The windows are almost finished."

Lucy nodded approvingly. "Well, it's good to see. That place hasn't looked that good since the feud."

As Lucy scurried away to refill coffees, Tess turned to Noah. "The feud?"

Noah looked surprised. "Your mom and Morna. They never told you?"

"No. Mom never talked about Peregrine Cove. It was like it never happened."

Noah's laugh held little humor. "That sounds about right. And I guess Morna didn't want to speak ill of your mother."

Tess imagined he was right. Lucy returned with a pot to refill their cups, catching the tail end of the conversation. "Discussing ancient history, are we?"

"Apparently not ancient enough," Noah replied. "Tess didn't know about the Bradford sisters' famous feud. Care to fill her in?"

Lucy glanced around, then pulled up a chair. "It wasn't just that Elizabeth left Rob for your father," she said to Tess, her voice lowered. "Although that was some drama. It's that Morna took Rob's side."

"She chose sides?" Tess asked, trying to reconcile this with her memories of her even-tempered aunt.

"Before Elizabeth left, they had words, or Elizabeth did, words that couldn't be unsaid. Morna was hurt," Lucy clarified. "Rob was devastated, and Morna got that." Lucy's weathered hand covered Tess's briefly. "The rift never did heal, although after you were born, Morna tried, for your sake."

That revelation settled in as Tess tried to imagine how much of her own life had been shaped by this hidden history. She'd spent years defining herself in opposition to her mother, Elizabeth's restlessness, versus her own painstakingly constructed stability. But what if she had more in common with Morna than she realized? The thought was both comforting and terrifying.

"Did my mother forbid Aunt Morna from contacting me after we left?" Tess asked, fragments of memory rearranging themselves.

Lucy and Noah exchanged glances.

"Not exactly," Lucy hedged.

"Not officially," Noah added, "but effectively."

The confirmation landed like a physical blow. "So, all those years when I thought Aunt Morna had lost interest in me ..."

"She wrote to you," Noah said. "Birthday cards, Christmas. She'd ask me about schools in Boston, trying to understand your world from a distance."

"I never got them." Tess's voice sounded hollow to her own ears.

"Elizabeth was ... protective of her new life," Lucy said diplomatically.

Protective? Tess thought bitterly. *Or possessive?*

They finished their coffee in contemplative silence, the weight of the past settling around them like evening fog rolling in from the harbor. As they walked back toward the cottage, the sky deepening to purple above them, Tess began to see Peregrine Cove, and her place in it, through new eyes.

"Noah," she said as they reached the cottage drive, "why did you really stay after the funeral? You could have just had a realtor handle the property until I figured out what to do with it."

He paused, hands in his pockets, face half-lit by the porch light. For a moment, she thought he might deflect, but then his shoulders relaxed with an exhaled breath. "Because Morna asked me to. She knew you'd come back eventually, and she wanted ...she hoped ..."

"That I'd stay," Tess finished for him.

"That you'd at least have the choice she thought your mother took from you." Noah looked out toward the darkening water, then back to her. "But it's still your choice, Tess. Whatever you decide about the cottage, about Peregrine Cove, it should be because it's what you want, not what anyone else wanted for you."

The statement held an unexpected generosity, acknowledging her agency in a way few others had. She studied him in the gathering darkness, this man who'd once been the center of her world, then a painful memory, and now, he was more.

"Thank you," she said softly.

His smile was gentle and genuine. "Good night, Tess."

As Noah walked to his truck, the familiarity of his gait stirred something both old and new inside her. As she turned to enter the cottage, no longer just Aunt Morna's but slowly becoming hers, Tess realized that Noah's fear might not be that she would leave again. His deeper fear was that he would be left behind, just as his father had been, watching someone choose a different life, a different future.

And her own fear? It wasn't just about being trapped in Peregrine Cove. It was the terrifying possibility that she might discover she belonged here. She'd always belonged here and had spent years running from the very place that could have been home.

CHAPTER 9

Tess's phone vibrated against the kitchen table, her mother's name flashing on the screen. She hesitated, her finger poised over the green icon. Three rings in, she answered.

"Hello, Mother."

"Tess, darling. How's the coastal adventure?" Elizabeth's voice carried that familiar lilt, the one that always made everything sound like a performance.

Tess tucked her feet beneath her on the worn kitchen chair. "It's going well. I've made great progress with the cottage renovations."

"Renovations?" The word dripped with disdain. "I thought you were just fixing it up to sell."

"That was the original plan, but—"

"But you're considering staying." It wasn't a question.

Tess twisted a loose strand of hair around her finger, a nervous habit she'd had since childhood. "I'm keeping my options open."

A silence stretched between them, filled only by the

distant sound of Elizabeth's long, measured exhale. Tess could almost see her releasing cigarette smoke in perfect rings, a party trick she'd perfected decades ago.

"You sound different," Elizabeth said. "More like your aunt every day."

The comparison sent a conflicting rush through Tess's body, pride and panic in equal measure. "Is that such a bad thing? Aunt Morna was incredible."

"Incredible at sacrificing herself for that town and that cottage of hers, all for a family legacy nobody cared about." Elizabeth's voice sharpened. "She could have been anything, gone anywhere."

"She chose to stay."

"Did she? Or did she just fall into the role everyone expected? The dutiful Bradford woman, keeper of traditions."

Tess's gaze drifted to the window, where she could just make out Noah in the garden, examining the stone wall that needed repair. His sleeves were rolled up, exposing tanned forearms as he tested each stone. Even in this simple task, his reverence for the property was evident.

"I'm not falling into anything, Mother. I'm making my own decisions."

Elizabeth laughed, the sound brittle. "My darling, you've spent your entire life running from permanence. Now, suddenly, you're considering roots in the same soil that trapped generations of Bradford women. Ask yourself why."

"I'm not trapped."

"Maybe not yet." Elizabeth paused. "Do you know what your grandfather once told me? 'Pierce men trap you with their devotion. What they call roots, I call chains.' He was right."

"Noah isn't—" Tess caught herself, realizing she'd just inadvertently revealed more than she'd intended.

"Noah?" Her mother's voice turned silky with interest. "Oh, Tess. History really does love to repeat itself."

"It's not what you think."

"It never is until suddenly it's exactly what everyone but you saw coming." Elizabeth sighed dramatically. "Just promise me you'll remember you have choices, Tess. That cottage isn't your destiny unless you allow it to be."

"What are you so afraid of, Mother?"

Elizabeth paused. "That you'll make the same mistake I almost did—choosing safety over the unknown. But the truth is, I was just scared to keep looking for what I really wanted."

And how did that work out for you? Tess bit her tongue.

By the time she ended the call, her hands were trembling. She placed her phone face down on the table and pressed her palms against her eyes. Her breath came in short gasps, each one shallower than the last, as she tried to push back the familiar tightness in her chest.

Not now, she silently pleaded with her body. *Not a panic attack now.*

She forced herself to stand, to move to the sink, to fill a glass with water. The cool liquid slid down her throat as she attempted to regulate her breathing. In for four counts, hold for seven, out for eight, a technique her therapist had taught her years ago when the attacks first started.

The question rattled around her mind with merciless precision: Was staying her choice, or was she falling into patterns set long before she was born?

The back door creaked open, and Noah stepped inside, bringing with him the scent of earth and sea air.

"That wall's going to need more work than I thought." Noah washed his hands at the sink. When he turned, water dripping from his fingertips as he reached for a towel, his expression shifted. "Tess? What's wrong?"

She shook her head, not trusting her voice.

Noah crossed the kitchen in two strides, reaching for her but stopping short of actually touching her. "Is it something I can help with?"

The genuine concern in his eyes made the tightness in her chest worse. This was exactly what her mother had warned about—the unwavering devotion that could so easily become a beautiful prison.

"Just a call from my mother," she managed. "She has a gift for getting under my skin."

Noah nodded, understanding without pushing. "Parents have that superpower." He leaned against the counter, giving her space, and changed the subject. "I've been thinking about the kitchen renovation. We should keep Morna's cabinets."

Tess's head snapped up. "What?"

"The cabinets. They're original to the house, handcrafted pine from the 1930s. We can refinish them, maybe replace the hardware, but keeping them would preserve a piece of the cottage's history."

Just like that, the panic that had been receding surged back with renewed force. "No!"

Noah blinked in surprise at her vehemence. "No?"

"I love the memories here, but I want something more functional." Tess gestured around the kitchen. "These cabinets are impractical. They're too deep, the shelves are fixed, and they don't utilize the space efficiently."

"But they have character. History."

"History isn't always worth preserving," she snapped, her mother's words echoing in her mind.

Noah stiffened. "This isn't just any old house, Tess. This cottage has been in your family for generations. Each piece tells a story."

"Maybe I want to write my own story!" The words burst from her with unexpected force. "Maybe I don't want to be confined by decisions made decades ago by people I never even met."

A flush crept up Noah's neck. "No one's confining you. I'm just suggesting we honor the craftsmanship and intention that went into this place."

"By keeping everything just like it's always been?" Tess threw her hands up. "That's not renovation, Noah. That's preservation. And I'm not a museum curator."

"There's value in preservation—"

"There's also value in progress! In change!" The conversation spiraled away from cabinets into territory far more personal. "Just because something is old doesn't automatically make it worth keeping."

Noah's eyes darkened. "And just because something requires commitment doesn't mean you should run from it."

The accusation was too direct to ignore.

"Is that what you think I'm doing? Running?"

Noah ran a hand through his hair, frustration evident in every line of his body. "I think you've spent your whole life with one foot out the door. Maybe the problem isn't the cabinets. Maybe it's the fact that committing to anything, even a design choice, feels too permanent for you."

Each word struck with brutal accuracy, as if he'd peeled back her protective facade and found the truth she'd been hiding even from herself.

"You don't know that."

"I know you better than you think." His voice softened dangerously. "I've watched you these past several days. You love this place. I can see it in the way you trace the woodwork, how you sit in Morna's reading nook, how you breathe deeper here than you do anywhere else. But you're terrified of admitting it because then you'd have to face what that means."

"And what exactly does it mean since you've got me all figured out?" Tess could hear the defensive edge in her voice but couldn't seem to soften it.

"It means you might belong somewhere, that you might be part of something bigger than just yourself. And that scares the hell out of you."

Tears threatened, hot and unwelcome. "You have no right—"

"You're just looking for excuses to justify leaving again."

"And you've got abandonment issues." The words exploded from her, raw and unfiltered.

They both froze, the accusation too revealing to be about her aunt. This was about Tess's mother, the woman who'd walked away from Peregrine Cove and torn Tess away with her. As painful as that memory was for her, bringing up Noah's loss of his mother was beneath her.

In the sudden silence, Tess could see it all with painful clarity. They were both acting out old scripts. His fear of abandonment was making him cling too tightly to traditions, while her fear of confinement made her resist anything permanent.

Their eyes locked across the kitchen, the air between them charged with understanding and a heat that had nothing to do with anger. Noah took a step toward her, and Tess moved to meet him, drawn by something stronger than her instinct to retreat.

They were inches apart when a sharp knock at the front door shattered the moment.

"That'll be the inspector," Noah said, his voice rough. "I called him to check the foundation before we go any further."

"Right. The inspector." Tess smoothed her hair, grateful for the interruption even as part of her wondered what might have happened. "I'll get it."

The next hour passed in a blur of technical terms and careful examinations. The inspector, a jovial man with weathered hands and endless stories about local buildings, seemed oblivious to the tension between them. By the time he left with promises to email his official report, the emotional intensity had receded, leaving in its wake an awkward awareness.

Noah lingered on the porch steps after the inspector's truck disappeared down the lane. The late afternoon sun cast long shadows across the garden, turning the ordinary scene into something from an impressionist painting, all soft edges and golden light.

"I'm sorry." He remained facing away from her. "That was unfair. I shouldn't have made it personal."

Tess leaned against the porch railing. "It's always been personal, hasn't it? This cottage, the renovations. It's never just been about fixing a house."

He turned to look at her with an expression that was open in a way that made her heart constrict. "No, it hasn't."

"I don't want to keep the cabinets," she said quietly.

Noah nodded, accepting. "Okay."

"But," she continued, "I've been thinking about using some of the wood from them to create a new kitchen island. Something that bridges old and new."

His eyes widened, hope replacing resignation. "You'd do that?"

"It seems like a reasonable compromise." Tess shrugged, trying to appear casual despite the significance of what she was offering. "We can honor the past while still creating something new. The island could incorporate some of the original detailing, maybe even Aunt Morna's carved initials from the pantry door."

"We can honor what has been without being trapped by it." Noah's words carried weight beyond their discussion of kitchen renovations.

The simple sentence cut through her defenses, offering a perspective she hadn't considered—that acknowledging the past didn't necessarily mean surrendering to it.

"I might be able to sketch some ideas," he offered. "Find a way to blend the traditional elements with more modern functionality."

Something unfurled inside Tess as if a tightly wound fear was beginning to loosen. "I'd like that."

A comfortable silence settled between them as the sun dipped lower, painting the sky in streaks of pink and gold. At that moment, Tess realized she'd been seeing permanence all wrong—not as chains binding her to one spot, but as roots giving her the stability to grow. "My mother called today. She said I'm becoming more like Aunt Morna every day."

Noah studied her. "Is that what triggered all this?"

Tess nodded. "She meant it as a warning. To her, Aunt Morna's life was a cautionary tale about a woman who sacrificed her potential for tradition."

"And what do you think?"

She considered the question, really considered it. "I'm not sure anymore. Growing up, I saw Aunt Morna's life through my mother's lens, limited and resigned. But being here, I've started to wonder if maybe it was something else entirely."

"Like what?"

"Like purpose. Connection." Tess gazed out at the cottage grounds, at the garden Aunt Morna had tended, at the stone walls built by hands long gone. "Maybe staying wasn't her sacrifice. Maybe it was her choice."

Noah moved closer, his shoulder nearly touching hers. "And what about you? What would staying mean to you?"

It was the question she'd been avoiding since she first arrived, the one that lurked beneath every decision about the cottage renovations. Not just whether to stay or go, but what each choice said about who she was and who she wanted to become.

"I don't know yet," she answered honestly. "But I'm starting to think I might want to find out."

Noah's hand found hers on the railing, his touch

tentative, offering connection without demand. "I happen to think you'd make a hell of a Peregrine Cove resident. You've got the stubbornness for it."

Tess laughed despite herself as she gave his hand a brief squeeze before letting go. "I'm not stubborn. I'm determined."

"Semantics." He grinned, but his eyes remained serious. "Whatever you decide about the cottage, about staying, make sure it's what you want, not what you think Morna would want or what your mother fears. This is your legacy to shape, not theirs."

As twilight deepened around them, Tess let his words sink in. Legacy wasn't just what was handed down to you, but what you chose to carry forward. Perhaps the true inheritance Aunt Morna had left wasn't the cottage itself, but the freedom to make it and her life entirely her own.

"Kitchen island sketches tomorrow?" she asked, ready to take one small step toward something that felt surprisingly like home.

Noah smiled, the last rays of sunlight catching in his eyes. "It's a date."

And for once, the word "date" didn't make Tess want to run. Instead, she found herself looking forward to tomorrow, the next day, and maybe all the days after that.

CHAPTER 10

"All clear!" Noah's voice rang out with genuine excitement as he waved the inspection report. "Foundation's solid as a rock. A few minor issues to address, but nothing structural."

Tess took the papers, scanning the official letterhead with relief. "That's great news."

"This calls for a celebration." Noah's eyes held a glint of mischief that made her pulse quicken. "Pack a light jacket and some sunscreen. I'm taking you sailing."

Tess glanced up from the report. "Sailing? It's been so long, I think I've forgotten how."

He leveled a wry look. "It's like riding a bike." He checked his watch. "The tide will be ideal in about an hour. I'll grab some provisions from home and meet you at the marina. Slip seventeen."

Before she could protest, he was out the door, leaving Tess standing in the cottage's entryway, the inspection report still in her hands.

Sailing. The word itself conjured images of freedom, of movement without roots or foundations.

Perhaps that was what she needed after days of weighing every decision against generations of history.

An hour later, Tess made her way down the weathered wooden dock, counting slip numbers as she went. The marina was quieter than she'd expected, with only a handful of people preparing their vessels or returning from morning excursions. The salt-laden breeze played with her hair as she spotted Noah loading a cooler onto the sleek sailboat, modest in size but impeccably maintained.

"There she is," he called, straightening as Tess approached. "What do you think of the *Mary Eleanor*?"

Tess took in the boat's clean lines, the polished wood trim contrasting against the white hull, and the neatly furled sails waiting to be released. "She's beautiful."

Noah ran his hand along the boat's edge with unmistakable affection. "Twenty-seven feet of pure joy. Not the biggest girl in the harbor, but she handles like a dream."

"Mary Eleanor," Tess read the name, his mother's name, painted in elegant navy script on the stern.

Noah's expression shifted from a momentary vulnerability to a quick smile. "She loved the water."

The simple statement held volumes beneath it. Tess wanted to ask more but sensed it wasn't the moment. Instead, she accepted Noah's outstretched hand and stepped onto the boat, feeling it adjust to her weight beneath her feet.

"First rule of sailing: Respect the sea." Noah handed her a life vest. "She gives incredible freedom, but she demands caution in return."

Tess slipped the vest on, watching as Noah moved

around the boat with practiced efficiency, checking lines and equipment. His movements were fluid and confident, a stark contrast to the hesitation he sometimes displayed at the cottage when discussing changes to Aunt Morna's home.

"Ready to cast off?" He looked at her, and something in his gaze made her feel as though they were embarking on far more than a simple afternoon sail.

"Ready as I'll ever be."

With Noah's patient instruction, Tess helped release the lines and secure them to the dock. The engine hummed to life, a gentle vibration beneath their feet as they eased away from the marina. The coastline of Peregrine Cove transformed from their new perspective, with its collection of weathered buildings, the rise of green hills behind, and the white speck that was Aunt Morna's cottage on its bluff.

"It looks different from out here," Tess said. "Smaller, somehow."

Noah nodded, guiding the boat through the harbor. "That's the gift of sailing—perspective. Problems that seem enormous on land have a way of shrinking when viewed from the water."

Once they cleared the harbor, Noah cut the engine. "Now comes the magic. Ready to raise the mainsail?"

What followed was a dance of instruction and movement. Noah positioned himself behind Tess, his arms reaching around to guide her hands to the correct lines, his voice close to her ear as he reminded her of each step. The physical proximity sent waves of awareness through her body, but there was something else too, a trust building between them as the sail rose and caught the wind with a satisfying thump.

The boat heeled slightly, responding to the wind's embrace. Tess gasped, instinctively grabbing Noah's arm.

"It's okay," he assured her, his hand covering hers briefly. "She's just finding her balance."

And indeed, Tess could feel it, the initial tilt giving way to a new equilibrium as the *Mary Eleanor* found her stride, cutting through the water with growing momentum. The sensation was exhilarating.

"Now the jib," Noah instructed, moving toward the front of the boat. Together, they unfurled the smaller sail, and as it filled with wind, the boat surged forward with renewed purpose.

The transformation in Noah was remarkable. On land, he often carried a weight about him—the responsibilities of the town, the pull of history and tradition. Here on the water, years seemed to fall away. His smile came easier, his laughter more readily. He moved with the boat as if they were in sync, anticipating each shift in the wind before it arrived.

As they sailed parallel to the coastline, Noah pointed out landmarks and shared stories about each cove and inlet. His knowledge wasn't just that of a local; it was intimate and personal, filled with the understanding of someone who had explored every hidden corner of this stretch of coast.

"Over there." He pointed to a small sandy beach nestled between rocky outcroppings. "That's where I found a message in a bottle when I was nine. I was convinced it was from a shipwrecked sailor, but it turned out to be from a fourth grader in New Jersey doing a science project on ocean currents."

Tess laughed. "What a disappointment."

"Actually, we became pen pals for a while. The old-fashioned kind, with actual letters and stamps."

"Of course you did." That was so Noah to find connection even in the most unexpected circumstances.

The afternoon unfolded in a rhythm dictated by wind and water. Noah taught her the basics of tacking, how to read the wind on the water's surface, and the names of each line and sail. With each new skill mastered, Tess grew more confident, not just at handling the boat, but in their partnership navigating it together.

When they were far enough from shore that Peregrine Cove was just a distant outline, Noah dropped anchor in a protected cove. The boat settled into a gentle rocking as he retrieved the cooler he'd brought aboard.

"Lunch," he announced, producing sandwiches wrapped in wax paper, a container of fresh berries, and two bottles of local craft beer. "Nothing fancy, but everything tastes better on the water."

They ate, sitting side by side on the cushioned bench, their shoulders occasionally brushing as the boat swayed. The isolation created an intimacy that they'd never experienced in town, where every interaction seemed scrutinized and weighed down with history and expectation.

"Does your dad take this out anymore?" Tess asked, nodding toward the boat beneath them.

Noah's expression softened. "No. About a year after my mother died, he gave it to me as a graduation present. He never said it, but this boat was their thing, and he couldn't bear to sail anymore." He took a swig of his beer. "Anyway, I was twenty-two, just finished college. It needed some work. Dad hadn't sailed it since Mom died, so I welcomed the project." His eyes fixed on the horizon. "I used to dream about traveling after graduation, maybe see the world before settling back in Peregrine Cove. But then Mom got sick, and everything changed."

Tess waited, sensing he had more to say.

"Pancreatic cancer. By the time they caught it, there wasn't much they could do." His voice remained steady, but Tess could see the cost of that control. "Six months from diagnosis to the end. I stayed home that last year of college, commuting to classes when I could, but mostly just being with her."

"I'm so sorry, Noah." The words seemed inadequate against such loss.

He nodded in acknowledgment. "After she was gone, the thought of leaving seemed ... impossible. Dad was a wreck. The fishing business needed running, and I just couldn't imagine walking away from everything she'd loved." He gestured toward the boat. "So, I stayed. I could stay rooted in Peregrine Cove, but still find freedom when I needed it."

The revelation revealed so much about Noah—his dedication to the town, his resistance to change, and the careful balance he maintained between duty and desire.

"That's why the cottage renovations are so important to you," Tess realized aloud. "It's not just about preserving history. It's about protecting what's left of your world before everything changed."

Noah looked at her with startled recognition. "I never thought of it that way, but ... yeah. After Mom died, I became terrified of change. Everything good in my life has been taken without warning. Keeping things the same became a way of feeling safe. And Morna ... she was like a second mother to me."

The honesty between them made Tess want to offer the truth in return.

"I grew up with a purpose—my mother's," she said quietly. "Every minute of every day was scheduled, whether I was at boarding school or at home on vacation. I didn't think anything of it because all of my friends were the same. They told us we were lucky to have so many opportunities. Of course, the underlying point was to overachieve. It never occurred to me that the adults all just wanted us out of their hair."

"Wow." Noah's eyebrows rose. "So the Cove must have been—"

"Another world? Yes." Tess smiled at the observation. "A world I didn't fully appreciate until I'd lost it."

"So that explains how you've structured your life."

Tess shot him a look of surprise. Was that how he saw her—as over-scheduled and unaware of what truly mattered in life as she was as a child?

Noah hastened to add, "I'm sorry. Did I say something ..."

"No ... Well, yes. I hadn't connected those dots before, but you might have a point. I guess I've lived my life the way I was prepared to." She let out a bitter chuckle. "They don't call it prep school for nothing." She traced a finger along the boat's railing. "The irony is that I've unwittingly lived my mother's dreams for me. I stay busy, keep my life uncluttered by personal ... distractions." She tossed a self-deprecating look at Noah. "You should see my apartment. It takes minimalism to a whole new level."

"So Morna's cottage must be a huge change."

Tess nodded. "Yeah." She tamped down unexpected melancholy. "Because it feels like home." She looked out at the vast expanse of ocean surrounding them. "What scares me most isn't being trapped in Peregrine Cove; it's discovering I belong there, then having it ripped away somehow. If I never fully commit, I can't fully lose, right?"

The confession was more revealing than she'd intended, yet somehow exactly what needed to be said. Noah's hand found hers on the bench between them, his calloused fingers warm against her skin.

"Some things are worth the risk," he said softly.

Their eyes met, and at that moment, there was no denying the current between them. Noah leaned closer. His gaze dropped to her lips, and Tess met him halfway, drawn by something stronger than her practiced caution.

A sudden gust of wind rocked the boat, the boom swinging slightly with a creak of protest. The moment shattered as both instinctively reached to secure loose items, their bodies shifting from intimacy to practicality in an instant.

"We should head back." Noah's voice sounded rougher than before. "The wind's picking up, and I promised you a sunset view from Peregrine Point."

The sail back was quieter, a new awareness humming between them as they worked together to navigate the strengthening breeze. Tess watched Noah's hands on the tiller, remembering their warmth against her own, and wondering what might have happened if the wind hadn't interrupted.

True to his word, Noah brought them to a perfect

vantage point as the sun began its descent. He dropped anchor once more, and they sat side by side, watching as the sky transformed into a canvas of impossible colors, deep oranges and pinks reflecting on the water's surface, turning everything to gold.

"Worth the trip?" Noah asked, his shoulder pressed against hers.

"Absolutely." Tess couldn't remember the last time they'd been so connected, so attuned to a single moment. "Thank you for bringing me out here."

"Thank you for trusting me enough to come." His voice was sincere, almost solemn in its gratitude.

As darkness fell, they reluctantly raised anchor and made their way back to the harbor, the boat's navigation lights creating a small pool of illumination in the growing night. They worked in companionable silence, each anticipating the other's needs as they prepared to dock.

Back at slip seventeen, Noah secured the *Mary Eleanor* with practiced efficiency. He helped Tess onto the dock, their hands lingering together a moment longer than necessary. The marina was quiet now. Most sailors had long since returned to shore, leaving them in a pocket of privacy beneath the first emerging stars.

"I had a wonderful time." Tess was suddenly shy in a way she hadn't been all afternoon.

Noah stood before her, his expression unreadable. He seemed on the verge of speaking, hesitating before finding his words.

"I don't just want the cottage to stay the same, Tess." His voice was low, meant only for her. "I want something to finally change for the better."

The implications of the admission were unmistakable. Before Tess could respond, Noah leaned forward and placed a gentle kiss on her cheek, his lips warm against her wind-cooled skin.

"Goodnight," he said softly, then turned and walked away down the dock, leaving Tess watching his retreating figure with her heart racing and her certainties unraveling.

Standing alone beneath the vast night sky, surrounded by boats straining gently against their moorings, Tess faced the truth she'd been avoiding since arriving in Peregrine Cove. What scared her wasn't the prospect of being trapped here; it was discovering she belonged here and always had, that the restlessness she'd inherited from her mother had been leading her in circles when her destination had been waiting all along.

The realization was both exhilarating and terrifying. Like sailing into uncharted waters, it promised both freedom and danger in equal measure. And like the moment the wind filled the *Mary Eleanor's* sails, Tess felt herself tilting toward a new equilibrium, one that might, if she had the courage to trust it, carry her exactly where she needed to go.

A DAY PASSED before Tess worked up the courage to seek Noah out. She found him in his workshop, bent over a piece of cherry wood, his plane making long, even strokes that curled into perfect shavings. The familiar sound of his methodical work brought back a flood of memories from their teenage summers when she'd sit on an overturned crate and watch him help his grandfather.

"Noah."

He looked up, surprise flickering across his face before settling into a cautious welcome. "Tess. Everything okay?"

"Are you busy?" She held up a thermos and a paper bag. "I brought coffee and Lucy's blueberry scones."

His smile was tentative but genuine. "I could use a break."

They walked without speaking toward the old oak tree behind the cottage, where the rope swing still hung from the massive branch, though the rope was newer than the one from their youth. The evening light filtered through the leaves, casting dancing shadows on the ground beneath.

"It's been a long time since we sat here," Tess said, settling onto the swing's wooden seat. The ropes creaked familiarly under her weight.

Noah leaned against the tree trunk, his expression growing distant. "August twenty-eighth. The night before you left for boarding school."

The precision of his memory made her chest tighten. "You remember the exact date?"

"I remember everything about that night." He was quiet for a long moment. "You were wearing that yellow sundress with the tiny white flowers. Your hair was in a braid, but pieces kept escaping. You'd been crying."

Tess closed her eyes, the memory rushing back with painful clarity. "My mother had just told me I wasn't coming back to Peregrine Cove for Christmas. That from then on, my summers would be spent in enrichment programs or internships. It felt like a prison sentence."

"But you didn't tell me."

She opened her eyes, finding his gaze fixed on her with an intensity that made her breath catch. "I couldn't find the words. That night, I was going to tell you something else. Then my mother dropped her bomb, and my whole life exploded. What could I say? All my feelings ...the words ... It all felt like pieces too broken to fix."

Noah pushed away from the tree, moving closer. "What words?"

For a moment, she lost herself in his gaze. "That I loved you." The words came out in a rush, fifteen years too late. "Not like a friend or a summer companion. I was seventeen and head-over-heels in love for the first time—with you—and I was terrified you didn't feel the same way."

Something shifted in Noah's expression. Pain and wonder warred across his features. "Tess ..."

"I wrote you a letter," she continued, her voice stronger now. "That first week at school. I poured my heart out and told you everything I wished I'd said on this swing. But I never sent it. I couldn't. I mean, what was the point when we couldn't be together? Plus, I was too scared. My mother made it clear that you were off-limits. She took away my phone, for God's sake!" She let out a chuckle. "Imagine me with no phone. The other girls thought I was some sort of freak." Her throat tightened as sadness threatened to overwhelm her. "And then when you didn't write back to any of my other letters, I was glad I'd kept it to myself."

Noah was quiet for so long that Tess began to regret her confession. Then he spoke, his voice rough with emotion.

"I waited for you."

"What?"

"That night, after you went inside, I sat on this swing until dawn." He gestured to the worn rope above them. "I kept thinking you might sneak back out, that we'd have one more chance to ... I don't know. Say the things we were both too scared to say."

Tess's throat constricted. "Noah ..."

"I didn't know at the time I wouldn't see you again. And then, when you left—like an idiot, I came back here every night for two weeks. I sat right there and imagined what I'd say when you came home for Christmas." His laugh was bitter. "But you didn't come home. So, I had to accept that you'd moved on."

"I wanted to come home." The words were thick with tears she'd held back for fifteen years. "Every holiday, every break, I begged my parents to let me visit. But Mom always had other plans—trips to Europe, cultural experiences in New York, college prep programs. She was so determined to keep me away from what she called 'small-town distractions.'"

"Meaning me."

"Meaning you." Tess wiped at her eyes with the back of her hand. "I should have fought harder, found a way."

Noah moved to sit beside her on the swing, the old wood creaking under their combined weight. "We were kids, Tess. Kids from different worlds, with parents who had their own agendas."

"But what if we hadn't been? What if I'd sent that letter? What if you'd written back? What if I'd come home that Christmas?"

The questions hung between them, heavy with fifteen years of what-might-have-beens.

"Do you want to know what I would have said?" Noah asked quietly. "If you'd snuck back out that night?"

Tess lifted her eyes to meet his, afraid to hope for the answer.

"I would have told you that I'd been in love with you since we were fifteen. That watching you discover who you were becoming was the best part of my summers. That I was terrified of you leaving, but even more terrified of holding you back." He turned to face her fully. "And I would have asked you to wait for me. To give us a chance when you came back from school."

"And I would have said yes." The admission came out in a whisper. "I would have waited."

They sat in silence as the sun sank lower, painting the sky in soft pastels. The swing moved gently in the evening breeze, and Tess was struck by how right it felt to be here beside him, finally sharing the words they'd carried alone for so long.

"I kept that letter," she said eventually. "All these years, in a box with my other keepsakes. I used to take it out sometimes and wonder what would have happened if I'd been brave enough to send it."

"What did it say?"

Tess smiled through her tears. "Everything I just told you. And that you were the first person who ever made me feel like I was enough, exactly as I was. That leaving you felt like leaving half my heart behind."

Noah's hand found hers, his fingers intertwining with hers, just as they had when they were teenagers. "I wish I'd known. All those years, I convinced myself you were better off without me."

"And I convinced myself you'd forgotten me."

"No." His thumb traced circles on her palm, a gesture so familiar it felt like coming home. "There were nights I'd lie awake wondering where you were, what you were doing, if you ever thought about this place. About us."

"Every day," Tess confessed.

The sun had nearly set now, the first stars beginning to appear in the darkening sky. Noah stood and offered her his hand.

"What are you doing?"

"Something I should have done fifteen years ago."

He helped her to her feet, then stepped closer, his hands framing her face with infinite gentleness. In the fading light, he looked exactly like the boy she'd fallen in love with, but his eyes held the depth of the man he'd become.

"Tess Bradford," he said, his voice steady despite the emotion she could see in his expression, "I love you. I've loved you since we were kids."

This time, she didn't hesitate. "I love you too, Noah Pierce. I always have."

When their lips met, it was with the sweetness of first love and the passion of a long-awaited reunion. Fifteen years of separation dissolved in that kiss, along with all the fear and uncertainty that had kept them apart.

When they finally broke apart, breathless and smiling, Noah rested his forehead against hers. "I've waited a long time for that."

Tess looked around at the swing where they'd almost kissed as teenagers, at the cottage where she'd learned what home really meant, at the man who'd held her heart across time and distance.

"Me, too," she whispered.

As they walked back to the cottage hand in hand, the swing swayed gently behind them in the evening breeze, a witness to love lost and found again, to the truth that some things are worth waiting for, no matter how long the journey home.

CHAPTER 11

Tess adjusted her blouse for the third time, smoothing nonexistent wrinkles as she waited for the Zoom call to connect. Her laptop sat on her aunt's old writing desk, angled to hide the cottage's exposed beams and vintage wallpaper—a deliberate framing that maintained the illusion she was working from a sleek Boston apartment rather than a century-old cottage on the Maine coast.

The chime of the connecting call sent a jolt of anxiety through her. Three familiar faces appeared on the screen: Lawrence, the firm's managing partner; Daniel, her direct supervisor; and Greg, the project coordinator who'd been handling her clients in her absence. None of them were smiling.

"Tess, good to see you," Lawrence began, his tone professional but cool. "I trust you're doing well?"

"Yes, thank you," she replied, instinctively straightening her posture. "The estate matters are progressing, though there's still quite a bit to—"

"That's precisely why we've called," Daniel cut in,

his fingers tapping an unseen surface. "It's been two weeks. We need to know your return date."

The directness of the question, though expected, still caught Tess off guard. In the back of her mind, she'd been postponing this very conversation, letting the days blend together as she lost herself in cottage renovations and quiet evenings with Noah.

Tess hesitated. "I was hoping we might discuss extending my leave. There are still several aspects of the estate that require my—"

"Tess." Lawrence's interruption was gentle, but firm. "You're one of our best assets, but the Harrington project has been on hold waiting for you to return, and the Westbrook campaign is at a critical stage. They specifically requested you."

Pride fluttered briefly at the recognition before sinking under the weight of what was coming.

"We've been accommodating," Daniel added, "but clients are beginning to ask for status reports and ... Well, either you're part of this team, or you're not."

Tense silence followed the ultimatum. A familiar tightness gripped Tess's chest—the prelude to panic that she'd come to know all too well.

"I know. I understand the position this puts the firm in," she managed. "But I just need a little more time to—"

"Tomorrow." Lawrence's harsh tone softened slightly. "I'm sorry to press, but we need an answer by tomorrow. If you can't return immediately, we'll need to make some staffing adjustments."

He didn't have to say more. She was losing her projects, and maybe her job.

Greg, who had remained silent until now, leaned

forward. "Tess, your clients miss you. The Harringtons ask about you every time I speak with them."

The meeting concluded with awkward pleasantries, promises to reconnect the following day, and Tess's halfhearted assurance that she understood the urgency. When the screen went dark, she sat motionless, staring at her reflection on the black laptop screen.

Outside, September had transformed Peregrine Cove. The maples lining the main street blazed scarlet and gold, and the morning air carried the first hints of fall's chill. But Tess barely registered the beauty as she paced the cottage, her mind racing through impossible calculations.

Her career in Boston represented a decade of hard work, connections, and achievements. The thought of surrendering it sent waves of vertigo through her. And yet, the idea of leaving the cottage, leaving Noah, created an entirely different kind of pain that was sharp and immediate.

Without quite forming a plan, Tess pulled a small overnight bag from the closet. She packed mechanically: a change of clothes, toiletries, her laptop. The cottage seemed to watch her movements with silent disapproval, each creak of the floorboards an accusation.

Noah had run out to the hardware store. She could leave without having to explain, without a goodbye that would inevitably become messy with emotions she wasn't ready to name. A clean break. Wasn't that what her mother had always advocated? *'Cut ties before they become chains?'*

She scribbled a vague note and left it on the kitchen counter: "Had to take care of some business in Boston.

Back soon." The inadequacy of the words struck her even as she wrote them, but anything more honest would require confronting feelings she was desperately trying to outrun.

Twenty minutes later, Tess was in her car, driving away from Peregrine Cove with a single glance in the rearview mirror at Aunt Morna's cottage perched on its bluff. The fall foliage created tunnels of gold and red along the coastal highway as she pushed southward toward Boston, toward the life she had meticulously constructed over the years.

She rehearsed what she would say to Lawrence and Daniel in person, gracefully negotiating a compromise, perhaps splitting her time between Boston and Peregrine Cove until the estate was settled. How she would salvage both worlds, even as a voice in the back of her mind whispered that some choices couldn't be straddled.

Fifty miles from Peregrine Cove, a scenic overlook appeared—one of those roadside viewpoints where tourists stopped to photograph the Atlantic's vastness. Without consciously deciding to, Tess pulled over and came to a stop at the edge of the cliff.

The ocean stretched before her, endless and indifferent to her human-scale crisis. The wind whipped her hair as she stepped out of the car, drawing her cardigan tighter around herself against the chill. Below, waves crashed against rocks in a rhythm that was ancient and unchanging.

Reality crashed in with similar force: she was repeating her mother's pattern of running when faced with difficult choices. The parallel was so obvious it was almost laughable. Elizabeth had fled Peregrine Cove to escape what she'd seen as the suffocating embrace of small-town life. Now Tess was fleeing in the same direction and with the same instinct to avoid commitment, maintain mobility, and keep one foot perpetually out the door.

"I'm just like her," Tess whispered, the wind snatching the words away.

But was that really who she wanted to be? A woman defined by what she ran from rather than what she embraced?

She thought of Noah's words on the dock after their sailing trip. *'I want something to finally change for the better.'* The vulnerability in his eyes, the hope he'd offered despite his own fears of abandonment. She thought of Aunt Morna's cottage no longer as a family burden, but as a foundation for something new.

Tess sat on a weathered wooden bench, pulling out her phone. Her fingers hovered over the screen before she made the call she'd been avoiding.

"Lawrence? It's Tess. I've made my decision."

Noah discovered the note at six that evening, returning to the cottage with takeout from the local diner and plans to surprise Tess after what he knew would be a difficult call with her firm. The sight of her neatly written words sent a cold wave of familiarity washing over him. How many times in his life had he discovered that he'd been abandoned and left with the same empty space where someone had been?

He set the food containers down with mechanical precision, then moved through the cottage with growing dread. Tess's closet confirmed his fears: half-empty hangers, a missing suitcase, the absence of the leather portfolio she kept her important documents in.

"Not again," he murmured, sinking onto her bed and overwhelmed by the betrayal.

The rational part of him tried to argue that her note promised her return. "Back soon" were her exact words. But experience had taught Noah that people who left rarely came back, at least not in the ways that mattered. His mother had always planned to return from her treatments, too.

He considered calling Tess, but stopped himself. No, he'd already scared her away. What would calling her do? If Tess needed space to make her decision, his pressure would only push her further away. Besides, what right did he have to make claims on her time, on her future? They'd shared a few weeks of renovation work, an afternoon of sailing, and countless moments of tension that hovered between conflict and attraction. It wasn't exactly a foundation for demands.

Still, as dusk gathered, and the cottage grew shadowy, Noah couldn't bring himself to leave. He settled on the porch steps, a silent vigil he couldn't quite justify to himself. The paper bag of takeout sat forgotten on the kitchen counter as the last colors of sunset bled from the sky.

Stars were just beginning to appear when headlights swept up the gravel drive. Noah straightened, breath catching as Tess's car came to a stop beside his truck. For a long moment, she remained inside, her silhouette visible through the windshield. Then, as if coming to a decision, she emerged, an overnight bag slung over her shoulder.

She stopped short when she spotted him on the steps.

"You came back," he said, disbelief evident in his voice.

Tess approached slowly, stepping through the fall leaves as they swirled close to the ground. In the dim porch light, her expression was a study in contrasts—exhaustion and exhilaration, uncertainty and resolve.

"I quit my job. I'm staying in Peregrine Cove. For the full year."

The declaration was heavy with implications. Noah stood, hands looking uncertain at his sides.

"What changed your mind?" he asked.

Tess set her bag down, her shoulders relaxing as if she'd set down a much heavier burden.

"I realized what matters," she admitted. "And it's not in Boston. That life was never mine to begin with. It was someone else's dream for me."

Noah wanted to move toward her, to close the distance, both physical and emotional, between them, but caution held him back. "Are you sure? Your career in Boston—"

"Will still be there in some form if I want it later." She shrugged, the gesture containing more certainty than resignation. "But this, the cottage, Peregrine Cove, this opportunity won't wait. And I'm tired of letting fear make my decisions."

The porch light cast a warm glow around them, creating an island of illumination in the gathering darkness. Something shifted within him. A tension he'd carried for weeks, perhaps years, began to uncoil.

A smile broke through his guarded expression. "Well, I happen to know a good contractor who can help you fix up the place."

Tess laughed, the sound dispelling the last of the

awkwardness between them. "Is he available for dinner? I skipped lunch, and I'm starving."

"I might have some cold takeout from Lucy's in the kitchen."

"Perfect."

As they moved inside together, the cottage seemed to welcome them with familiar creaks and sighs, the old house settling into the cool autumn night.

Tess was at her desk, tying up loose ends from work, when her phone rang.

"You're making a mistake." Elizabeth's voice through the phone was sharp with disapproval. "A colossal mistake."

Tess held the receiver away from her ear momentarily, drawing a steadying breath before responding. "I appreciate your concern, Mother, but it's done. I've made my decision, and it's what I want."

"You're throwing away your career for a house and a town that will suffocate you just like they did me."

The criticism stung but didn't sway her as it once might have. Tess curled deeper into Aunt Morna's reading chair, watching moonlight filter through the windows. Noah had left an hour before, after they'd shared their reheated dinner and made plans to continue the kitchen renovations the following day.

"I'm not throwing away anything," Tess countered. "I'm choosing to invest my time in something different right now."

"And the Pierce boy? I suppose he has nothing to do with this sudden commitment to small-town life?"

A flush crept up Tess's neck. "Noah is part of it," she admitted. "But not in the way you're implying. This isn't some romantic fantasy, Mother. It's about finishing something I start instead of always keeping one foot out the door."

Elizabeth was silent for a long moment. When she spoke again, her voice had lost some of its edge. "You sound like Morna. She always believed in seeing things through, even when the world was offering better options elsewhere."

"Maybe that wasn't weakness," Tess suggested gently. "Maybe it was a different kind of strength."

"Perhaps." The concession seemed to cost Elizabeth something. "Just don't forget you have options, Tess. Promise me that. A cottage can be sold. A career can be rebuilt. But years spent living someone else's dream— those you never get back."

After the call ended, Tess sat in the quiet cottage, letting her mother's words settle alongside her own certainties. There was truth in Elizabeth's warning, even if it came filtered through her own regrets. Choices did close doors, and every commitment narrowed the field of future opportunities.

Yet something in Tess had shifted irreversibly during that moment of clarity at the ocean overlook. Her tendency to keep her alternatives open had its own cost, never completely inhabiting a single moment or connection.

Later, restlessness drove her to the porch swing despite the fall chill. Wrapped in one of Aunt Morna's handmade quilts, Tess rocked gently, listening to the distant sound of waves and the occasional rustle of falling leaves.

Headlights appeared on the lane leading to the cottage, familiar now as Noah's truck made its way toward her. He hadn't mentioned returning tonight, and Tess felt a flutter of surprise as he parked and approached, a thermos in hand.

"Couldn't sleep," he explained, climbing the porch steps. "Thought you might be up too."

"How did you know?"

He smiled, gesturing toward the cottage. "Your reading light was on when I drove by earlier. And you strike me as someone who might need quiet reflection time after making life-altering decisions."

"Wow, you get me." She cast a sideways smirk at him and shifted on the swing to make room. "Join me?"

Noah settled beside her, the swing adjusting to their combined weight with a gentle creak. He opened the thermos, and the rich aroma of hot chocolate filled the cool air.

"Second thoughts?" he asked guardedly, pouring the steaming liquid into the thermos cap and offering it to her.

"Not about staying," she answered, her certainty surprising even herself. "Though plenty about what comes next. I've never been without a five-year plan before."

Noah nodded, understanding in his expression. "It's disorienting. After Mom died, all my careful plans disintegrated. For months, I was as lost as if I were navigating without a compass."

"How did you find your way?"

He considered the question, his shoulder warm against hers as the swing moved rhythmically. "I started building smaller maps instead of trying to chart the entire ocean at once. Today's route, this week's journey. Eventually, I could see farther ahead again."

Tess sipped the hot chocolate, letting its warmth spread through her. "That's good advice."

"I have my moments." His smile was visible even in the dim light. "So, what's on tomorrow's map?"

"Kitchen cabinets," she declared. "Definitely time to tackle those cabinets."

They fell into a comfortable conversation about renovation plans, design choices, and the upcoming town harvest festival. As they talked, everything seemed to fall into place. A new horizon was opening where before there had only been walls. It felt right.

Overhead, stars wheeled in their ancient patterns while the leaves gently rustled. Behind them, the cottage stood stable and sure, its foundations deep in the rocky Maine soil. For the first time in her adult life, Tess didn't find herself calculating escape routes or contingency plans.

Tomorrow would arrive with its own challenges. Her resignation would need to be formalized, finances rearranged, and explanations given to friends and colleagues. But tonight, rocking gently beside Noah with fall's chill held at bay by shared warmth, Tess allowed herself to be present and rooted in a decision that felt, against all expectations, like freedom.

CHAPTER 12

"You're what?" Tess nearly dropped her phone as she gripped the kitchen counter for support, as heat rose in her face.

"I said I'm coming to visit," Elizabeth repeated, her tone suggesting this was the most reasonable thing in the world. "I'll leave first thing in the morning, stop at Red's to pick up some lunch, and I've already booked a room at that little B&B in town—The Harbor something-or-other."

"The Harbor House," Tess corrected, her mind racing. "Mother, this isn't a good time. The cottage is completely torn apart with renovations and—"

"Well then, that's perfect timing. I'll be able to see what you've sacrificed your career for." The edge in Elizabeth's voice could have cut glass. "Darling, I won't get in the way. I'll just be there as another set of eyes to help you think clearly."

"But—"

"You know, quitting your job was an impulsive decision, but not an irreversible one."

Tess recognized the strategy. Elizabeth presented herself as a concerned ally while positioning herself to steer Tess toward a better way of thinking—hers. It was a familiar dance, one they'd performed countless times over the years.

"I don't need you to talk sense into me." Tess hadn't meant to take such a sharp tone. "I know what I'm doing. And, frankly, it's done."

"Wonderful. Then you won't mind showing me this marvelous new life you've chosen." Elizabeth's voice turned honey-sweet. "I'll see you tomorrow, darling. I'll text when I'm on my way."

The call ended before Tess could voice another protest. She set her phone down with deliberate care, then surveyed the disaster zone that was her aunt's cottage.

The kitchen renovation was half-complete, with new cabinets installed on one wall while the others still sat in their boxes. Plastic sheeting separated the living spaces, and tools littered every surface. The dust had become a permanent resident, settling on every available surface despite their best efforts to contain it.

Panic rose in Tess's throat. Elizabeth would see this chaos and instantly categorize it as evidence of failure, poor planning, and amateur execution. It wouldn't matter if it was perfect. Her mother had a gift for finding weakness in any endeavor.

The back door opened, and Noah walked in carrying a box of new cabinet hardware. He took one look at Tess's face and set the box down.

"What's wrong?" he asked.

"My mother is coming. Tomorrow." Tess pressed

her palms against her eyes. "To 'help me think clearly' about my terrible life choices."

Noah leaned against the counter beside her, close enough that she could feel his warmth. "Ah, a rescue mission."

"Exactly." Tess dropped her hands, gesturing at the construction chaos surrounding them. "And the cottage looks like a war zone. She's going to take one look and see confirmation of everything she already believes— that I'm making a huge mistake, that I'm in over my head, and that I've thrown away my career for ...for ..."

"For a pile of sawdust and exposed wiring?" Noah offered, with a hint of a smile.

Despite herself, Tess laughed. "Yes, exactly."

Noah eyed the kitchen thoughtfully. "We can get the place presentable by tomorrow. Not finished, but organized enough to show the vision. What time does she arrive?"

"She's leaving early and stopping at Red's to pick up lunch. At least that's a plus. And, depending on how long the line is, she could be here any time after noon."

"Okay." Noah was already moving, gathering scattered tools and organizing them on the workbench they'd set up. "We can install the rest of the upper cabinets and countertops this afternoon, sweep and clean tonight, and finish the backsplash in the morning."

His calm efficiency both soothed and irritated Tess. "How are you not panicking right now?"

Noah looked up from sorting screws, a question in his eyes.

"My mother is coming," Tess emphasized, as though he might have missed this critical fact. "Elizabeth Bradford. The woman who found Peregrine Cove so suffocating she fled at the first chance she got and dragged me with her. The woman who believes this town, this cottage—" *and you*, she almost said it but caught herself, "—are just weights that will drag me down."

Noah's expression shifted subtly. "I remember your mother, you know. I remember how she always seemed separate somehow, like she was visiting another country —or planet."

The observation was so accurate, it momentarily silenced Tess. That was how Elizabeth had always approached Peregrine Cove, as an anthropologist might study a distant culture with detached interest but never belonging.

"She's going to hate everything we've done here," Tess said.

Noah crossed to her then, gently taking her shoulders in his hands. "Then let her hate it. This isn't her cottage. It's yours. And what we're building here ..." he gestured to the half-finished kitchen, "is *your* home and *your* life, not hers."

The sincerity in his eyes anchored her, pulling her back from the edge of panic. Tess took a deep breath and nodded. "You're right. Okay. Let's make this place presentable."

What followed was fourteen hours of concentrated effort. Noah called in reinforcements. His father arrived with dinner and stayed to help install light fixtures, while Maya from the hardware store delivered a rush order of cabinet pulls and offered to return in the morning with flowers "to soften the construction edges," as she put it.

By midnight, exhaustion had replaced Tess's anxiety.

The kitchen, while still under renovation, now showed the promise of its eventual glory. The new cabinets and gleaming quartz countertops had been installed on two walls, and a custom island, crafted partly from Aunt Morna's old cabinets, stood proudly in the center, its warm wood tones balancing the modern elements surrounding it.

"Not bad for a day's panic-driven work." Noah collapsed onto the sofa beside Tess. He handed her a glass of wine from the bottle Maya had thoughtfully included with dinner.

"Thank you." She meant it for more than just the wine. "I couldn't have done this without you."

Noah's eyes met hers over the rim of his glass. "You're not alone, Tess. That's the point of a community like Peregrine Cove."

The simple truth of his statement settled around her with the warmth of a blanket. Before she could respond, Noah stood, stretching his tall frame with a grimace of exhaustion.

"Get some sleep," he advised. "You'll need your energy for tomorrow."

After he left, Tess wandered through the cottage, seeing it with fresh eyes, or rather, anticipating how Elizabeth would see it. The blend of old and new, tradition and innovation. In every choice they'd made, there had been respect for the past without being imprisoned by it. The realization steadied her as she drifted to sleep.

❧

ELIZABETH BRADFORD ARRIVED at precisely two

fifteen the following afternoon and stood by her car as she eyed the cottage exterior with narrowed eyes.

"Just for one night?" Tess asked, nodding toward the three pieces of luggage in the back seat of the Mercedes as she hugged her mother stiffly.

Elizabeth waved a dismissive hand. "One never knows how long these things might take."

Slack-jawed, Tess pondered what that might mean.

"Well." Elizabeth turned her attention to Tess for the first time. "You look ... rustic."

Tess glanced down at her jeans and t-shirt, which had been her de facto uniform while they worked on the cottage. At least she'd applied makeup this morning.

"It's good to see you too, Mother."

Elizabeth's smile didn't quite reach her eyes. "Show me this project that's consumed you, then."

The tour began with the exterior, where they'd repaired the stone walls and restored the garden beds. Elizabeth offered perfunctory praise, though her gaze lingered critically on the areas still awaiting attention. Inside, she moved through the spaces with the calculated assessment of someone looking for flaws.

"So, this is what you've chosen over your career," she said coolly, running a manicured finger along the old cabinet wood on the new kitchen island.

"I haven't abandoned my career," Tess countered. "I'm redirecting it. There's significant demand for design services in the coastal communities nearby."

Elizabeth arched a perfect eyebrow. "Vacation rentals and fishermen's cottages? Hardly the caliber of clients you had in Boston."

"Different, but no less important." Tess had rehearsed the retort throughout the morning.

Before Elizabeth could respond, a knock at the back door interrupted them. Noah's father entered, carrying a box of specialized trim pieces they'd ordered for the archway between the kitchen and dining room.

"Delivery for—" He stopped short, recognition flickering across his weathered face. The air seemed to thicken with decades of unspoken history. "Lizzie."

The use of the childhood nickname landed like a physical blow. Elizabeth's posture stiffened almost imperceptibly, her social mask sliding firmly into place.

"Rob," she acknowledged. "Still working at the hardware store, I see."

Rob set the box on the counter with deliberate care. "Yeah."

"Hmm." She glanced down her nose as she nodded.

The loaded pause that followed communicated volumes. Tess glanced between them, witnessing a silent conversation built on shared history she could only guess at.

"The cottage looks good." Rob turned to include Tess in the conversation. "Noah says you've got a real eye for balancing the old with the new."

"Thank you." A surge of pride moved through her. "We've tried to honor Aunt Morna's vision while making it functional for today."

"Morna would approve," Rob nodded. "She never believed in preserving things just for tradition's sake. She believed homes should evolve with the people living in them."

Elizabeth's laugh was light but cutting. "How convenient, since nothing in this town ever seems to evolve otherwise."

Rob met her gaze steadily. "Some find freedom, where others find prison, Lizzie."

Elizabeth's perfectly composed expression faltered for just a moment before she recovered.

"Yes, well. Perspective is everything, isn't it?" She turned deliberately away from Rob, focusing on Tess. "Darling, why don't we have that tea you promised? I'm absolutely parched after the drive."

Rob recognized the dismissal for what it was. He nodded to Tess. "Tell Noah I dropped off those trim pieces. He'll know what to do with them."

After he left, Elizabeth's poise collapsed into a genuine scowl. "Of all the people in this town, that man has changed the least. Still carrying that self-righteous devotion to this place like it's some kind of virtue."

"He seems perfectly nice to me," Tess ventured, putting the kettle on. "He and Noah have been incredibly helpful with the renovations."

Elizabeth's eyes sharpened. "Yes, let's talk about Noah, shall we? Is he the real reason you're staying, Tess? Because if so, you should know men like him are anchors. They'll keep you in place until you drown."

The accusation struck at Tess's most vulnerable uncertainty, the fear that her growing feelings for Noah were clouding her judgment about staying in Peregrine Cove. But even as the doubt flickered, she recognized her mother's tactic for what it was: an attempt to reframe Tess's agency as manipulation by others.

"Or maybe they're foundations that let you build something lasting," Tess countered, setting tea mugs on the counter with more force than necessary. "Not everyone who chooses to stay somewhere is trapped, Mother. Some people actually want roots."

"You've never wanted roots before. You've spent your entire adult life specifically avoiding them."

"Maybe I was running from the wrong thing." The words emerged before Tess had considered them fully, but once voiced, they resonated with the truth. "Maybe I wasn't running from commitment. Maybe I was running from the fear that if I did commit to something —a place, a person, a path—I'd turn into you, always looking over my shoulder for the better option that might be somewhere else."

Elizabeth recoiled as if slapped. "That's unfair."

"Is it? You've never stopped running, Mother. Even when you settled in Boston, you changed apartments every few years, changed jobs, changed social circles. Nothing was ever quite right, never quite enough."

"I sought better opportunities—"

"You sought to escape," Tess interrupted, her voice surprisingly steady despite the rapid beating of her heart. "From what, I don't know. But I do know I don't want to spend my life that way anymore."

"You sound like Morna. She always believed in her simple life rooted here, even when the world was offering better options elsewhere."

"Maybe that wasn't weakness," Tess suggested gently. "Maybe it was a different kind of strength."

"Perhaps. But I spent years wondering what I'd given up by staying with your father, by choosing the safe path. I don't want you to wake up at fifty wondering about the roads not taken."

The kettle whistled, piercing the charged silence between them. Tess turned away to prepare the tea, giving them both a moment to regain their composure. When she turned back, Elizabeth was seated at the kitchen island, her expression uncharacteristically vulnerable.

"You really believe you'll be happy here?" she asked, and for once, the question seemed genuine rather than leading.

Tess placed a mug of tea before her mother. "I believe I want the chance to find out. On my terms."

The confrontation left both women shaken but established something new between them—respect, perhaps, or at least recognition of boundaries that hadn't existed before.

Elizabeth retreated to her B&B room for the evening, citing travel fatigue, though Tess suspected she needed space to regroup after their unexpected confrontation. The reprieve gave Tess time to process the day's emotional turbulence.

Just after sunset, Noah arrived with to-go containers from the local seafood restaurant. "Peace offering," he explained. "Figured you might need sustenance after surviving Hurricane Elizabeth."

"How did you know she'd gone back to the B&B?"

Noah grinned. "Small town. Mrs. Farnsworth, who runs Harbor House, texted my dad that your mother had checked in early and requested the 'least rustic room available.'"

The thought of her mother's movements being community knowledge should have bothered Tess, but instead, she found it oddly comforting. Visibility meant connection, even if Elizabeth would see it as invasive surveillance.

"Want to eat by the water?" Noah suggested. "Might help clear your head."

They walked to the small private beach below the

cottage, a narrow strip of sand accessible by wooden steps built into the bluff. The full moon cast a silver path across the dark water, and the October air held just enough chill to make their shared blanket necessary rather than merely pleasant.

"Your mother's still beautiful," Noah said as they finished their meal, leaning back on his elbows to gaze at the star-filled sky.

"And controlling," Tess replied, the insight crystallizing her determination not to repeat Elizabeth's pattern of constant flight. "Even her visit isn't really a visit. It's another escape plan, just not her own this time."

Noah turned to study her profile in the moonlight. "Does that scare you? That you might have that same instinct?"

Tess considered the question seriously. "It used to. I thought it was inevitable—genetics or conditioning or whatever. But now I'm not so sure."

"What changed?"

"I'm still figuring that out," she admitted. "But I think ... I think maybe I've been running away from things my whole life, while my mother has been running toward something she can never quite reach—an idea of freedom or fulfillment that's always just over the next horizon."

Noah's hand found hers on the blanket between them, his work-roughened fingers warm against her skin. "And what are you running from, Tess Bradford?"

The question hung in the moonlit air. Tess turned her hand to interlace her fingers with his, the simple connection anchoring her to the present moment.

"I'm not running anymore," she said softly. "I'm staying still long enough to find out where I belong."

The waves continued their ancient rhythm against the shore, voices from the past and present mingling in the sound. Family ghosts might walk these beaches and inhabit the corners of the cottage, but for the first time, Tess didn't feel haunted by them. Instead, she felt accompanied by those who had come before, by the man beside her, and by her own emerging certainty that some roots were not chains but lifelines, tethering her not to limitation but to connections that mattered.

CHAPTER 13

The summer sea breeze held a hint of coming rain as Tess followed Noah across the yard to his workshop. Elizabeth's visit the previous week had cleared the air. Since then, Tess had thrown herself into cottage renovations with renewed purpose, determined to complete the essential work before the harsh Maine winter arrived in force.

"We should move any materials that can't handle temperature fluctuations into storage," Noah explained, unlocking the workshop door. "The insulation here should protect anything sensitive."

Tess nodded, pulling her jacket tighter. "The paint, for starters. And I'd rather not leave the new cabinet hardware where it might get damp."

The workshop was larger than it appeared from the outside, with high ceilings and an organized chaos that spoke of Noah's methodical mind. One half contained his carpentry tools, arranged with precision on pegboards and shelves. The other half held supplies for various projects, all neatly labeled and categorized.

"There's space on those back shelves," Noah pointed, rolling up his sleeves. "We'll need to consolidate some things first."

They worked companionably, Tess organizing supplies while Noah shifted larger items to create the needed space. The physical labor was satisfying after days of phone calls and paperwork related to her career transition. She'd been laying the groundwork for freelance design work in the area, surprising herself with her own enthusiasm for this new professional direction.

"Can you grab that box of hardware samples?" Noah called from where he was rearranging storage bins. "It should be behind the workbench."

Tess crouched to peer behind the heavy wooden bench. Several boxes were stacked in the shadowy space, but one immediately caught her attention, not because it matched Noah's description, but because her name was written on it in faded marker.

"Tess?"

She didn't respond, staring at the cardboard box with *Tess Bradford* written in a younger Noah's handwriting. Curiosity mingled with confusion as she pulled it forward.

"Did you find it?" Noah appeared beside her, then froze when he saw what had captured her attention.

The silence between them stretched taut as Tess looked up at him with questioning eyes. Noah's expression shifted from surprise to resignation tinged with apprehension.

"What is this?" she finally asked.

Noah exhaled slowly. "Your letters."

With careful movements that were simultaneously tentative and inevitable, Tess opened the box. Inside, arranged chronologically with characteristic precision, were dozens of envelopes. She recognized her own handwriting immediately, the careful script of her teenage years, evolving subtly with each postmark date. Many of the envelopes appeared worn, opened, and refolded multiple times.

"These are all the letters I wrote you from boarding school." Her voice sounded distant to her own ears. "You kept them."

Noah remained motionless, his body tense. "Yes."

Tess lifted one of the envelopes, noting its worn creases and tattered edges. "This looks like it's been read many times."

"It has." The admission emerged quietly, heavy with implication.

The pieces aligned in Tess's mind with devastating clarity. "You read these. All of them." It wasn't a question, but a realization. "Even though you never wrote back."

Noah's gaze dropped to the box and then returned to meet hers. "I tried writing back at first, but I was too angry and hurt. Eventually, I just ...collected them."

The blood drained from her face as the full weight of his words sank in. Not deception, but something perhaps more painful: he had heard her yet opted for silence.

"You read them all?" Her voice gained strength, propelled by a sudden wave of indignation. "Even when I begged you to write back, even when I asked if I could visit?"

Noah's face showed the cost of his confession, old guilt etched in the tightness around his eyes. "Yes."

Tess stood abruptly, needing the physical distance,

and letters tumbled back into the box with the sudden movement. "Why would you do that? Why read them if you had no intention of responding?"

"I told myself I'd stop," he admitted, rising to face her. "After each one, I'd promise myself it would be the last I'd open. But then another would arrive, and I couldn't help myself." A pained smile ghosted across his face. "Reading them was like watching you build a life that didn't need me anymore. But I couldn't stop torturing myself with them."

The raw honesty in his voice collided with her rising anger, creating a turbulent emotional undertow. Tess shook her head, struggling to process this new understanding of their shared past.

"Those letters weren't about building a life without you," she countered, gesturing sharply toward the box. "They were about trying to keep you in my life despite everything that happened. I was reaching out to the one person who had always understood me."

"That's not how it felt at the time." Noah's voice hardened. "The first few letters were all about your exciting new school, your sophisticated new friends, your brilliant teachers. Everything you were gaining by leaving."

"Because I was terrified!" The words burst from her with unexpected force. "I was trying to convince us both that I was okay, that being sent away wasn't destroying me. Do you have any idea how lonely I was?"

Noah flinched but held his ground. "And do you have any idea what it was like to be the one left behind? To watch your best friend get whisked away to a better life while you stayed in the town everyone couldn't wait to escape from?"

Their erupting argument uncovered years of misunderstanding. Her letters had chronicled not excitement but loneliness, not abandonment but desperate reaching out. His silence had stemmed not from indifference but from a wounded pride too vast to overcome.

"You could have written back," Tess insisted, her voice breaking. "You could have told me how you felt."

"I started to. Several times." Noah ran a hand through his hair in frustration. "But every draft sounded pathetic. 'Dear Tess, I miss you so much it hurts to breathe sometimes'? 'Dear Tess, the town seems empty without you?' I couldn't bear to be that person, the sad friend left behind while you thrived."

The image of a teenage Noah struggling over unsent letters sent a sharp pang through Tess's chest, but the hurt of his prolonged silence still burned too freshly to fully embrace compassion.

"So instead, you chose to be nothing." The words came out more bitterly than she'd intended. "You chose to let me think you'd forgotten me."

"I was seventeen and hurt!" His control slipped, revealing the depth of emotion beneath. "And by the time I might have been mature enough to handle it differently, the pattern was set. Too much time had passed, too many letters had gone unanswered."

Tess crossed her arms, a protective gesture against the ache spreading beneath her ribs. "Then why keep them? Why not throw them away if reading them was such torture?"

The question seemed to strike something fundamental in Noah. His shoulders sagged, defense giving way to a vulnerability that seemed to physically diminish him.

"Because they were all I had left of you," he admitted quietly. "I read the last one so many times the paper started to tear."

The raw honesty in his confession shifted something in Tess's perspective. She knelt beside the box again and lifted the final envelope. The postmark date was from the spring of her senior year, the last letter she'd written before giving up on ever receiving a response. The paper was indeed worn thin at the folds, the ink slightly smudged from handling.

"Which one?" Her anger gave way to a different kind of pain, a shared wound rather than opposing injuries. "Show me the ones you read most."

Noah hesitated, then kneeled beside her. With gentle movements, he sorted through the box.

"It's kind of obvious from the frayed edges. This one, for instance." He pulled out a letter from her sophomore year. "You wrote about a meteor shower you watched from your dorm roof. You said it made you think of summer nights at the cove when we'd sneak out to stargaze."

He picked up another. "This one came after your first Christmas away. You wrote that the fancy dinner at your friend's Manhattan penthouse made you miss burned marshmallows at the town bonfire."

One by one, Noah showed her the letters that had meant the most to him—moments when her words had pierced his defensive armor, glimpses of the Tess he'd known beneath the prep school polish she'd described acquiring.

Together, they began to read select passages, witnessing her transformation from hopeful to increasingly despondent as each unanswered plea passed. The pain was there in black and white, a chronicle of teenage heartbreak documented in increasingly desperate attempts to maintain a connection that had once seemed unbreakable.

I don't understand why you won't write back, Noah. I miss you.

I overheard Mom tell my dad that you're working at the hardware store. What else is going on in your life? I'd love to hear from you.

This will probably be my last letter. I guess some friendships aren't meant to last forever, even when it feels like they should. I'll always remember you the way we used to be—best friends. At least, that's what I thought we were.

The final letter lay between them, its edges softened by countless readings. Tess couldn't bring herself to open it again. The memory of writing those words and surrendering hope was still too vivid despite the years that had passed.

Noah broke the heavy silence. "I convinced myself you were better off, that your silence when you returned for brief visits confirmed that you'd moved beyond Peregrine Cove. Beyond me."

"I thought you were angry that I'd left," Tess countered. "That you resented me for going to boarding school when we'd always talked about going to college together."

"I was angry," he admitted. "But not at you, at the situation, and at your mother for taking you away. And I hated that I couldn't be what you needed."

"What I needed was my friend," Tess said. "That's all I ever needed from you."

Noah's gaze fell to the scattered letters. "For years, I steeled myself against your return visits. I built walls that your reappearance at Morna's funeral nearly broke through. When you came back this summer, I promised myself I wouldn't let those walls down again."

"But you did."

"Not intentionally." A ghost of a smile crossed Noah's face. "You're very determined when renovating things—cottages, career plans, people ..."

"I wasn't trying to renovate you."

"No, but you made me want to renovate myself." His eyes met hers plainly. "I thought I was protecting myself all these years," he confessed. "Instead, I was just making sure I stayed broken."

Their shared history was reframed in this new light, both victims of pride and fear rather than indifference. The realization didn't erase the damage done, but it offered a new context for understanding it.

"We can't get those years back," Tess said, "but maybe we can stop losing more."

The tentative reconciliation acknowledged both the harm inflicted and the hope of healing, leaving them in fragile new territory. Noah began returning the letters to their box, treating each one with reverence.

"I think you should have these." He offered the box to her. "They've always been yours, anyway."

Tess shook her head. "Not yet. I'm not ready to read them all again. The memories are still too raw."

She selected the final letter, the one he'd nearly read to pieces, and held it out to him. "But I think we should both read this one. Together. When we're ready."

Noah accepted the envelope with careful hands, understanding the significance of the gesture.

They finished their original task in subdued collaboration, creating space for the cottage materials without returning to their earlier easy conversation. The discovery had shifted something fundamental between them, removing a long-festering misunderstanding while exposing the tender wounds beneath.

As they walked back to the cottage, the December wind picked up, carrying the scent of snow not yet fallen. Tess wrapped her arms around herself against the chill.

"I should get back," Noah said as they reached the porch steps. "Dad asked me to stop by this afternoon to give him a hand with some things around the house."

Tess nodded, not trusting herself to speak. As he turned to leave, she found her voice.

"Noah?"

He paused, looking back.

"Thank you for keeping them. The letters. Even if you couldn't answer them, thank you for not throwing them away."

Something vulnerable and honest passed between them, an acknowledgment that sometimes preservation itself is an act of love, even when expression fails.

"Some things you can't let go of," he said, "even when holding on hurts."

As he walked away, Tess remained on the porch, watching his retreating figure. In his workshop, the box of letters sat waiting, proof that the thread connecting their hearts couldn't be broken. It had survived distance, time, and every attempt to sever it. And now, here they were, home again.

Like Aunt Morna's cottage with its solid bones beneath years of neglect, some foundations remain sound enough to build upon if only one has the courage to clear away the debris of the past and begin again.

CHAPTER 14

The *Mary Eleanor* cut through water that had lost its summer sparkle as the late August light filtered through a haze that spoke of changing seasons. Tess adjusted the jib sheet as Noah called out from the helm, their movements synchronized in the way that came from weeks of sailing together. Their sailing outings had evolved into a shared ritual of stolen afternoons when work allowed and the wind was right.

"Perfect," Noah said as the sail filled properly. "You're getting good at reading the wind."

Tess settled beside him, close enough that their shoulders touched as the boat heeled gently to starboard. "I had a good teacher."

The compliment earned her one of his slow smiles, the kind that still made her pulse quicken even after months of these quiet moments together. They'd grown comfortable in each other's presence, the tentative friendship of early summer deepening into something neither was quite ready to name.

Above them, a lone maple leaf spiraled down from the overhanging branch of a tree on the distant shore, landing on the water's surface with barely a ripple. Tess watched it float past, carried by the current toward the open sea.

"First one I've seen fall," she murmured.

Noah's gaze followed hers. "Summer's ending."

The words held more weight than their simplicity suggested. In a few weeks, the tourists would depart, leaving Peregrine Cove to its year-round residents. The cottage would need winterizing. And Tess would have to decide whether the temporary arrangement that had become so natural was something more permanent.

"Does summer's end make you sad?" she asked, studying his profile as he adjusted their heading.

"Not sad, exactly." Noah considered the question, his eyes on the horizon. "More like ...aware. Summer goes so fast here. You learn to pay attention to the signs."

They sailed in comfortable silence toward their usual anchorage, a protected cove where they'd taken to sharing lunch and conversation away from the curious eyes of the town. As Noah dropped anchor, Tess noticed other signs of the season's shift—the different quality of light, softer and more golden than June's brightness, the way the water had lost its summer warmth and taken on the deeper blue of the approaching fall.

"I brought something," Noah said, reaching into the cooler he'd packed. Instead of their usual sandwiches, he produced a thermos and two mugs. "Hot cider. Seemed like the day for it."

The gesture was small but thoughtful, quintessentially Noah in its quiet consideration. As he poured the steaming cider, fragrant with cinnamon and cloves, Tess felt something shift inside her chest—a recognition of how completely this man had learned to read her moods, her needs, and her unspoken wishes.

"Thank you." She accepted the warm mug gratefully, wrapping her fingers around its heat. "This is perfect."

They sat side by side on the cushioned bench, the boat rocking gently in the sheltered cove. Around them, the world seemed suspended in that magical hour when afternoon begins its slide toward evening and everything was tinged with the shimmer of gold.

"Can I ask you something?" Tess said, breaking the comfortable quiet.

"Sure."

"Do you ever think about leaving? Peregrine Cove, I mean. Seeing what else is out there?"

Noah was quiet for so long that Tess wondered if she'd overstepped some invisible boundary. When he finally spoke, his voice was thoughtful.

"I used to. Right after college, I had plans. Boston, maybe New York. I figured I'd work for some big firm." He took a sip of cider, his eyes distant with memory. "Then Mom got sick, and those plans didn't seem as important anymore."

"Do you regret staying?"

"No." His answer was immediate and certain. "I've found something here I never would have found in a city."

"What's that?"

Noah turned to look at her, his sea-glass eyes holding hers with an intensity that made her breath catch. "Peace. Purpose. The knowledge that what I'm building matters to the people who'll use it."

A pause, then softer: "And now you."

His words hung between them, heavy with implication. Tess's heart began to race as the careful boundaries they'd maintained now seemed gossamer-thin.

"Noah—"

A gust of wind chose that moment to sweep through the cove, setting the boat to dancing. Instinctively, Noah reached for her arm to steady her, but then his hand lingered. The touch was so gentle that Tess found herself leaning into it without conscious thought.

"You can feel summer ending," she whispered, though she wasn't sure if she meant the season or this perfect, suspended moment between friendship and something deeper.

"Maybe," Noah said, his thumb tracing the line of her cheekbone with infinite care. "But not yet."

The space between them seemed to shrink, drawn together by gravity and longing and the weight of everything unspoken. Tess could see the gold flecks in his eyes and could feel the warmth of his breath against her face. One small movement, one slight lean forward, and they would cross the line they'd been walking for months.

A splash nearby broke the spell—a fish jumping or perhaps a seal curious about their presence. They drew apart slowly, the moment dissolving like morning mist, but something had changed. The air between them hummed with new awareness and hope that, although unacknowledged, was there just the same.

"We should head back," Noah said, his voice

rougher than usual. "The weather's supposed to turn tonight."

Tess nodded, not trusting her voice. As Noah raised the anchor and prepared to sail them home, Tess watched him and wondered how a moment that felt so right could trouble her so.

The sail back to the harbor was quieter than their outward journey, both lost in their own thoughts as the *Mary Eleanor* cut through water that reflected the first hints of sunset. The cottage came into view on its bluff, windows catching the late light, looking more like home than Tess was quite ready to admit.

As they secured the boat and gathered their things, Noah caught her hand, stopping her as she prepared to step onto the dock.

"Tess."

She turned, finding his expression serious, almost vulnerable.

"Whatever happens," he said, "whatever you decide about ...everything. These afternoons—" He gestured toward the boat, toward the cove where they'd just shared something unnamed but significant. "They've been the best part of my summer. The best part of a lot of years, actually."

The confession was simple, honest, and quintessentially Noah in its lack of pretense. Tess felt something crack open inside her chest like a wall that was beginning to crumble.

"Mine too," she whispered.

They walked back to the cottage in the gathering dusk, as the afternoon light hinted that summer was surrendering to something new. Neither spoke of what had almost happened in the cove, but it lived between them now like a bridge half-built, waiting for one of them to be brave enough to finish the crossing.

That night, as Tess lay in bed listening to the wind pick up outside her window. Summer would end, yes, but that meant fall would soon follow. In nature, nothing truly ended. It simply transformed to become something richer and deeper.

Perhaps the same could be true for whatever was growing between her and Noah Pierce. Perhaps some things were worth the risk of hanging on through the seasons.

Outside, the wind carried the scent of the sea and its eternal rhythm of waves against stone. Inside, Tess gazed out at the moon's path that led over the water and wondered where her own path would lead.

CHAPTER 15

"I'm just saying you need to lean into what makes you unique," Tess explained, sketching rapidly on a napkin as Lucy watched from behind the café counter. "Every coastal town has lobster rolls and saltwater taffy, but only Peregrine Cove has your grandfather's secret recipe for hot chocolate that people drive an hour for."

Lucy tilted her head, considering the rough logo Tess had drawn of a steaming mug with the café's name arching above it in an elegant, vintage-inspired font. "Winter warmth from Maine's coolest coast," Tess had written beneath it.

"It's good," Lucy admitted, wiping her hands on her apron. "Really good, actually. But advertising costs money, and winter's always tight."

"That's why you need coordinated social media," Tess countered, flipping to a fresh napkin. "Targeted, not expensive. And if several businesses collaborate on a cohesive campaign, you all benefit from the increased visibility."

Three weeks into her stay in Peregrine Cove, Tess had grown increasingly aware of the economic challenges facing the small coastal town. Summer brought reliable tourism, but the long, harsh winters saw many businesses barely breaking even. It was a pattern common to seasonal destinations, but one that seemed particularly entrenched here.

"You should tell all this to the Chamber meeting tonight." Lucy poured Tess another coffee. "Seriously. They've been debating winter revenue strategies for years without much progress."

Tess hesitated, stirring her coffee absently. "I'm not sure they'd welcome input from an outsider."

Lucy's eyebrow shot up. "All the weeks living in Morna's cottage, and you're still calling yourself an outsider? Besides, your marketing background gives you credibility they'd respect."

Before Tess could form a rebuttal, the café door opened, bringing a rush of sea air and Noah. He nodded to several regulars before claiming the stool beside Tess.

"What are we plotting?" he asked, noticing the napkin sketches.

"Tess is saving our economic future," Lucy declared, setting a mug of coffee before him without being asked. "She's got ideas for boosting winter tourism."

Noah regarded Tess with interest. "Let me guess. You're telling Lucy to highlight what makes her place distinct instead of trying to compete with Camden's coffee scene."

"Something like that," Tess admitted, surprised by his insight.

"It's good advice." He sipped his coffee. "The Chamber's been stuck in a 'more of the same except louder' approach for years."

Lucy leaned across the counter conspiratorially. "Which is why I told her to come to tonight's meeting."

Noah's expression brightened. "You definitely should. Dad's presenting the annual fishing season report, so I'll be there anyway for moral support."

The casual assumption that she might naturally attend a community meeting and belong in the discussions stirred something warm in Tess's chest. It wasn't just Noah. Over the past few months, she'd found herself increasingly woven into the town's daily rhythms. Shopkeepers greeted her by name, neighbors stopped to chat about the cottage renovations, and she'd somehow acquired a regular order at not just Lucy's Café but also the bakery and the diner.

"Alright," she conceded, gathering the napkin sketches. "But I'm just observing, not presenting anything formal."

Lucy's triumphant smile suggested she knew better.

Five hours later, Tess stood before Peregrine Cove's Chamber of Commerce, twenty pairs of eyes fixed on her as she outlined her impromptu presentation.

What had begun as casual attendance had evolved rapidly when the topic turned to seasonal revenue strategies, and several members, Lucy prominent among them, had volunteered Tess's marketing expertise. With minimal preparation time, she'd organized her thoughts into a cohesive pitch, drawing on both her professional background and her growing understanding of the town's unique character.

"The mistake most seasonal destinations make is

trying to be something they're not during the off-season," she explained, her confidence building as she spoke. "Peregrine Cove doesn't need to compete with mountain ski resorts. It needs to offer what urbanites crave in winter—an authentic Maine experience."

She outlined a coordinated campaign highlighting cozy accommodations, local craftsmanship, comfort food with a distinctive Maine character, and the raw beauty of the winter coastline. "Weekend getaways, not week-long vacations," she emphasized. "Targeted at professionals within a three-hour drive seeking brief escapes from city pressures."

Her proposed strategy included unified social media themes, cross-promotion between businesses, and creating several seasonal holiday anchor events to draw initial visitors who would then spread word-of-mouth recommendations.

"The key is cohesion," Tess concluded. "Individual businesses benefit from a strong town identity. 'Winter in Peregrine Cove' becomes the brand, with each establishment offering its unique facet of that experience."

The room remained silent for a moment after she finished speaking. In the third row, Noah caught her eye, his expression conveying a quiet pride that steadied her nerves. Beside him, Rob Pierce nodded appreciatively, jotting notes in a small leather-bound book.

Walter Simmons, the seventy-something Chamber president who ran the local bookstore, cleared his throat. "That's a mighty sophisticated proposal, Ms. Bradford. But some of us have been in business here for decades. Fancy marketing doesn't change the basic reality of Maine winters."

Several older members murmured agreement, though Tess noticed Lucy and the other younger business owners exchanging encouraging glances.

"With respect, Mr. Simmons," Tess responded, "I'm not suggesting we change reality. I'm suggesting we change perception. The very elements that might seem like liabilities—the quieter streets, charming shops, and, yes, the dramatic winter weather. Sitting by a warming fire with a cup of cocoa while the sea waves crash against the rocks beneath brooding clouds—these can be assets when framed correctly."

She pulled up a mock social media post she'd quickly created on her laptop. The image showed Lucy's Café window, frost patterns decorating the edges, and a steaming mug visible in the golden interior light while snow fell outside. The caption read, "Some warmth is worth the journey. #PeregrineCoveWinter."

"Simple, authentic, and aspirational," Tess explained. "Not promising something we can't deliver but highlighting what we genuinely offer."

A thoughtful silence followed, broken when Maya from the hardware store spoke up. "I like it. Different from what we've tried before, but not so radical that it feels foreign to who we are."

Debate ensued, with questions ranging from practical budget concerns to philosophical discussions about Peregrine Cove's identity. Throughout, Tess fielded each query with the confident expertise that had made her successful in Boston while maintaining a collaborative tone that acknowledged the Chamber members' deeper knowledge of their town.

To her surprise, Walter Simmons eventually rapped

his knuckles on the table decisively. "I propose we establish a tourism revitalization committee to develop these ideas further, with Ms. Bradford as chair, if she's willing."

The motion carried with majority support, though Tess noted a few abstentions among the older members. As the meeting adjourned, various business owners approached her with questions and suggestions, their initial skepticism giving way to cautious optimism.

"That went better than expected," Noah commented when he reached her side, helping her gather her materials.

"I wasn't planning to become a committee chair," Tess admitted, still processing the rapid evolution of her casual advice into formal responsibility.

"Peregrine Cove has a way of pulling people in deeper than they intend." Noah's tone was light, but his eyes searched hers for a reaction.

Before she could respond, Walter approached them, extending his hand to Tess. "Impressive presentation. Reminds me of conversations we had with your mother years ago. Elizabeth always had big city ideas for our little town."

Something in his tone made Tess tense. "Thank you, though I hope my approach feels more aligned with Peregrine Cove's existing character."

Walter nodded, seemingly satisfied with her diplomatic response. "We'll see how it develops. Good evening to you both."

As they gathered their coats and prepared to leave, Tess overheard a conversation between Walter and Edith Caldwell, who owned the gift shop adjacent to his bookstore.

"Just like her mother—full of big plans," Edith remarked, her voice carrying in the nearly empty room. "Let's see if she sticks around to implement them."

The comment stung with its casual dismissal of her commitment, but before Tess could decide whether to acknowledge it, Noah spoke up.

"Tess isn't just passing through." Noah was firm but respectful. "She's investing in Peregrine Cove's future. The cottage renovations alone show her commitment to preserving what matters here while bringing a fresh perspective."

Edith had the grace to look abashed. "No offense intended, Noah. Just an observation based on experience."

"Sometimes new patterns emerge," he replied, then turned to Tess. "Ready?"

The night breeze carried a damp chill as they stepped outside. Stars, sharp and brilliant, glittered above them. For several blocks, they walked in comfortable silence while Tess processed both the meeting's outcome and Noah's defense of her.

"Thank you." Tess turned to Noah. "For what you said back there."

Noah shrugged. "It was true."

"Still. It means something, your speaking up for me like that." She glanced sideways at him. "Especially given our history."

They turned onto the path that led to the bluff where the cottage stood, following the beam of Noah's flashlight. The town lights receded behind them, leaving only stars and the distant rhythm of the waves on the rocks.

"I meant what I said," he confessed after a long

moment, "but sometimes I wonder if I'm fooling myself again."

The honest vulnerability in his admission, rather than creating distance, drew Tess closer. She stopped walking, turning to face him.

"I'm here, Noah," she said quietly.

His eyes searched hers, hope warring with the caution of experience. "Good ..."

"But?" she prompted, sensing his unspoken reservation.

Noah's smile was tinged with self-awareness. "But we've both changed. I'm not the boy who collected your letters, and you're not the girl who wrote them. Sometimes, I wonder if we're getting to know each other now or just chasing memories."

The question hit at something Tess had been considering herself—the complex intertwining of their past and present connections. Were they building something new or merely trying to repair what had been broken?

"I think it's both. I couldn't have stayed for a memory, Noah. I'm staying for what's real now—the cottage, yes, but also the community and the possible future I see here." She paused, gathering courage. "And you—the person you've become."

They had reached her porch, the cottage windows dark but welcoming. Noah set her presentation materials down on the top step.

"And who have I become?" he asked softly.

"Someone who builds things to last," Tess replied. "Someone who defends what he believes in. Someone who's learned to bend without breaking."

The air between them seemed to crystallize,

charged with all the words they hadn't yet said. Noah stepped closer, his hand tentatively reaching for hers.

"Tess," he began, his voice rough with emotion.

She closed the distance between them, her free hand finding his shoulder as she rose slightly on her toes. Their lips met in a kiss that began warily, a question rather than a declaration, but deepened as years of missed connection and months of growing attraction converged.

When they separated, both a bit breathless, Tess rested her forehead against his. "I need to be sure this isn't just about the past," she whispered.

Noah nodded, understanding in his eyes despite the longing evident in his expression. "We have time." The statement carried profound meaning between them.

Their second kiss was briefer but no less significant, like a promise rather than a culmination. As Tess gathered her things and unlocked the cottage door, Noah remained at the bottom of the steps, watching with an expression that lingered long after she'd closed the door.

In the quiet darkness of the cottage, Tess leaned against the wall, fingertips touching her lips where the memory of his kiss lingered. For the first time in her adult life, she was putting down roots, not out of obligation or momentum, but by deliberate choice.

The realization was both terrifying and exhilarating, that belonging somewhere wasn't the trap she'd always feared, but perhaps the foundation from which true freedom might grow. Not her mother's restless flight nor Aunt Morna's steadfast permanence, but something uniquely her own—a life built on a chosen commitment rather than either rebellion or resignation.

Outside, the sea breeze whispered through pine

branches while distant waves found their way to the shore. Tess moved through the darkness with newfound certainty, no longer feeling like a visitor in the space that was, with each passing day, becoming undeniably hers.

CHAPTER 16

"They've upgraded it to a Category 3," Noah said, his voice tight as he set down his phone. "There's a mandatory evacuation for the beachfront properties."

Tess looked up from the stack of documents she'd been sorting, and her stomach dropped at the grim set of his jaw. All morning, they'd been monitoring the hurricane's approach while preparing the cottage—boarding windows, securing loose items from the yard, and filling bathtubs with water. The sky outside had transformed from summer blue to an eerie yellowish gray, and the air was unnaturally still.

"What about us? We're not on the beach. We're on high ground, tucked away in our own little inlet."

"But we're still in the evacuation zone." Noah ran a hand through his hair, disheveled from hours of storm preparation. "And these old cottages weren't built for this kind of wind."

"Yeah, but it's lasted this long." Tess glanced around the living room that had become more familiar to her in weeks than her Boston apartment had in years. Aunt Morna's photographs, the hand-knit throws, the books lining the built-in shelves all seemed suddenly fragile and ephemeral. Having just come to feel home again here, she couldn't bear the thought of losing it all. "How long do we have?"

"Six hours, maybe less, before it really hits." Noah checked his watch. "Most people are heading to the high school shelter. We should think about—"

A sharp knock interrupted him. Eileen from the bakery stood on the porch, her normally cheerful face drawn with concern.

"Tom sent me to check if you need help getting to the shelter." Eileen peered past them into the cottage. "Most folks are heading there now."

Tess felt Noah's eyes on her, waiting for her decision. Three weeks ago, she would have already been in her car, driving inland to safety without a second thought. Now, the idea of leaving this place, even temporarily, made her chest ache.

"Thank you, but I think we'll stay put," she heard herself say. "The cottage has weathered a century of storms."

Eileen's eyebrows shot up, but she nodded. "Tom figured you might. He says to tell you the cellar's your best bet if it gets bad. These old places have good bones." She handed over a paper bag. "Cinnamon rolls. Might as well face a hurricane with something sweet."

After she left, Noah turned to Tess. "Are you sure about this? We can still go."

Tess looked at him, taking in the concern etched on his face and the way he stood a little closer to her than was strictly necessary, as he'd been doing increasingly over the past weeks. There was something in his eyes she couldn't quite read, something beyond the immediate worry about the storm.

"I'm sure," she said. "I want to stay here." *I want to stay here with you*, she thought, the realization hitting her with unexpected clarity.

As the afternoon progressed, the world outside transformed. The wind began as a whisper, then a moan, building to a howl that made conversation difficult. Rain arrived not in drops but in horizontal sheets that slammed against the boarded windows. The cottage, so solid and reassuring for weeks, began to creak and groan around them like a living thing in distress.

"We should move to the cellar," Noah said after a particularly violent gust made the whole structure shudder. "It's safer below ground."

The cellar was surprisingly clean, but chilly. Noah had stocked it earlier with blankets, lanterns, bottled water, and a battery-powered radio that now spat static-filled updates about the hurricane's path. They sat side by side against the stone foundation wall, shoulders touching, the lantern casting long shadows across the floor.

"I've never been in the direct line of a hurricane before," Tess admitted, trying to keep her voice steady as something heavy crashed outside.

Noah's hand found hers. His fingers, warm and strong, interlaced with her own. "First time for everything."

Above them, the storm unleashed its full fury. The sound was unlike anything Tess had ever experienced. It wasn't just the wind, but the sound. It felt like a living, breathing monster that screamed and clawed at their sanctuary with terrible power. The foundation trembled with each new assault, while dust sifted down from the ceiling beams.

"Tell me something." Tess was desperate for any distraction from the apocalyptic sounds above. "Tell me something I don't know about you."

Noah was quiet for so long that she thought he might not answer. "I almost asked you to marry me once."

Tess turned to him, certain she'd misheard. "What?"

"The summer just before you left. We were at the annual bonfire at Lighthouse Point." His profile in the lantern light was sharp, his eyes fixed on some distant memory. "We were sharing our dreams about college and the future."

"I remember that night." Tess recalled the scene from sixteen years ago—the heat of the fire, the salt-water drying on her skin, the bittersweet ache of the approaching end of summer.

"You were wearing that blue dress with the little white flowers. Your hair was all wild from swimming. We were talking about all the places we wanted to travel to. We even talked about backpacking through Europe together."

Tess grinned at the memory. "I remember."

Noah's thumb traced circles on her palm. "And I had this ridiculous thought. When we got to Paris, we'd visit the Eiffel Tower, and I would propose to you. And suddenly I didn't want to wait. I almost blurted it out right then and there. Let's get married!"

The cellar seemed to shrink around them, the storm forgotten. "But you didn't."

"No." His voice held no bitterness, only a quiet certainty. "Come on, Tess. Your parents had money. You could follow your dreams, but I'd never be able to keep up. And I loved you too much to be the thing that held you back. I guess I hoped you'd come back and stay so we could be together."

The confession hung in the air between them, stripped of pretense by the storm's violence. Something broke loose inside her, some final barrier she hadn't even realized she'd been maintaining.

"I've spent sixteen years running," she whispered. "From myself. From feelings I couldn't control. From the terrifying possibility that what I really wanted wasn't in Boston or New York or any of the places I kept convincing myself were home."

A tremendous crash directly above made them both jump. The radio squawked to life with an emergency alert. The hurricane had made landfall, with winds exceeding 115 miles per hour.

Noah pulled her closer with a strong, steady arm around her shoulders. "We're okay. The cottage has good bones, remember? And this cellar is built into solid rock."

But the tension in his body and the tightness in his voice contradicted his attempt to reassure her. For the first time, Tess considered the very real possibility that they might not survive the night. The thought sent a surge of panic through her, not just for their lives, but for all the things they'd left unsaid.

"I dated a man in Boston for three years," she said abruptly.

Noah glanced at her, clearly thrown by the change of subject. "Okay?"

"He was perfect on paper. Successful stockbroker, cultured, ambitious. He wanted to marry me." She swallowed hard. "I kept finding reasons to delay. I told myself I wasn't ready, that there was still too much I wanted to accomplish first."

"What was the real reason?" Noah asked.

"He kissed me once, and I felt ...nothing." The memory surfaced with painful clarity. "I stood there thinking about the way my shoes were getting ruined and whether I'd have time to stop for coffee before my next meeting."

The storm seemed to pause for breath, a momentary lull that only highlighted how fragile their shelter was.

"And then there was Michael, who loved sailing, David, who wanted to move to a small coastal town and open a restaurant, and James, who kept suggesting weekend trips to the shore." Tess laughed, the sound edged with wonder at her own blindness. "Do you see the pattern? Because I didn't. Not until this moment."

"Tell me," Noah urged, his voice barely audible over the renewed assault of the wind.

"They were all echoes. Incomplete reflections of something I'd been missing for sixteen years." Tess turned to face him, their knees touching in the confined space. "They were all poor substitutes for you."

The lantern flickered as another violent gust shook the house to its foundations. Something large fell upstairs, the crash reverberating through the cellar. Instinctively, Noah pulled Tess against his chest, his body curving protectively around hers.

At that moment, with destruction raging above them and the future uncertain, a clarity she'd been searching for her entire adult life came to her.

"It was you. It's always been you. I've been looking for you everywhere," she whispered against his shirt. "In every relationship, every city, every career achievement. Trying to recapture what we had that summer when everything seemed possible."

Noah's hand came up to cradle her face, his palm warm against her cheek. His eyes searched hers in the dim light, disbelief warring with hope.

"But ... if we make it through this." His voice was rough with emotion. "If we wake up tomorrow and the cottage is still standing, what then? Will you go back to Boston?"

The question was charged with sixteen years of missed opportunities and paths not taken. "No." Tess was certain. "I'm done running. I'm done pretending I belong somewhere I don't."

She leaned forward, eliminating the last inches between them. "I love you, Noah Pierce. I think maybe I always have."

The kiss that followed wasn't gentle or hesitant. It was desperate, hungry, the physical expression of years of sublimated longing. Noah's hands tangled in her hair as he pulled her closer, his mouth hot and insistent against hers. Tess matched his intensity, pouring into the kiss everything she'd been afraid to admit, even to herself.

When they finally broke apart, breathless, the storm seemed to have receded, though whether it had actually lessened or she'd just stopped hearing it, Tess couldn't tell.

"I should have said this the moment you walked back into town," Noah said, his forehead resting against hers. "I love you, Tess Bradford. I've never stopped."

The radio crackled with static, and then the announcer's voice broke through: "Breaking news. Hurricane Eliza has shifted course, moving offshore more rapidly than predicted. Coastal areas can expect continued strong winds and storm surge, but the most dangerous conditions should ease within the next few hours."

They both froze, absorbing the unexpected reprieve. Then Noah laughed, the sound rich with relief and perhaps even joy.

"Saved by a last-minute course change." He brushed a strand of hair from her face. "Just like you."

"What? I'm a hurricane?"

A wry smile crossed his face. "In a way. You were set on a path that would have taken you right back to Boston after settling the estate. Then something shifted." His eyes were soft in the lantern light. "And here you are, riding out a hurricane in a cellar with me."

Tess smiled, feeling lighter than she had in years, despite the storm still raging above them. "I think Aunt Morna would approve of my course correction."

"Approve? Morna orchestrated it!" Noah replied with a wry grin. "That woman played the longest game I've ever seen."

Another crash from above reminded them that they weren't entirely out of danger. Noah pulled her close again, his heartbeat steady against her ear. They stayed that way, wrapped in each other and the strange intimacy created by shared peril, as the hurricane gradually relinquished its hold on their small corner of the coast.

Sometime in the darkest hours of the night, with the storm reduced to fitful gusts and occasional downpours, Tess felt Noah's lips brush her temple.

"Whatever damage we find in the morning," he murmured, "we'll face it together."

It was the simplest of promises, but to Tess, who had spent her adult life maintaining careful independence, it was revolutionary. As she drifted toward sleep, still nestled in Noah's arms on their makeshift bed of blankets, she realized that for the first time in sixteen years, she wasn't planning her next escape.

CHAPTER 17

Dawn crept over the horizon in auras of pale gold, shedding light on the damage the storm had exacted overnight. Tess pushed open the cottage's front door and stepped gingerly onto the porch. The hurricane had veered offshore at the last moment and spared them the direct hit that had been predicted, but the outer bands had still packed enough punch to leave a significant mark.

Her breath caught as she surveyed the landscape. One of the massive old oaks had fallen across the front yard and crushed the porch railing and steps, yet miraculously stopped short of the main structure. Branches and debris littered the garden that Aunt Morna had tended so lovingly over the decades.

"Another foot, and it would've gone through the roof," Noah said quietly, coming to stand beside her.

They'd spent the night huddled in the cottage cellar as the storm raged above, a battery-powered radio their only connection to the outside world. The forecaster's announcement that the hurricane had shifted course had brought a relief so profound that Tess had found herself weeping as she buried her face against Noah's shoulder. Neither had managed to sleep through the howling wind and their own racing thoughts.

In those tense hours, with the storm's fury shaking the very foundation of the cottage, something had broken open between them, revealing a vulnerability neither had intended. Noah had held her close in the dim light of their emergency lantern, his heartbeat steady against her ear despite the fear she knew he must feel. It was there, with the world seeming to end around them, that Tess had finally stopped running from herself.

"I'm scared," she'd admitted in a whisper, nearly lost beneath a particularly violent gust.

His arms had tightened around her. "I know."

"Not just of the storm. Of this. Us." She'd looked up at him then, finding his eyes in the shadows. "Of how much it would hurt to lose you."

The memory of that raw confession lingered between them now as they stood in the harsh light of morning, surveying the damage that seemed so much more manageable than what they'd feared in those dark hours.

The garden that had been Aunt Morna's pride was flattened, with branches and debris scattered across the lawn. But the cottage itself stood firm, a testament to the craftsmanship of another era, or perhaps simple luck.

"It could have been so much worse," Tess whispered, relief flooding through her.

Noah took her hand, his palm rough against hers. "You're safe, and the house is still standing. That's all that matters."

Those simple words echoed back to their night in the cellar, how they'd clung to each other in the darkness, confessing long-held feelings as the storm raged overhead. A blush rose up her neck as she remembered the intensity of their kiss and the way Noah had held her, as if she might disappear.

"Last night," she began, unsure if the emotions of the storm would hold up in daylight. "What you told me about our last summer ..."

Noah's hand tightened around hers. "I meant every word. I've carried that thought in my mind for sixteen years."

"And I meant what I said, too," Tess replied, her voice stronger. "About all those relationships that never worked because they were just poor substitutes for what I really wanted." She turned to face him. "For whom I really wanted."

He turned to her then, his eyes searching her face. Whatever he saw there made his expression soften.

"I've been alone most of my life," he said. "I thought I preferred it that way. Then you arrived, and solitude wasn't enough."

A truck pulled into the driveway, interrupting the moment. Men in ServePro uniforms climbed out, ready to assess the damage.

"Ms. Bradford? We're here for the emergency cleanup. Your insurance company dispatched us."

The next few hours passed in a flurry of activity. The ServePro team walked the property with clipboards while Noah and Tess salvaged what they could from the crushed porch. By afternoon, the insurance adjuster had come and gone, assuring Tess that everything would be covered.

"Small-town efficiency," Noah explained with a small smile.

As the cleanup crew departed with a promise to return the next day, Tess stood in the yard and looked over the property. The cottage appeared wounded but dignified.

"It's still home." She surprised herself with the certainty in her voice.

Noah fixed his eyes on her. "Is it?"

The question held more weight than just the immediate aftermath of the storm. Tess knew he was asking about her life, her future, whether her place was here in this coastal town or back in the urban world she'd come from. Quitting her job had bought her a year to settle the trust, but what came after that was uncertain.

She thought of her apartment in Boston, sterile and stylish, where neighbors passed in hallways without speaking. And then there was her office with its deadlines and constant pressure. Any new job would bring with it similar stress. Then she looked at Noah, with his steady presence and eyes that seemed to see through her facade.

"I spent my whole life planning for a future that always seemed just out of reach," she said slowly. "Always telling myself that happiness was one promotion, one project, or one achievement away. But last night, when I thought I might die, I didn't regret the reports I hadn't filed or the meetings I might miss."

She stepped closer to him, and her heart beat so hard she was certain he must hear it.

"I regretted the fear that kept me from admitting what I wanted. Who I wanted."

Noah's breath caught. "And what do you want, Tess?"

She looked into his eyes and wondered whether she dared put it in words. "I want this. This life. This place." She reached up, touching his face with trembling fingers. "You."

The simplicity of it was terrifying and liberating all at once. There was no hedging now, no escape routes, and no cautious distance.

He drew her into his arms and held her as if she were precious and fragile. He pulled away just enough to lean in for a kiss. As their lips nearly touched, his phone rang.

He glanced down at the screen. "It's my landlord."

Tess cringed. *That can't be good.*

Noah ended the call. "We need to go." They hopped into his truck.

THEY HAD BARELY TURNED the corner into the harbor district when Noah went still. Even from a distance, the damage was evident. The two-story building housing his apartment above the boatyard office had a gaping hole where the roof should have been. Debris littered the small parking area, and yellow caution tape fluttered in the breeze.

"No," Noah whispered, quickening his pace. Tess hurried to keep up, her heart sinking as they drew closer, and the full extent of the destruction became clear.

The hurricane's path through town had been erratic, sparing some structures while decimating others. Noah's building had taken a direct hit, leaving the second floor exposed to the elements like a dollhouse with its roof removed.

A town emergency worker intercepted them before they could cross the caution tape. "Sorry, folks. The building's been condemned. No entry without structural engineers present."

"That's my apartment," Noah said, his voice oddly flat. "All my things are in there."

The worker's expression softened with recognition. "Pierce, right? I'm sorry, man. We secured what we could, but the rain damage alone ..." He shook his head. "Insurance rep's been by taking photos. They'll contact you."

Noah nodded mechanically, his eyes fixed on what remained of his home. Tess placed a hand on his arm, feeling the tension in his muscles.

"Is there anything that can be salvaged?" she asked the worker.

"Maybe some items on the lower shelves, away from the exterior wall. But honestly? Most of it's a total loss."

Noah moved toward the tape as if in a trance. "I just need to see—"

"I can't let you in, Noah," the worker said firmly. "It's not safe. The whole structure could come down."

Tess watched as Noah absorbed this reality, his shoulders slumping almost imperceptibly. He'd been so focused on helping everyone else—her with the cottage, his father with storm preparations, and elderly neighbors with evacuation—that he'd hardly had time to secure his own belongings.

"Where will you stay?" she asked as they walked away from the building, the worker having moved on to other tasks.

Noah ran a hand through his hair, looking suddenly lost. "Dad's, I guess. His place is inland, so it didn't get hit as hard."

The thought of Noah returning to his father's house, where Rob's disapproval of their relationship hung in the air, was unsettling. Without thinking, the words tumbled out. "Stay with me. At the cottage."

Before Noah could voice the doubts that were clear on his face, Tess continued. "Look, your place is a mess, and my cottage is fine. And—bonus—it has a roof." Her smile faded. "Stay with me. Not because you have to, but because you want to. And because I want you to."

Noah looked at her, surprise evident in his expression. "Tess, I couldn't—"

"Why not? It makes sense. You've been helping repair it for months. The cottage owes you." She attempted a light tone, though her pulse quickened at the implications of what she was offering. Her smile faded. "I owe you. And I want you to stay."

A complex series of emotions crossed Noah's face—gratitude, hesitation, and an intensity that made Tess's heart skip. "What would people say?"

She rolled her eyes, trying to keep things casual despite the significance of the moment. "People have already been talking about us since the festival dance. We might as well give them something to actually talk about."

That earned a small smile, though his eyes remained troubled. "My dad wouldn't be thrilled."

"And my mother would probably have a conniption," Tess agreed. "But it's not about them. It's about us and what makes sense right now." She paused, realizing she needed to make something clear. "It's temporary, of course. Just until you figure out your next steps or your apartment is repaired."

The word "temporary" was layered with unspoken complications. The cottage renovations and her stay in Peregrine Cove existed in this undefined interim period. Neither of them had defined what they were to each other in practical terms, despite the confessions shared during the storm.

"Temporary," Noah repeated, the word carrying a weight his tone couldn't quite disguise. "Right."

They stood in silence, the wreckage of his apartment behind them, the uncertain future ahead.

"It makes sense," Tess added, feeling the need to clarify her intentions. "The cottage has plenty of space, and with all the repairs needed after the storm, having you there would make everything easier."

Noah studied her face, seeing through her attempt at casualness. "Is that the only reason you're asking?"

The directness of his question caught her off guard. In the aftermath of the hurricane, with emotions still raw from their shelter confessions, dancing around the truth seemed exhausting.

"No," she admitted quietly. "It's not the only reason."

His expression softened. "Then yes. I'll stay at the cottage." He took her hand, interlacing their fingers. "Temporarily."

The way he said it, with gentle irony and a hint of challenge, made something flutter in Tess's chest. They both knew this arrangement would test the boundaries they'd maintained, even as the distance between them had narrowed over the past months.

"We should probably not mention this to your father right away," Tess suggested as they turned to walk back toward the cottage.

"Or your mother," Noah agreed. "Some things are better shared after they're already done."

Tess felt a mixture of anticipation and apprehension as they walked hand in hand. "This is going to complicate things, isn't it?"

Noah's thumb traced a small circle on her palm. "Tess, things between us were complicated the moment you drove back into town." His smile was both tender and wry. "But some complications are worth it."

As they made their way toward the cottage that was no longer just Aunt Morna's, not quite fully Tess's, and now partly Noah's, at least for the time being, the word "temporary" lost its meaning. She'd spent her adult life creating exit strategies, keeping one foot out the door in every situation. Yet here she was, inviting Noah into her space without a clear endpoint in sight.

It should have terrified her. Instead, beneath the practical concerns and logistical questions, hope took root, as if this arrangement, born of disaster and necessity, might be the beginning of something neither temporary nor easily defined.

But as they crested the hill overlooking the cove, the reality of their situation reasserted itself. The cottage stood partially damaged on its bluff, surrounded by debris. Tess had a life in Boston on hold, with an apartment and responsibilities accumulating in her absence. Noah had lost his home, but not his ties to Peregrine Cove, his business, and his community commitments.

"We'll figure it out." Noah seemed to read her thoughts.

Tess looked at their intertwined fingers, then up at the weathered cottage that had brought them together against all odds.

"We always do," she replied, squeezing his hand.

Neither of them mentioned that "always" wasn't a word they'd earned the right to use just yet. But for the first time in her life, Tess wasn't afraid of the possibility.

THAT NIGHT IN THE COTTAGE, they moved around each other with a new awareness. The tension that had built between them since her arrival, accelerated by their desperate connection before the hurricane, had transformed into something deeper. They now recognized what they could be together.

When the electricity flickered out again, Noah lit some candles that cast the simple room in golden light. At his small table, they sat and ate sandwiches they'd brought from town, as their knees touched under the table.

"Tell me what you're thinking." He studied her face in the warm candle glow.

"I'm thinking about Aunt Morna. She knew this would happen."

"That you'd fall in love with the cottage?"

Tess held his gaze. "That I'd finally stop running from what I've wanted since I was eighteen." She smiled softly. "She must have known that whatever we had back then wouldn't fade away."

"Of course she knew. Morna knew everything," Noah agreed, his voice warm with affection. "She told me once that some people need to leave a place before they can truly find their way home."

"Wise woman."

Later, they stood by the window and watched the harbor waters reflect the emerging stars. Behind her, Noah stood with his arms wrapped around her waist and his chin resting on her head.

"I'm not good with words," he softened his tone. "But I need you to know something."

Tess leaned back against him, feeling the solid strength of his chest. "What's that?"

"Yesterday, when I thought about losing you, afraid you might decide this place wasn't worth the trouble, it felt like watching a storm surge coming. I wasn't sure how I'd make it."

The simple admission, spoken in his straightforward way, moved her more than any elaborate declaration could have.

"I'm not leaving." She turned in his arms to face him. "That part of my life is over. This is my life now."

When he kissed her, it wasn't with the desperate urgency of the hurricane night but with a deliberate tenderness that spoke of time and intention. It wasn't a kiss stolen in the face of disaster but one given freely, with the promise of tomorrow and all the days after.

His hands framed her face, and his thumbs gently stroked her cheekbones as if memorizing their shape. Tess leaned into his touch and allowed herself to be present in a way she'd never managed before. She no longer needed to calculate the outcome or protect herself from potential pain, but she let herself feel each sensation as it unfolded.

"I've wanted to do that since the day you arrived in town," Noah confessed, his forehead resting against hers. "Standing there with your Boston high heels and that look of determination mixed with absolute terror."

Tess laughed softly. "I was so focused on how I didn't belong here and getting everything done so I could leave."

"And now?"

She slid her hands up to his shoulders and reveled in his solid warmth. "Now I can't imagine being anywhere else."

Later, on the small balcony outside his apartment, they shared a bottle of wine and watched the harbor returning to life. Fishermen were assessing their boats for damage, shop owners were sweeping debris from the sidewalks, and children were running through puddles despite their parents' protests.

"It's amazing how quickly people bounce back," Tess said.

Noah leaned against the railing beside her. "People here understand that nature gives and takes. You adapt, or you don't survive."

"Is that why you stayed?"

He was quiet for a moment, considering. "I guess. I've seen people leave, but I never understood why, because here I was free. What else could I need? Well, except for one thing."

A wave of sympathy and guilt rushed through Tess.

Noah continued. "Leaving here wouldn't change anything, so I stayed."

The admission was honest and unvarnished. Tess had spent her entire adult life avoiding this kind of vulnerability in herself and in others. She'd chosen men who were as emotionally unavailable as she was, whose relationships could be easily compartmentalized alongside their work and ambitions.

What Noah offered was honest, messy, and sometimes unsettling, but it was real.

"I used to think people who talked about love were deluding themselves," she said quietly. "I thought it was just chemicals and convenience, something people invented to make themselves feel less alone."

"And now?" His question was gentle, without pressure.

"Now I think I've spent my whole life being wrong." She met his gaze unflinchingly. "I love you, Noah. Not because it's convenient—God knows it's not —but because somehow, in the middle of all this chaos, you've become the one steady thing I can't imagine living without."

The words, once spoken, were like a weight lifted rather than a burden assumed. Noah's eyes darkened, and he pulled her to him with an urgency that contrasted with his earlier restraint. This kiss was deeper, hunger mingling with tenderness, the first true acknowledgment of where the night would lead them.

Outside, the harbor waters lapped gently against the shore, a rhythmic reminder that even the most violent storms eventually yielded to calm. Inside, as they moved from the balcony to the living room, the lamplight painted their bodies in gold as they shed layers and abandoned inhibitions.

"Are you sure?" Noah asked, his voice rough as they paused at the threshold of his bedroom.

Tess answered by taking his hand and leading him toward the bed, her heart racing not with uncertainty but with the thrill of choosing what she wanted.

LATE IN THE NIGHT, Noah traced lazy patterns on Tess's bare shoulder. "You realize the whole town is going to know about this by tomorrow?"

Tess laughed, surprising herself with how little she cared. "Those people need a hobby."

He smiled against her hair. "Morna would be smug as hell right now."

"Yeah, she would! She planned this whole thing, didn't she? Leaving me the cottage, knowing you'd be the one to help me with it."

"Morna played the long game," Noah agreed. "But even she couldn't have predicted the hurricane."

"Maybe not the actual storm," Tess mused, settling more comfortably against his chest. "But I think she knew it would take that kind of upheaval to bring me to my senses."

They fell silent and listened to the distant sounds of the sea. Tess knew there would be challenges ahead. The cottage needed repairing, and her career needed reimagining, but now she had something more important to build. For the first time in her adult life, she wasn't planning escape routes or safeguarding against disappointment.

She was here at this moment, her body curved

against Noah's, building something neither of them could have envisioned alone.

It wasn't the story she had expected when she'd first driven down that coastal road with Aunt Morna's letter on the passenger seat. It was better, if messier, but more authentic and filled with a richness she'd denied herself for too long.

"Tomorrow," Noah whispered against her skin as she drifted toward sleep, safe in his arms, "we begin something new."

CHAPTER 18

Tess woke to the unfamiliar sound of cabinets opening and closing in the kitchen. For a disorienting moment, she couldn't place herself. The bedroom was hers, but the muffled percussion recital beyond the door belonged to someone else's life. Then the memory rushed back. With Noah's apartment destroyed, she'd impulsively offered him hers. Now his belongings, what few had survived the hurricane, now occupied her spare room.

She stretched beneath Aunt Morna's quilt, listening to the quiet efficiency of Noah's movements downstairs. Three days into their temporary arrangement, a rhythm had already established itself. Noah rose early to make coffee, and Tess joined him after catching those precious extra minutes of sleep that had become her small luxury since leaving Boston's frantic pace.

The clock read 6:47 a.m., later than Noah usually let her sleep. Curious, she slipped from the bed, pulled on her robe, and padded downstairs. The sight that greeted her in the kitchen made her pause in the doorway.

Noah stood at the counter with his back to her and arranged two plates with what appeared to be an actual breakfast instead of the hurried toast or cereal they'd managed in the previous days. Sunlight streamed through the windows and shone on his still shower-damp hair, illuminating the focused set of his shoulders as he worked.

"You didn't have to do all this," Tess said, stepping into the room.

Noah turned, a smile warming his face. "Morning, sleepyhead. I found eggs and that fancy bread you like in town yesterday." He gestured toward the table, already set with mugs of steaming coffee. "I figured we deserved a real breakfast."

The simple domesticity of the moment caught Tess off guard. How many mornings had she spent in Boston gulping coffee while reviewing emails, then rushing out the door without speaking to another soul? The contrast with this quiet kitchen, filled with morning light and the rich aroma of coffee, couldn't have been starker.

"What's that expression?" Noah asked, setting the plates on the table.

Tess realized she'd been staring. "Just ... adjusting. It's nice having someone else in the house." The words felt like an unexpected admission of a desire for commitment.

They settled into breakfast, discussing their plans for the day. Noah mentioned a town meeting that evening about hurricane recovery efforts. The easy back-and-forth reminded Tess of their teenage summers when conversation flowed without effort or pretense.

"I was thinking." Noah collected their empty plates. "Maybe we could rearrange the living room furniture. That couch would get better light if we moved it under the bay window."

"I've been thinking the same thing," Tess admitted, surprised at their synchronicity. "And maybe we could move Aunt Morna's reading chair to that corner? It's always looked cramped where it is."

Noah's grin lit up his face. "Great minds! We could do it this afternoon after I pick up some groceries."

The casual planning for their shared space was both new and somehow familiar, as if they were piecing together old fragmented dreams of what their life could be.

By MID-AFTERNOON, they had transformed the living room. The heavy sofa now faced the bay window, catching the best of the winter light. Aunt Morna's reading chair occupied a cozy corner near the bookshelves. They'd even swapped two smaller side tables, creating a more balanced flow to the room.

"It looks bigger this way." Tess stood back to admire their work. "More welcoming."

Noah nodded, wiping the dust from his hands. "Amazing what a fresh perspective can do."

They stood side by side, shoulders almost touching, and contemplated the space they'd reconfigured together. At that moment of shared satisfaction, a strange sensation took hold, as if the cottage were exhaling and settling around them like a contented cat.

This wasn't just Aunt Morna's house anymore, or even just Tess's. It was beginning to feel like theirs.

"What now?" Noah asked, turning to her with an expectant smile.

Before Tess could answer, a sharp knock at the front door interrupted. Through the window, she glimpsed a familiar sedan parked in the driveway.

"Mom?" Tess couldn't hide her surprise as she opened the door.

Elizabeth Bradford stood on the porch, looking elegant as always in a camel-colored coat and boots far too fashionable for Peregrine Cove's muddy November streets.

"You haven't returned my calls in days, and I saw the hurricane coverage on the news." Elizabeth stepped inside without waiting for an invitation. "I thought I should see for myself if you were all right."

Her critical gaze swept the living room, taking in the obviously rearranged furniture and equally obvious signs of Noah's presence—his jacket tossed over a chair, his laptop open on the coffee table, and a mug sitting beside Tess's on the side table.

"Noah," Elizabeth acknowledged with cool politeness when she spotted him. "I didn't realize you were here."

"Mrs. Bradford." Noah nodded, a certain wariness entering his posture. "Good to see you again."

Tess glanced between them, feeling the sudden tension crackle in the air. "We were just rearranging some furniture," she explained, hearing the defensive note in her own voice. "The room needed refreshing."

"Clearly." Elizabeth removed her coat, handing it to Tess with practiced elegance. "Lucy mentioned I might find you both here, although she neglected to mention the extent of the arrangement."

"Noah's apartment was destroyed in the hurricane," Tess explained, hanging up her mother's coat. "He's staying here temporarily while he figures out his next steps."

"How convenient." Elizabeth's perfectly shaped eyebrow arched as she surveyed the room again, this time with greater deliberation. Her gaze lingered on the obvious signs of cohabitation—Noah's books mingled with Tess's on the coffee table, their jackets hanging side by side, the subtle but unmistakable presence of a man's belongings integrated with Tess's own.

"I'll put on some coffee," Noah said, a clear excuse to give mother and daughter some privacy.

Once he'd disappeared into the kitchen, Elizabeth turned to Tess, keeping her voice low. "So, this is why you've been ignoring my calls? You've been playing house with Rob Pierce's son?"

"I haven't been ignoring your calls," Tess countered, matching her mother's hushed tone. "And we're not playing house. We're busy dealing with the aftermath of a hurricane."

"Apparently." Elizabeth settled onto the newly positioned sofa, her posture perfect even in censure. "Darling, I understand the appeal of a rugged handyman after a disaster, but surely you could have maintained some propriety?"

"This isn't about propriety, Mom." Tess struggled to keep the frustration from her voice. "Noah lost his home. I had space. It was the decent thing to do."

Elizabeth's smile held no warmth. "There's decent, and then there's shacking up. This—" she gestured to the evidence of their shared life "—looks decidedly more like the latter."

In the kitchen, Noah was taking longer than coffee preparation strictly required, his consideration for their privacy both appreciated and somehow disappointing. Tess wished he were beside her to form a united front against her mother's cool judgment.

"I don't need your approval." Tess kept her voice even. "Noah and I are adults, making our own decisions."

"Clearly," Elizabeth replied. "I just hope you've considered what you're sacrificing. Your career in Boston won't wait forever, and temporary arrangements have a way of becoming ... complicated."

Tess was taking a moment for a few calming breaths when Noah returned with a tray bearing coffee and cookies. His eyes met Tess's, but his expression was neutral.

"I hope you still take it with cream, Mrs. Bradford." Noah offered Elizabeth a mug.

The forced politeness of the next few minutes was excruciating. They discussed the hurricane damage in town, the recovery efforts, the unusually sunny weather —anything but the obvious. Elizabeth sipped her coffee with practiced grace as her eyes cast an occasional sweep over Tess and Noah's shared living space with barely concealed disapproval.

The sound of another vehicle pulling into the driveway broke the stilted conversation. Tess moved to the window, and her stomach sank as she recognized Rob's truck.

"It's your dad." Panic edged her voice.

Noah's eyes widened. "He mentioned he might stop by to drop off some tools he found in storage."

Before any of them could fully prepare, a knock sounded at the door. Noah opened it to reveal his father, whose expression shifted from casual greeting to wary alertness when he spotted Elizabeth sitting on the couch.

"Rob." Elizabeth set down her coffee mug with deliberate precision and turned with a pasted-on smile. "What a surprise."

"Elizabeth." Rob nodded stiffly from the doorway, looking unsure of whether to enter. "I didn't realize you were in town."

"Evidently, there's quite a bit you didn't realize." Elizabeth's gaze pointedly shifted to Noah and the obvious signs of his residence in the cottage.

The tension in the room thickened to an almost unbearable degree. Tess shot Noah a helpless glance, only to find his face set in the same careful neutrality he'd worn since Elizabeth's arrival.

"I heard around town Noah was staying here." Rob directed his comment to Tess while stepping into the room. "I thought I might check to see how things were going."

"Things are going fine," Noah answered before Tess could, his tone deliberately light. "We were just having coffee with Mrs. Bradford."

"Were you?" It wasn't so much a question as a flat acknowledgment, loaded with subtext.

Elizabeth smiled thinly. "What a surprising coincidence, both of us checking on our children on the same day."

"Not much coincidence in a town this size," Rob

countered, shifting his weight uncomfortably. "Word travels."

"Yes, I imagine it does." Elizabeth's tone could have frosted glass. "Just like it did years ago."

The reference to their shared past hung in the air like smoke, acrid and suffocating. Tess felt Noah move closer to her.

"Some things don't change." Rob's voice was gruff but controlled. "Small towns have long memories."

"And limited horizons," Elizabeth added with a pointed glance between Tess and Noah.

"Mom," Tess warned, her patience finally snapping.

The sharpness in her tone seemed to surprise everyone, including herself. Elizabeth raised an eyebrow but remained silent.

"Noah's here temporarily," Tess continued, feeling the need to address the unspoken concerns directly. On impulse, she added, "But that could change." She'd meant it as a jab toward her mother. But when, from the corner of her eye, she saw Noah shoot her a look of surprise, she added, "It's our decision." Her eyes darted between her mother and Rob.

Rob had the grace to look abashed. "I'm just concerned about history repeating itself," he muttered.

"We're not you," Noah said quietly, the simple statement somehow more powerful for its gentleness. "Either of you."

A strange expression crossed Elizabeth's face—not quite regret or even acknowledgment, but something that suggested she'd received the message.

Rob cleared his throat uncomfortably. "Well," he said after an awkward pause, "I should get going. Just wanted to drop these off." He handed Noah a small box of tools that seemed more like a pretext for checking on the living situation. "Maya's organizing a meal train for the Henderson family. Their roof still isn't fixed."

"We'll sign up," Tess replied, grateful for the shift to safer ground.

Rob nodded. "Thursday's open."

Tess said, "I'll take it."

"Great. Thursday it is." Rob turned with obvious reluctance to Elizabeth. "Good to see you, Lizzie."

The childhood nickname seemed to catch Elizabeth off guard. For a brief moment, her perfect composure wavered, revealing a flicker of vulnerability—something Tess had rarely seen in her mother.

"You, too, Rob," she replied, her voice softer than before.

After Rob left, an uncomfortable silence fell. Elizabeth stood, smoothing her immaculate slacks with practiced hands.

"I should go, too. I have a dinner reservation in Camden." She collected her coat, her movements precise and controlled. "Tess, would you walk me to my car?"

Outside, a warm breeze stirred the leaves. Elizabeth paused at the driver's side door, looking unusually serious.

"Be careful, Tess." Her mother was quieter than before. "I'm not saying he isn't a good man. Rob was a good man, too. But good men from small towns often can't imagine why anyone would want more."

"I'm not like you, Mom." Tess crossed her arms. "I'm not running from anything or using Noah as an excuse to stay. I'm choosing to be here in the Cove—

with Noah—because they matter to me. And I'm happy."

Elizabeth's expression shifted to surprise, then reluctant recognition. She studied Tess's face for a long moment before speaking.

"Just be sure you're choosing freely, not reacting to my choices." She touched Tess's cheek briefly, the gesture unexpectedly tender. "We often define ourselves in opposition to our parents, darling. That can be just as limiting as any other kind of prison."

The insight, unexpected from a woman Tess had always considered self-absorbed, left her momentarily speechless. Elizabeth slipped into her car with practiced elegance, rolling down the window for a final observation.

"And Tess? He looks at you the way Rob once looked at me. Be certain of what you want before that look becomes an expectation you can't meet."

With that, she drove away, leaving Tess standing in the driveway, her mother's words echoing in her mind. The cottage door opened behind her, and Noah's footsteps crunched on the gravel.

"Are you okay?" he asked, coming to stand beside her.

"Not really," Tess admitted, turning to face him. "That was ..."

"A lot," Noah finished when she trailed off. "Parents have a special talent for making adult children feel fifteen again."

Or younger. Tess laughed.

They stood side by side in the fading afternoon light, watching Elizabeth's car disappear down the road. The weight of the past hour, the unresolved tension and unexpected insights, settled around them like the November chill.

Noah broke the silence. "I should probably tell you Dad invited us to dinner on Sunday."

"Of course he did." Tess laughed. "Your father manages to convey disapproval and dinner invitations in the same conversation."

"Family talent," Noah agreed, his smile warming his eyes. "We don't have to go."

Tess considered this, then shook her head. "No, I think we should. Running away only gives them more power."

Noah's expression shifted to something more serious. "Is that what your mother was doing? Running away?"

The question cut closer to the bone than Tess expected. "I think she was running toward something she thought she wanted. But yes, also away from what scared her."

"And what scares you, Tess?"

The directness of the question was pure Noah—no hedging, no games. It was one of the things she'd come to value most about him.

"That I'm making choices based on rebellion instead of what I really want," she admitted, the truth surprising even her. "That I'm staying in Peregrine Cove just to prove my mother wrong about small towns and limited horizons."

Noah nodded, absorbing this without defensiveness. "And what do you really want?"

Tess looked at him and took in the concern in his eyes, the patience in his stance, and the quiet strength that had become her anchor through storm and aftermath. "I want to find out if what we're building here is real, not just a reaction to the hurricane or our parents' history or Aunt Morna's wishes. Something that's ours —something real."

Noah's expression softened, something like hope flickering in his eyes. "I want that too."

They stood in the fading light, neither moving to close the small distance between them, yet somehow more connected than if they had. Around them, the wind rustled through pine branches, carrying the distant sound of waves on the shore.

"We should go in," Tess said after a moment.

Noah nodded, but neither moved immediately. "Can I ask you something?"

"Of course."

"Are you okay with me staying here? Really okay? Because I can find somewhere else if—"

"No," Tess interrupted, surprising herself with her vehemence. "Don't go."

The words were full of meaning neither had fully acknowledged until this moment. Noah's hand came up, hovering near her cheek without quite touching.

"I don't want to push you into something you're not ready for," he said.

Tess closed the distance between them, her lips finding his with a certainty that surprised them both. Unlike their desperate kiss during the hurricane, this was deliberate, a choice made with clear eyes and full hearts. Noah's arms encircled her, drawing her closer as the kiss deepened, months of building tension finally finding release.

When they parted, breathless, Noah rested his forehead against hers. "Are you sure?" he asked, his voice rough with emotion. "This isn't just a reaction to your mother's visit?"

Tess smiled, recognizing the echo of Elizabeth's warning. "This is the one thing I am sure of." She traced the line of his jaw with gentle fingers. "Being here together feels right in a way nothing else has."

Noah's smile bloomed slowly, transforming his face from cautious hope to certainty. "It does, doesn't it?"

Back inside the cottage, they moved through the evening routine they'd established over the past days—preparing dinner together, washing dishes side by side, discussing books and town gossip. Yet everything seemed different now, charged with new awareness and possibility.

Later, as moonlight spilled through the cottage windows, Tess curled against Noah as they sat watching a movie together.

"What are you thinking?" Noah asked, his fingers tracing lazy patterns on her bare shoulder.

Tess considered the question, sorting through the complex emotions of the day, from her mother's unexpected visit and Rob's awkward appearance to simple moments together like this. "I'm thinking that sometimes the right path isn't the one you planned. It's the one that finds you when you stop running."

Noah's arms tightened around her until she could hear his steady heartbeat beneath her ear. Outside, the wind carried the distant sound of the waves on the shoreline, but inside, a quiet peace settled upon them. The last of Tess's resistance dissolved, not in surrender, but by choice.

For the first time in her adult life, she embarked on a path that was completely and undeniably her own.

CHAPTER 19

October light slanted through the kitchen windows as Tess sifted flour into a mixing bowl. Outside, the coastal Maine landscape was beginning to change. It was subtle at first, but the late afternoon sun slanted early and low through the windows, and the rustling leaves were beginning to change. Before long, they would fall, shifting the world into the muted palette of winter. But for now, the cottage was warm with domesticity. A steaming mug of coffee sat on the counter, Noah's sweater lay draped over a chair, and their mingled voices and movements created a harmony that had become so natural neither of them remarked on it anymore.

"We're low on firewood." Noah glanced out the back window toward the dwindling stack. "I'd like to see that woodshed full by the end of the month. I'll split some more this afternoon."

The casual "we" slipped out without thought, and neither of them paused to acknowledge it. Without looking up from the pie crust she was preparing, Tess said, "There's still time before the snow flies."

Noah wrinkled his face in disagreement. "The local forecast is calling for an early winter."

Two months after the hurricane, what had begun as an emergency arrangement had evolved into something neither of them openly questioned. Noah's presence in the cottage seemed less like a temporary solution to his destroyed apartment and more like a piece that had always been missing and had finally settled into place.

"Dad dropped another hint yesterday." Noah leaned against the counter beside her. "Something about having cleared out the spare room at his place."

Tess's hands stilled in the flour. "Oh?" She tried for a neutral tone but didn't quite achieve it.

"Yeah." Noah picked up a stray apple peel, turning it absently between his fingers. "He said he'd put fresh sheets on the bed in case I wanted to 'come home for a while.'"

The unspoken question hung between them, tangled with their careful avoidance of defining what this living arrangement had become. Temporary, they'd told everyone, including themselves. Yet each day that passed made the prospect of separation more unthinkable.

"What did you tell him?" Tess asked, returning her attention to the pie dough with more focus on working the butter into the flour than the task required.

Noah shrugged, the movement bringing his shoulder lightly against hers. "That I appreciated the offer, but I was comfortable with the current arrangement."

Something loosened in Tess's chest. "And he was okay with that?"

"He didn't push," Noah replied, then added with a wry smile, "which, for my father, is practically a blessing."

Tess laughed, the tension dissolving as quickly as it had formed. This was what had surprised her most about living with Noah—the easy rhythm they'd established, the way they could navigate potentially fraught conversations without the drama she'd always associated with relationships.

Tess reached for her phone. "Speaking of parents, my mother called about Thanksgiving."

Noah's expression shifted subtly. "I'm guessing I wasn't mentioned in the invitation?"

"Not explicitly, no." Tess wiped flour from her hands. "Just the usual 'we expect you'll come to Boston' directive, as if the past months haven't happened."

"You should go." Noah paused. "Family traditions are important."

Tess looked up at him, studying the controlled neutrality of his expression. In the weeks they'd been living together, she'd learned to read the subtle indicators of his emotions—the slight tension around his eyes that signaled concern, the measured tone that hid disappointment.

"What if we created our own tradition?" she suggested, the idea forming as she spoke. "Here, at the cottage. We could invite both our families."

Noah's eyebrows rose. "That's ...brave."

"Or possibly insane," Tess acknowledged with a small laugh. "But maybe it's time we stopped letting our parents dictate the terms of our relationships, with them or with each other."

Noah considered this, then a slow smile spread across his face. "You know what? Let's do it. Worst-case scenario, we create a holiday disaster we'll be laughing about for years."

Neither addressed the casual reference to their shared future and the years stretching ahead of them, but the thought warmed her.

"I'll call my mother back," Tess said as she reached for her phone.

"And I'll talk to Dad," Noah added, already moving toward the door. "Though something tells me convincing him will be the easier task."

As Thanksgiving Day approached, Tess's prediction proved accurate. Elizabeth had declined the invitation with a mixture of disapproval and barely veiled disappointment, citing previous commitments but making it clear that she considered Tess's decision to host her own Thanksgiving a personal betrayal of their family tradition. To Tess's surprise, her father had been noticeably silent on the matter, neither supporting Elizabeth's position nor offering to attend himself.

Rob Pierce, on the other hand, had accepted with a gruff "sounds fine" that left Noah staring at his phone in mild disbelief after their conversation ended.

"He didn't argue or question it at all?" Tess asked as they prepared the guest bedroom the evening before Thanksgiving.

"Not a word," Noah replied, still sounding puzzled.

"He just asked what time and if he should bring anything."

"Wow. Did I just see a pig fly past the window?" Tess murmured, smoothing fresh linens over the bed. "Maybe our parents are finally accepting that we're adults capable of making our own decisions."

Noah's laugh held a touch of skepticism. "Whoa, there. Let's not get carried away with optimism."

As Tess fluffed the pillows, she found herself contemplating the guest room, formerly Aunt Morna's room, now transformed into a space for visitors. Noah had moved into Tess's room so gradually that neither had marked a formal transition. First, his reading glasses lay on her nightstand, then a drawer was emptied to make room for his clothes. Then one night, the question of where he would sleep wasn't even discussed.

"We've come a long way." The thought brought a smile to her face.

Noah glanced around the room, then back to her, something warm in his gaze. "In more ways than one."

Their eyes met across the neatly made bed, and Tess felt the now-familiar flutter in her chest—the pleasant disorientation of finding herself just where she wanted to be with no effort.

THANKSGIVING DAY dawned clear and cold, with sunlight glinting off frost-covered grass. Tess and Noah moved about the kitchen in their established morning dance—coffee brewing, oven preheating, the turkey already prepared and waiting. The familiar rhythm of working together had taken on a festive air, punctuated by stolen kisses between tasks and the occasional burst of music from the old radio Aunt Morna had kept on the windowsill.

As the dinner preparations grew frenzied, flour dusted Tess's cheek, and hair escaped its hasty bun. "Remind me why we thought hosting was a good idea?"

Noah grinned as he wiped a smudge from her face with his thumb. "Because we're gluttons for punishment? Or maybe we've just lost our minds."

"Both seem plausible," she agreed, leaning briefly into his touch before turning back to the potatoes she was peeling.

By four o'clock, the cottage was transformed. The dining table was set with Aunt Morna's best china, candles waited to be lit, and the rich aroma of roasting turkey and sage stuffing filled the air. Tess had just emerged from a quick shower and changed into a simple burgundy dress when the first knock sounded at the door.

Rob Pierce stood on the porch with a bottle of wine in one hand and an uncertain expression that melted into relief when Noah greeted him.

"The place looks nice." Rob stepped inside and glanced around at the newly decorated cottage. "Different."

Tess recognized the comment for what it was—an acknowledgment not just of the physical changes to the space, but of their new lives in the cottage now under their joint care.

"Thank you for coming." Tess took his coat. "We're glad you could make it."

Rob nodded. His usual gruffness softened somewhat. "Smells good. Like when Morna used to host."

The comparison, clearly intended as high praise, warmed Tess unexpectedly. She caught Noah's eye over his father's shoulder, and both shared a pleasantly surprised look.

Dinner progressed more smoothly than they'd dared to hope. Rob was on his best behavior, making an obvious effort to engage Tess in conversation about her work, the cottage renovations, and even her plans for the garden in the spring. The notable absence of her parents hung in the air but remained unmentioned as they worked their way through turkey, stuffing, cranberry sauce, and Rob's favorite—sweet potato casserole that Tess had prepared using Aunt Morna's recipe.

"This is exactly how she used to make it." Rob helped himself to a second serving. "You got the brown sugar crust just right."

"Tess has been going through Morna's recipe box," Noah explained with evident pride in his voice. "She's discovered all sorts of traditional dishes."

"Noah's done his share of cooking, too," Tess added, nodding toward Noah. "He's surprisingly adept in the kitchen."

Rob's eyebrows rose. "He never showed much interest in cooking before."

"Morna taught me some things," Noah replied, his hand finding Tess's under the table.

The casual intimacy of the gesture wasn't lost on Rob, whose expression shifted to something more thoughtful than disapproving. Before he could respond, however, the sound of a car in the driveway interrupted their meal.

"Are we expecting someone else?" Rob asked, glancing toward the window.

Tess shook her head, already rising from her seat. "No, but—"

The words died on her lips as she recognized the vehicle coming to a stop beside Rob's truck. It was her parents' car, with her father at the wheel and her mother sitting rigidly in the passenger seat.

"Oh," she breathed, looking at Noah with wide eyes. "It's my parents."

Noah sprang up and moved to her side. "Both of them?"

Rob's expression had changed from his earlier warmth to wary caution. "I can go if this is about to get complicated."

"No," Tess said with conviction. "No one's leaving. This is our home, and if they've chosen to come, they can deal with whoever happens to be here."

The knock came, and with a steadying breath, Tess moved to open the door. Her father stood on the threshold with Elizabeth slightly behind him, both dressed for dinner as if they'd planned this visit all along.

"Dad? Mom? Hello." It was all she could do to hide her shock and dismay.

Thomas Bradford smiled with a combination of sheepishness and determination in his expression. "Happy Thanksgiving, Tess. We thought we'd surprise you." He glanced past her to where Noah stood, adding, "Both of you."

"Thomas insisted," Elizabeth added, her tone making it clear this had not been her preference. Her gaze moved to the dining table, where Rob still sat, and something flashed in her eyes—surprise quickly masked by her usually composed detachment. "Oh. I see we're interrupting."

"Not at all." Noah stepped forward with more grace than Tess could have managed in the moment. "We have plenty of food. Please, join us."

The next few minutes passed in a blur of rearranging chairs, setting additional places, and navigating awkward introductions. Noah's hand at the small of Tess's back provided steady support as she welcomed her parents into a home they'd never truly seen as hers, which she now shared with the son of a man her mother had once rejected.

"Rob." Thomas extended his hand across the table once they were all seated. "Been a long time."

"Thomas." Rob's tone was neutral but not hostile as he returned the handshake. "I didn't expect to see you here."

"That makes two of us," Elizabeth murmured, just loudly enough to be heard as she arranged her napkin in her lap.

Tess shot her mother a warning look. "We're glad you could make it." She tried to sound diplomatic. "I got a little ambitious in the kitchen, so there's more than enough food."

"It all looks wonderful." Thomas seemed genuinely warm as he helped himself to the dishes being passed around. "Your mother mentioned you were hosting, and I thought it was high time we saw this cottage everyone's been talking about."

The careful phrasing of "your mother mentioned," and not "we were invited," told Tess precisely how this surprise visit had come about. Her father had taken matters into his own hands, forcing Elizabeth's participation through what must have been considerable negotiation.

Conversation during the meal tiptoed around potential landmines, with Elizabeth limiting herself to polite inquiries about the food and weather while Rob responded with equally safe topics. But as second helpings were served and the wine glasses refilled, something unexpected began to happen. Thomas engaged Rob in a discussion about fishing techniques that evolved into a surprisingly animated debate, complete with gestures demonstrating proper casting form.

"You're using too much wrist," Rob insisted, demonstrating the motion. "It's all in the forearm rotation."

"That might work for saltwater," Thomas countered, "but for fly-fishing in streams, you need that wrist action. I should take you up to my spot in the White Mountains this spring and show you what I mean."

The casual invitation and Rob's equally casual acceptance left Tess nearly slack-jawed and Noah staring in surprise. Elizabeth, too, seemed taken aback, watching the exchange with an expression that shifted between disbelief and discomfort.

As Noah began clearing plates to prepare for dessert, Thomas rose to help him, leaving Tess momentarily alone with Rob and her mother, a scenario she would have considered nightmarish just weeks ago.

"The cottage looks lovely," Elizabeth said after an awkward silence. "You've made some ... interesting changes."

"Thank you," Tess replied, recognizing the olive branch, however tepid. "We've tried to honor what was here while making it our own."

The "our own" slipped out naturally, and Tess saw

her mother register it, a slight tightening around her eyes the only indication of her reaction.

Rob cleared his throat. "Tess has done wonders with the place. Morna would approve."

The unexpected compliment from Rob seemed to surprise Elizabeth as much as it did Tess. She studied him across the table with a softening expression.

"Yes," she agreed quietly. "Morna always did have faith in Tess's ability to find her way."

In the kitchen, Noah and Thomas worked side by side, the older man rolling up his sleeves to help with the dishes while Noah sliced the apple pie.

"This was a pleasant surprise," Noah said when the silence had stretched long enough to become uncomfortable. "Your visit, I mean."

Thomas smiled ruefully. "Elizabeth wasn't thrilled with the idea. But I told her it was time we all grew up a bit." He glanced toward the dining room, where his wife sat in an uncharacteristically subdued conversation with Rob and Tess. "Some old patterns need to be broken, you know?"

Noah nodded slowly, understanding more than Thomas might have intended. "Thank you for coming. It means a lot to Tess."

"I can see that." Thomas's gaze was direct now. "And I can see that you mean a lot to her, too."

Noah's shoulders tensed as he prepared for the protective father speech he'd been expecting since Tess's parents had arrived.

Instead, Thomas surprised him. "She's happy. Happier than I've seen her in years." He picked up a stack of clean plates. "That counts for quite a bit in my book."

"Mine too," Noah said.

When they returned to the dining room with dessert, the conversation had shifted to safer ground— the winter festival the town was planning, the repairs still ongoing at the harbor, and the unusually cold forecast for December. As pie was served and coffee poured, Noah noticed Tess watching her parents with a puzzled expression, as if she were trying to solve a riddle.

After dessert, Thomas suggested a walk to settle their meal. To everyone's surprise, Rob agreed to join him, the two men setting off down the path toward the water, their conversation continuing unabated as they disappeared from view.

Elizabeth declined the walk with a pointed glance at her impractical shoes, leaving her alone with Tess and Noah. After a moment of strained silence, she rose gracefully. "I think I'll freshen up," she said.

Once she'd disappeared upstairs, Tess turned to Noah, feeling thoroughly bewildered. "What just happened?" she whispered. "My father and your father are suddenly fishing buddies, and my mother is being almost civil. Did we slip into an alternate dimension?"

Noah shook his head, equally baffled. "I have no idea. But it's ... nice?"

"Weird," Tess countered, though a smile tugged at her lips. "Lovely, but definitely weird."

Through the window, they could see their fathers walking along the shore, Thomas gesturing emphatically while Rob nodded, hands in pockets but posture relaxed. The sight was so unexpected, so contrary to everything they'd feared about this day, that they could only watch in wonder.

Later, as Elizabeth and Thomas prepared to leave, Tess stood alone with her father on the porch. The evening had mellowed to a peaceful darkness, stars emerging in the clear sky above.

"Thank you for coming," she said, with genuine gratitude. "I know it wasn't easy to convince Mom."

Thomas smiled and wrapped an arm around her shoulders. "Your mother is complicated, but she loves you. She's just afraid of you making what she considers mistakes."

"You mean Noah," Tess clarified, glancing back toward the cottage where he was helping Elizabeth into her coat with careful courtesy.

"I mean, choosing a life she once walked away from." Thomas's voice held no judgment, only quiet understanding. "Elizabeth needs conflict to justify her restlessness. She always has. It's easier for her to believe Peregrine Cove is provincial and limiting than to admit she might have found happiness here."

The insight into her mother struck Tess with unexpected force. "I never thought of it that way."

Thomas squeezed her shoulder gently. "Give her time. She's coming around in her own way." He glanced toward the cottage with a softening expression. "I think Noah's a good man. Like his father."

"You and Rob seemed to hit it off." Tess was still marveling at the evening's unlikely turn.

"Time has a way of putting old rivalries in perspective." Thomas chuckled. "Besides, he really does know his fishing spots."

As they rejoined the others, Tess was struck by the tableau before her—Noah standing easily beside Elizabeth, Rob nearby, all of them somehow managing a civilized goodbye. Not friendship, certainly, but a tentative truce she would have considered impossible just hours earlier.

After her parents' car disappeared down the lane, Tess and Noah helped Rob gather leftovers to take home. The older man seemed thoughtful as he prepared to leave.

He paused at the door. "Your father knows his stuff about fly-fishing," he said directly to Tess. "He invited me up to his cabin in the spring."

"Are you going to go?" she asked, curious.

Rob considered it, then shrugged. "I might." He glanced between them with approval. "Dinner was good. Thanks for having me."

After he, too, had gone, Tess and Noah stood in the doorway of their cottage, watching his taillights fade into the darkness. The silence between them was comfortable, filled with the shared experience of a day that had defied all expectations.

"Well ..." Noah slid his arm around Tess's waist. "That was ..."

"A Thanksgiving miracle?" Tess leaned into him.

He laughed softly and pressed a kiss to her temple. "Something like that."

They went inside and closed the door to the November chill. The cottage welcomed them back. It was their home now, unquestionably. As they began cleaning up together, Tess paused to watch Noah as he wrapped the leftover pie, looking comfortable and sure in their shared space.

"What?" he asked, catching her gaze.

"I was just thinking about what my dad said," she

replied. "About my mother needing conflict to justify her restlessness."

Noah nodded thoughtfully. "That explains a lot."

"It made me realize something," Tess continued, moving closer to him. "I've spent so long being afraid of ending up like her. But what if I was actually more like Aunt Morna all along?"

"How so?"

"Aunt Morna knew where she belonged. She wasn't trapped here. She chose this place and this life." Tess gestured around them at the cottage that had become theirs. "Just like I'm choosing this. You. Us."

Noah set down the pie, turning to face her. "Does that scare you? Making that choice?"

Tess considered the question seriously, searching her heart for the old fear, the claustrophobic panic that had always accompanied thoughts of permanence. To her surprise, she found only certainty. "No. For the first time, the thought of staying put feels more like freedom than the thought of running away."

Noah's smile was slow and deep, reaching his eyes and warming them to the color of summer sea glass. "That sounds suspiciously like you're planning to keep me around."

"Suspicious indeed," Tess agreed, stepping into his embrace. "We might need to investigate further."

Later, as they lay in what had unquestionably become their bed, Tess thought about the day's unexpected revelations—not just about her parents and their complicated history with Rob, but about herself. The cottage around them creaked and settled in the night chill, its sounds no longer strange but familiar and comforting.

"What are you thinking?" Noah asked, his voice soft in the darkness.

Tess turned toward him, finding his outline in the dim moonlight filtering through the windows. "I'm thinking that sometimes the families we make choose us as much as we choose them."

Noah's hand found hers beneath the covers, their fingers intertwining with practiced ease. "I like that thought."

Outside, the first light snow of the season began to fall, silently dusting the cottage roof and the ground below. Inside, Tess drifted toward sleep, Noah's steady breathing beside her, no longer questioning whether this arrangement was temporary or permanent. Some questions answered themselves, given enough time and enough courage to hear the answers.

CHAPTER 20

As December painted the coastal landscape in muted earth tones, Tess found herself settling into the rhythms of Peregrine Cove's off-season with fewer tourists, longer conversations with shopkeepers, and cozy evenings by the fire with Noah. Her marketing consultancy flourished as word spread about her successful summer campaigns, and she began planning a winter tourism initiative that would launch after the holidays. The cottage, now fully winterized, seemed to sigh with satisfaction as the first snow dusted its roof and frost traced delicate patterns on the windows Noah had so carefully restored.

Tess adjusted her scarf against the chill as she hurried up Main Street toward the Chamber of Commerce. Under her arm, she clutched a portfolio containing weeks of research, mock-ups, and prepared proposals for Peregrine Cove's winter tourism campaign. The afternoon sun cast long shadows across the snow-dusted sidewalks, where Christmas decorations in shop windows glinted as they caught the midday sun.

She'd spent the morning rehearsing her presentation, with Noah patiently playing the role of skeptical Chamber members as she refined her pitch. Now, with the actual meeting minutes away, butterflies fluttered in her stomach, a sensation she hadn't experienced since her early days pitching to clients in Boston.

"This matters more," she realized, pausing outside the weathered brick building that housed the Chamber offices. In Boston, presentations had been about advancing her career, impressing colleagues, and securing accounts. Here, her work would impact people she now knew by name—the shopkeepers who greeted her each morning, the fishermen who saved their best catch for the local restaurants, and the artisans whose crafts she now displayed proudly in the cottage.

The Chamber meeting room was already half-full when she arrived. Walter Simmons, the bookstore owner who served as Chamber president, nodded her way as she shed her coat and arranged her materials at the front table. Lucy waved from her seat, giving Tess an encouraging thumbs-up.

"All set for the big reveal?" Lucy asked as Tess slid into the chair beside her.

"As ready as I'll ever be," Tess replied, smoothing invisible wrinkles from her presentation folder. "Though I'm starting to think selling ice to Eskimos might be easier than selling winter tourism to this crowd."

Lucy chuckled. "Don't let them intimidate you. Half of them are just resistant in principle to anything new."

As if on cue, Hank Morrell entered, stomping snow from his boots with unnecessary force. As harbormaster and third-generation Peregrine Cove resident, Hank considered himself the guardian of town traditions. His skepticism toward Tess's committee leadership had been barely concealed from the start.

"Here we go," Lucy murmured as Hank took a seat across from them, his expression already set in preemptive disapproval.

By the time Walter called the meeting to order, the room had filled with a cross-section of Peregrine Cove's business community, from enthusiastic younger entrepreneurs to cautious old-guard stalwarts. Tess scanned the faces, mentally cataloging likely allies and probable opponents as Walter moved through routine business.

"Next on the agenda," Walter announced, adjusting his reading glasses, "is the tourism committee's winter campaign proposal." He nodded toward Tess. "Ms. Bradford has prepared a presentation. The floor is yours, Tess."

Taking a steadying breath, Tess moved to the front of the room and set up her laptop and projector. The faces watching her reflected varying degrees of interest, skepticism, and curiosity. When everything was set up, she turned to address the room.

"Thank you all for the opportunity to share this proposal," she began, her voice growing more confident with each word. "For too long, Peregrine Cove has treated winter as something to be endured rather than celebrated. We shut down shops, reduce hours, and essentially hibernate until Memorial Day, missing months of potential revenue and community engagement."

She advanced to the first slide, a striking image of Peregrine Cove's lighthouse with frost patterns adorning its base and dramatic winter waves crashing behind it.

"What I'm proposing isn't about transforming Peregrine Cove into something it's not," she continued, moving through her prepared visual aids. "It's about highlighting what makes this place special year-round, particularly the authentic winter experiences visitors can't find in commercialized ski resorts or overcrowded Christmas markets."

For the next fifteen minutes, Tess outlined her vision—lighthouse tours showcasing winter storm watching, frost fishing expeditions guided by local fishermen during the harbor's quieter season, artisan workshops where visitors could create souvenirs alongside local craftspeople, and cozy accommodations marketed as peaceful winter retreats from urban hustle.

"We're not targeting week-long vacations," she explained, "but weekend getaways for professionals within a three-hour drive."

She concluded by showing mock-ups of coordinated social media campaigns and promotional materials, all centered around a "Winter in Peregrine Cove" theme that would unify individual businesses under a cohesive brand.

As she finished, the room remained quiet for a beat too long. Tess's confidence wavered until Lucy broke the silence with enthusiastic applause, quickly joined by several of the younger business owners. Hank, however, cleared his throat loudly.

"That's a mighty fancy presentation," he said, his tone making the word "fancy" sound like an accusation.

"But some of us have been surviving winters here for decades without turning the town into a tourist circus."

"With all due respect, Hank," Tess countered, "surviving winter and thriving during winter are two different things. I'm not suggesting we change what Peregrine Cove is, just that we share its winter beauty with visitors who would appreciate it."

"And who's going to run these 'authentic experiences?'" Margaret Winters from the gift shop asked. "Most of us can barely keep regular hours with the reduced staff we have in winter."

"That's where the coordinated schedule comes in," Tess explained. "No business would need to be open seven days a week. By staggering special events and creating a centralized booking system, we can manage visitor flow efficiently."

The debate continued, with concerns and questions flying from all directions. Some were practical, concerning budgets, implementation timelines, and marketing reach. Others revealed deeper anxieties over changing the town's character, disrupting winter's quiet rhythm, and inviting outsiders into what many considered a sacred recovery period after the summer tourist season.

Through it all, Tess maintained her composure, answering each challenge with data, providing examples from similar coastal communities, and affirming her sincere respect for Peregrine Cove's traditions. Yet with each passing minute, she felt the room's resistance hardening, particularly among the older members whose opinions carried significant weight.

"I just don't see why we need to fix what isn't broken," Harold Jenkins from the hardware store said, leaning back in his chair with arms crossed. "Winter's been quiet here since my grandfather's time, and we've all managed just fine."

"Managing isn't the same as growing," Tess pointed out. "And while many established businesses might weather slow winters, newer shops struggle. Three closed permanently last winter alone."

"That's the natural order of things," Hank interjected. "If they can't make it through a Peregrine Cove winter, maybe they don't belong here."

"Like some other recent arrivals," Margaret added under her breath, though loud enough for Tess to hear.

The thinly veiled reference stung more than Tess expected. Before she could respond, her eyes met Noah's, and his encouraging nod fortified her.

"The committee is recommending a trial program," Tess continued, refocusing on her proposal rather than the personal slight. "Three coordinated weekend events in January and February. They'd require minimal investment, trackable results, and a full evaluation before deciding whether to expand the program."

Walter rubbed his chin thoughtfully. "A trial does sound reasonable. Limited risk, potential upside. But I think we need to consider—"

"What I'd like to consider," Hank interrupted, "is whether someone who's just passing through should be driving changes that will affect those of us who've built our lives here." He looked at Tess. "No offense, but you've been here ten minutes."

Six months. Not to mention my childhood summers. Tess willed herself to be silent and hear him out.

He continued. "And we all know you'll be heading

back to Boston once you've had your fill of small-town charm." He cast a snide glance toward Noah.

The accusation landed like a physical blow. Tess opened her mouth to defend herself, but Noah's voice rang out from the back of the room before she could speak.

"That's unfair, Hank, and you know it." Noah stepped forward, his calm tone belying the intensity in his expression. "Tess has invested more in this town in six months than some lifelong residents. She's supported local businesses, volunteered for storm cleanup, researched our history, and now she's offering professional expertise that would cost thousands if we hired a consultant."

The room fell silent as all eyes alternated between Noah and Hank.

"And she's not just passing through," Noah continued, his gaze steady. "She's committed to Peregrine Cove's future, which is exactly what this proposal is about."

Noah's defense filled Tess with a flush of gratitude. His unwavering support, offered without hesitation in front of the entire business community, touched her in ways she hadn't expected.

"Noah makes a valid point," Walter said, stepping in diplomatically. "We should evaluate ideas on their merit, not on how long the presenter has lived here." He surveyed the room. "I propose we put the trial program to a vote. Three events, closely monitored, with a full review in March before any further commitment."

The vote passed, though not unanimously. Seven in favor, five opposed, with Hank and his allies recording their objections for the minutes. As the meeting adjourned, Tess gathered her equipment with a complex mixture of triumph and lingering hurt swirling within her.

Lucy squeezed her arm as she passed. "You did it! Don't let the grumps get to you. They'll come around when the cash registers start ringing."

Outside, snow had begun to fall in fine flakes drifting lazily in the early December twilight. Noah waited for her at the bottom of the steps with his hands in his pockets as flecks of snow collected in his dark hair.

"That was quite a defense in there," Tess said as she reached him. "Thank you."

"I was just stating facts," Noah replied with a shrug, though his eyes were serious. "Hank was out of line."

They fell into step together as they walked toward the harbor.

"It bothered me more than it should have," Tess admitted. "Being called a temporary visitor."

Noah glanced at her. "Because it hit close to home?"

The question was layered with meaning neither had addressed since she'd quit her Boston job. Tess considered deflecting, but instead admitted, "Because it's not true anymore. I don't know exactly what my future looks like, but I want Peregrine Cove to be part of it."

Noah nodded, satisfaction evident in his expression. "Your proposal was excellent. Professional, thoughtful, and respectful of the town's character."

"Not everyone saw it that way."

"Change is hard, especially in small towns." They reached the harbor railing and paused to watch the snow accumulate on the boats and docks. "They'll come around, Tess."

They stood in comfortable silence, watching darkness settle over the harbor, the snow falling more heavily now. Tess leaned against Noah as his arm slipped around her waist. Moments like this made her feel like she was home. Perhaps that was the most significant change in her life over the past months.

"Takeout dinner at the cottage?" she suggested as the wind picked up, carrying the scent of approaching snow.

Noah's eyes sparkled. "It's like you can read my mind."

AN HOUR LATER, Noah emerged from the kitchen with a bottle of sparkling wine and two glasses.

"What's this?" Tess asked, wide-eyed.

"A celebration!" He popped the cork and filled their two glasses. "Your first Chamber victory deserves proper acknowledgment."

They settled into conversation as easily as they did everything else these days, discussing the meeting and tossing around ideas for the first winter event.

"Did you ever imagine this?" Tess asked during a lull, gesturing vaguely between them. "Us, here, like this?"

Noah considered the question, his eyes reflecting the golden glow of the candle between them. "I imagined a lot of things over the years," he admitted. "None of them quite matched the reality."

"Better or worse?" she teased, though the question carried more weight than her tone suggested.

"Different," he said thoughtfully. "More complex. More real." He reached over and took her hand. "More worth waiting for."

The simple honesty of his answer moved her unexpectedly. This was what had been missing in her other relationships, this unvarnished truth and openness.

"I used to count the days," she confessed, her voice soft. "When I was a teenager, I'd count the days until I could come back here."

Noah's thumb traced gentle circles on her palm as he listened.

"Now I'm here, and sometimes it's hard to believe." The admission was significant—not a declaration of permanent roots, but an acknowledgment that the change was profound.

Noah smile deepened as if he understood.

"I've counted too," he said. "But different things. Days since you came back. Mornings waking up beside you. All the moments I want to remember."

"I have something for you." He reached into his jacket pocket. "An early Christmas gift."

He pulled out a key on a handcrafted wooden keychain shaped like a boat.

"What's this?" she asked, running her finger over the smooth wood.

"The key to my workshop," Noah explained. "I thought you might like a place to meet clients outside of your home. There's a desk by the window that catches the morning light perfectly."

The thoughtfulness, not just of the key, but of his recognition of her needs as she built her consulting business, touched her deeply. Noah wasn't asking for declarations or promises, just offering connection, integration, the weaving together of their separate lives.

"I love it." Tess closed her fingers around the key. "Thank you."

Later, as they brought down boxes of Aunt Morna's Christmas decorations from the attic, Tess paused and stared at an ornament.

"What are you thinking?" Noah asked, noticing her contemplative expression.

"That I've never really decorated for Christmas," she replied.

Noah's step faltered, and he stared as if she'd just landed from another planet. "What?"

She shrugged. "It was just my apartment, and I was always too busy." As she said it, she realized how lame her excuses sounded. "But it feels different this year."

The smile that spread across Noah's face was like the sun breaking through clouds. "I'm glad."

He didn't press for more. He squeezed her hand, smiled, and proceeded to unbox more ornaments as snow continued to fall. Christmas was coming this year to their home.

CHAPTER 21

Snow fell in large, lazy flakes amid the glow of white lights strung through the trees of Peregrine Cove's village green. Families gathered in anticipation as children bundled in colorful scarves and mittens chattered with glee in the December air. In the center stood a magnificent spruce tree adorned with garlands and bulbs. The annual Christmas tree lighting was about to begin.

Tess stood beside Noah. His arm was wrapped securely around her waist as they sang Christmas carols. As a brisk wind blew in from the sea, Tess nestled closer.

"Hot chocolate?" he murmured into her ear.

"Please!" She watched him make his way toward Lucy's stand, where steaming cups changed hands as fast as Lucy and her staff could serve them. The separation gave Tess a moment to absorb the surrounding scene. The familiar townspeople now greeted her by name. These were people whose shops were now part of her weekly routine. Beyond the village square, fishing boats bobbed gently in the harbor, all decorated with their own Christmas lights.

Six months ago, she would have been in Boston, attending some colleague's cocktail party or stopping by her parents' house for a dutiful holiday visit. But this place and these people were now part of her home.

"One hot chocolate with extra cinnamon, just how you like it." Noah returned with two steaming cups. He passed one to her, their gloved fingers brushing in the exchange.

She grinned. "You remembered!"

Noah shrugged, that half-smile she'd grown to love warming his face. "I always remember what matters."

She playfully rolled her eyes and nudged him, but his corny comment rang true. He did always remember what mattered to her, and it touched her deeply. This was what separated Noah from any other man she'd known. His attentiveness wasn't strategic. It was just who he was.

"Ladies and gentlemen," Mayor Thurlow's voice boomed through the speakers set up around the square, "it's time for our annual Christmas tree lighting!"

The crowd cheered, parents lifting children onto shoulders for a better view. Noah moved behind Tess, wrapped his arms around her, and rested his chin on her head. His casual intimacy felt as natural as breathing.

"Ten! Nine! Eight!" The countdown began, voices joining in unison across the square. Tess shouted along, caught up in the communal anticipation.

"Three! Two! One!"

The massive spruce blazed to life, thousands of white lights illuminating the square all at once. The crowd erupted in applause and cheers, and an unexpected lump came to Tess's throat. There was something magical about the moment, not just the beauty of the lights against the dark December sky, but the shared joy and the sense of belonging to this tradition.

"Beautiful," she whispered.

"Yes, you are," Noah replied softly, turning her in his arms to face him. His eyes reflected the tree lights as he gazed down at her.

Tess's heart fluttered in her chest, a sensation she'd once have dismissed as foolish romanticism but now recognized as the very real effect this man had on her. She stretched up on tiptoes and pressed a gentle kiss to his lips, unconcerned about the public display of affection. Peregrine Cove had already labeled them a couple. There was no use pretending otherwise. In fact, she didn't mind it at all.

"I have reservations at the Harbor Light," Noah said as they separated. "Our table should be ready soon."

"You've been secretly planning." Tess tucked her hand into the crook of his arm as they began walking toward the restaurant.

"No secret. It's Christmas Eve. It should be special," he replied.

The Harbor Light Restaurant was transformed for Christmas Eve, the elegant dining room aglow with twinkling lights, candles, and evergreen boughs. Their table overlooked the harbor, where the water reflected the moon and the shimmering lights from boats and distant windows. A single red rose waited in a crystal vase alongside a bottle of wine.

"Noah, this is lovely." Tess took her seat and

admired the view. "I'd have been just as happy with takeout at the cottage, but this ... it's perfect."

His expression softened as he playfully said, "It's just dinner out."

The meal unfolded at a leisurely pace—seafood chowder followed by locally caught lobster tails. They talked and laughed easily, sharing stories of Christmas traditions from their childhoods. Noah described his father's annual Christmas afternoon ice fishing expedition, while Tess recounted the formal dinners her mother insisted upon, even when there were no guests.

"I used to beg to open just one present on Christmas Eve," Tess recalled, smiling at the memory. "My father would pretend to consider it a terrible breach of protocol, then inevitably give in."

"And what would be waiting under your tree?" Noah asked, refilling her wine glass.

"As I grew older, the toys, dolls, and board games became mostly books. My father knew what I loved." Her smile softened with fondness. "What about you? Any Christmas Eve traditions?"

"My mom would read 'The Night Before Christmas' every year, no matter how old I got." Noah's expression held the particular mixture of joy and melancholy that always accompanied memories of his mother. "After she died, Dad and I ..." He paused, gathering himself. " ...kind of lost that tradition."

Tess reached across the table, covering his hand with hers. "Maybe it's time for some new traditions."

Noah turned his hand to interlace their fingers. "I had the same thought."

Something in his tone, a hint of future plans, of permanence, sent a flutter of anxiety through Tess's chest. She pushed it aside and focused instead on the warmth of his hand and the sincerity in his eyes.

"So ...traditions ...let's see ...I could eat my weight in Lucy's Christmas cookies. They're dangerous!" she said, aiming for lightness.

Noah smiled and added, "Christmas Eve dinners here." He gestured around them. "And watching the tree lighting together, of course." He hesitated as his thumb traced a gentle pattern on her palm, then said softly, "And waking up on Christmas morning together."

Each suggestion built upon the last, sketching an image of Christmases stretching into the future, all rooted in Peregrine Cove. The picture was beautiful, appealing, and suddenly overwhelming.

She managed a nod before taking a sip of wine to cover her uneasiness. Why was she feeling this tightness in her chest? This was Noah, the man she'd come to love, talking about spending holidays together. It should have filled her with joy, not this strange, creeping panic.

If Noah noticed her discomfort, he didn't comment on it. Instead, he changed tack, sharing a funny story about Rob's attempt to deep-fry a turkey one disastrous Thanksgiving. Tess laughed, grateful for the shift to safer ground, but the moment had left its mark. As dessert arrived, chocolate soufflé with raspberry sauce, she found her thoughts wandering, examining her unexpected reaction.

"What is it?" Noah said gently, noticing her distraction.

Tess offered a smile she hoped appeared more

genuine than it felt. "Just thinking about how different this Christmas is from any other I've had."

"Good different?"

"Very good different," she assured him, and that much was entirely true. "I've never felt so ..."

"So what?" he prompted when she hesitated.

"Present," she decided. "Usually, I'm already planning the next thing, the next trip, the next project. But tonight, I'm just here, with you, and it's enough."

Noah's expression softened. "That might be the nicest thing anyone's ever said to me."

The moment should have been perfect. Yet beneath Tess's contentment lurked that nagging anxiety, a persistent whisper asking questions she wasn't ready to answer. Was she ready to commit to Peregrine Cove permanently? To define herself as a small-town marketing consultant rather than a Boston executive? To build a life with Noah that would inevitably sink roots deeper with each passing season?

She loved him. Of that, she had no doubt. But loving Noah and permanently tying herself to Peregrine Cove were intertwined in ways she was still sorting through.

"There's something else." Noah reached into his jacket pocket. "A Christmas Eve gift. A tradition my father always kept with my mother."

Tess's pulse quickened as he placed a small box on the table between them. Not ring-sized, she noted with a mixture of relief and a bit of disappointment.

"You didn't have to."

"I wanted to," he interrupted gently, pushing the box toward her. "Open it."

Inside, nestled on a bed of white cotton, lay a delicate silver bracelet. From it hung a single charm, a miniature lighthouse crafted with exquisite detail.

"It's beautiful," Tess breathed, lifting it from the box.

"It's from Clarkson's Jewelry on Main Street," Noah explained, as he helped fasten it around her wrist. "Thomas Clarkson makes each charm by hand. I thought the lighthouse was fitting, not only because it reminded me of ours, but because lighthouses have guided sailors home for generations."

There it was again. Home. The word both comforted and unsettled her in equal measure. Noah's eyes held hers, and for a moment, Tess wondered if he was trying to tell her something beyond the obvious, that Peregrine Cove could be her permanent home.

"I love it." She held it up to admire the way the silver caught the candlelight. "Thank you."

Noah smiled, apparently pleased by her reaction. "I was thinking this could be a tradition, too. A new charm each Christmas Eve, marking another year together."

Another year. Years. The implied future stretched before her, beautiful and terrifying in its solidity. Tess's flutter of panic was stronger this time.

"I'd like that," she managed, thankful when the waiter appeared with coffee, providing a momentary diversion.

As they sipped their coffee, watching the lights on the harbor, Noah's hand found hers again across the table. "I've been thinking," he began.

Tess's anxiety spiked. *Please don't propose. Not tonight. Not when I'm suddenly questioning everything.*

"The winter festival committee is looking for

someone to design their promotional materials," Noah continued, oblivious to her internal crisis. "I mentioned your marketing background, and they're interested in talking to you. It could be a good opportunity to expand your local client base."

The relief that washed through Tess was so powerful she nearly sagged in her chair. "That sounds interesting," she said, meaning it. "I'll reach out to them after the holidays."

The conversation shifted to safer topics—the upcoming winter festival, Lucy's plans to expand the café's hours, and the new artist who'd opened a gallery near the harbor. Yet beneath the easy exchange, the unspoken question lingered. How long would she stay in Peregrine Cove? Would she really be here next Christmas, or was she just dreaming of something she couldn't follow through with?

By the time they finished their coffee, soft snow had begun falling again and dusting the harbor rails. They walked back to the cottage hand in hand through the now-quiet streets. Most residents had returned home for Christmas Eve celebrations with family. Holiday lights glowed in windows, and occasionally laughter or music spilled out from a doorway.

"It's like a Christmas card." Tess took in the picturesque scene.

"No, it's better," Noah replied, squeezing her hand. "It's real."

Once home, they hung their coats and kicked off their snowy boots in the mudroom. The tree they'd decorated together the previous weekend stood in the living room window with glittering lights and Aunt Morna's treasured ornaments. Presents waited beneath it. Some they'd purchased for each other, while others came from family and friends.

"Nightcap?" Noah suggested, moving toward the kitchen. "I think we still have some of that mulled cider."

"Perfect," Tess agreed, sinking onto the couch and tucking her feet beneath her.

As Noah busied himself in the kitchen, Tess found her gaze drawn to the bracelet on her wrist, the lighthouse charm catching the tree lights. It represented a future in Peregrine Cove, which was everything she should want. Everything she *did* want nearly all the time. So why did she still have this whisper of doubt?

"Here we go." Noah returned with two steaming mugs. He settled beside her on the couch, close enough that their shoulders touched. "To our first Christmas Eve together," he offered, raising his mug in a toast. "The first of many."

Tess nodded, even as a rush of uncertainty overwhelmed her. Had she just made a promise she wasn't sure she could keep?

If Noah noticed her momentary discomfort, he didn't show it. Instead, he draped his arm around her shoulders and drew her against his side as they sipped their cider and admired the tree.

"I've been thinking about getting a workshop close to town," he said casually after a comfortable silence. "I've been getting more online orders, and I really need more space."

"That makes sense," Tess agreed, relieved by the practical topic.

"There's a space available near the marina," he continued. "Good light, high ceilings, plenty of room."

He took another sip of cider. "And it even has a small office area that would be perfect for your consulting work, that is, if you'd be interested in sharing the space."

This was another step toward intertwining their lives. Tess's chest tightened. "It's a thought. Although I'm pretty comfortable working from the cottage for now."

Noah nodded, accepting her noncommittal response without pushing. She loved that about him. He could offer without ever demanding.

"I just thought I'd mention it," he said easily. "No rush to decide."

They finished their cider in comfortable silence as the Christmas tree lights bathed the room in warm light. Outside, snow continued to fall, coating Peregrine Cove in a perfect Christmas blanket.

Later, Tess lingered at the window and watched the soft glow of moonlight on the new-fallen snow. Noah's arms slipped around her waist from behind.

"Merry Christmas," he murmured against her ear.

Tess leaned back into his embrace. "Merry Christmas." His arms felt solid and warm. And right.

For this moment, here with this man, she was where she wanted to be. Tomorrow would bring its own questions and decisions. But tonight was perfect, despite the whispers of doubt and the uncertain future.

As Noah's lips found the sensitive spot beneath her ear, Tess closed her eyes, pushed all thoughts of the future aside, and surrendered to the present. Tonight belonged to the two of them alone. Whatever happened, this Christmas would remain a perfect memory of a love still finding its future.

CHAPTER 22

The Chamber of Commerce conference room was cold, as usual. Tess folded her arms and tried to focus on the discussion about their winter festival. The committee volunteers were initially full of enthusiasm for the event, but when it came down to the logistics and budget details, they were getting bogged down.

Tess was trying to keep them on course when her phone vibrated against the table. She glanced down and saw Noah's name above a string of random characters.

gjkkl helpp frll

She smiled slightly. He had obviously pocket dialed her while he was working. When she left, he'd mentioned something about working on the cottage, but she'd been so focused on her upcoming meeting that she couldn't remember what it was.

Turning the phone face down, she returned her attention to the current topic of advertising costs.

Ten minutes later, her phone buzzed again. Another text from Noah, this time just a single letter: *h*.

Something about it made her stomach tighten. One accidental text was normal. Two felt ... wrong. She sent a quick reply:

Everything okay?

No response.

She tried to concentrate on the meeting, but found herself checking her phone every few minutes. Nothing. She called his number discreetly, but it went straight to voicemail. Noah always answered with a quick call or text.

Her uneasiness grew until she couldn't ignore it any longer. She gathered her notes and caught Lucy's eye across the table.

"I'm sorry," she interrupted the meeting in the midst of a discussion of print versus digital marketing. "I need to step out. Family emergency."

Lucy's concerned gaze followed her to the door. "Do you need help?"

"I'll call if I do." Tess was already dialing Noah again as she hurried to her car. Still no answer.

The January air bit at her face as she started the engine. Her breath formed a cloud in the unheated interior. It's probably nothing, she told herself. Maybe he'd gone to pick up supplies and forgotten his phone. Maybe the cell signal at the cottage was acting up again.

But as she turned onto the coastal road, slick with recent freezing rain, the dread intensified. She and Noah had developed an easy pattern over the past months. They checked in with each other, coordinated schedules, and shared small observations throughout the day. This silence seemed wrong.

She turned into the cottage drive faster than was

wise on the icy pavement. Noah's truck was there in its usual place near the side of the house.

"Noah?" she called, hurrying from her car. No answer.

As she rounded the corner of the cottage, she found the extension ladder toppled on its side, one section partially detached where it had slid against the gutter. Tools were scattered across the frozen ground, including a hammer, pliers, and pieces of gutter guard.

"Noah!" The panic in her voice echoed back from the silent trees.

Then she spotted him—a crumpled form on the far side of the ladder, partially obscured by the porch railing. Her heart stopped, then thundered into a gallop as she scrambled toward him, nearly falling on the icy ground.

Noah lay on his side with one arm twisted beneath him and blood matting his hair above his right temple. His work coat was dusted with frost, and his lips were tinged blue on a too-pale face.

"Noah. Oh God, Noah." She dropped to her knees beside him, hands hovering, afraid to move him. "Can you hear me?"

His eyelids fluttered, then opened halfway, pupils dilated and struggling to focus. "Tess?" The word was slurred, barely audible.

Relief rushed through her, quickly followed by fresh terror at his condition. She fumbled for her phone, cursing her shaking fingers as she dialed 911.

"My—" Noah tried to shift, wincing sharply. "My phone ..."

She spotted it then, lying just beyond his

outstretched hand, its screen shattered. He'd been trying to reach it.

"Don't move," she ordered, pressing her free hand gently to his shoulder while giving their location to the dispatcher. "Help is coming. What were you doing out here?"

His eyes drifted closed, then snapped open with visible effort. "I was ... cleaning the gutters. You said they were clogged."

The guilt was instant and crushing. They had been for days. She was worried about water damage to their recent repairs, so she'd reminded him just that morning. "I said we should hire someone. The ice—"

"Why, when I could do it?"

"Yeah." She winced.

His voice wavered as his teeth began to chatter. "How'd you know?"

She thought of the garbled text message and the strange certainty that had pulled her from the meeting. "I just knew."

The wait for the ambulance stretched endlessly. Tess covered Noah with her coat, terrified to move him but equally terrified of the hypothermia setting in after what must have been—she checked her phone—nearly two hours exposed to the freezing temperatures. His periods of lucidity alternated with confused mumbling, and his grip on her hand became weaker.

"You're here," he murmured once as his eyes found hers with momentary clarity.

"Of course I'm here," she whispered, her throat tight. "I'll always be here."

The promise emerged without thought, startling in its certainty. At that moment, huddled on the frozen ground beside him, the precariousness of everything they'd built together crashed over her. How quickly it could all vanish by simple, terrible chance. The realization left her breathless.

~

THE EMERGENCY ROOM was a flurry of activity with bright lights, urgent voices, and forms thrust at her while Noah was swept away on a gurney behind swinging doors. She sank into a chair and stared at her hands, still smeared with his blood.

"Family?" a nurse asked, clipboard poised.

"Yes," Tess answered without hesitation. The single syllable encompassed everything that had changed since she'd first returned to Peregrine Cove.

Time blurred. She called Rob, who arrived white-faced and stiff-shouldered, with tight lines around his mouth, as if haunted by echoes of his own losses. Lucy appeared with coffee and a change of clothes, having closed the café early when word spread through town.

The diagnosis finally came—concussion, broken wrist, three cracked ribs, and hypothermia that was slowly resolving. The doctor's calm recitation of injuries felt surreal, as if he were discussing someone else, not the man whose unconscious form had terrified her beyond reason just hours before.

"He's lucky you found him when you did," the doctor concluded.

She didn't need to hear more.

Once Noah was stabilized, Tess went in to see him. His large frame looked strangely diminished against the white hospital sheets. His wrist was wrapped, awaiting surgery once the swelling went down. Monitors steadily beeped beside him. The blood had been cleaned from his hair, revealing a neat line of stitches.

When his eyes opened, her relief was so intense she had to grip the bedframe for support.

"Hey," he said, his voice rough.

"Hey yourself." She took his uninjured hand. "You scared the hell out of me."

"Sorry about the gutters."

A laugh escaped her, a half-sob. "Forget the gutters."

"I got your text," he murmured, his eyes heavy with medication. "I tried to answer. Couldn't ... reach the phone."

"I know." She stroked his cold fingers.

AFTER THREE NIGHTS in the hospital, Noah was released with strict instructions: limited movement, no work, regular rest.

"No more work on the cottage. Maybe ever," she told him, brooking no argument as she helped him into her car.

"Tess—"

"Don't 'Tess' me." She secured his seatbelt gently around his immobilized ribs. "And don't even try to do anything without me. You fell off a ladder. The last thing you need is to crack your head open trying to navigate the cottage on painkillers."

He didn't fight it, which concerned her more than his visible injuries. Noah Pierce never surrendered easily.

The first days of his recovery established a new routine between them. She converted the small living room into a temporary bedroom where she could keep an eye on him while she worked in the sunroom and managed her growing client list. Rob stopped by daily, with his gruff practicality, helping Noah with tasks he couldn't manage one-handed.

"He's stubborn," Rob told her one evening as they washed dishes side by side. "He must get it from his mother."

Tess smiled. "Not from you?"

A rare twinkle came to Rob's eyes as his weathered face softened. "He hasn't let anyone take care of him since Mary died. The closest anyone came to helping was Morna. She convinced him that she needed help with her garden and cooking."

The observation settled into her like a stone dropping through water, ripples expanding outward. That sounded so much like Aunt Morna. And Noah. How many years had he spent being the reliable helper, the fixer, the person others leaned on? The role had become so intrinsic to his identity that accepting help seemed to threaten his own sense of self.

In bed that night, listening to his measured breathing, Tess confronted the tangle of emotions the accident had unleashed—the terror of finding him injured, the fierce protectiveness that had risen in her at the hospital, and the bone-deep certainty that she would do whatever was needed to help him heal.

These weren't the feelings of someone fulfilling an obligation or playing at domesticity until a better option appeared. These were the feelings of a woman who had found her place, her home, and a man that she couldn't live without.

The realization should have frightened her. This was the kind of attachment her mother had warned against, the roots that Elizabeth had characterized as chains. Instead, a profound sense of peace settled upon her, as if some restless part of herself had finally settled.

"You don't have to babysit me, you know." Noah's voice broke the comfortable silence of the cottage living room, where they'd spent the evening reading by the fire. Two weeks into his recovery, color had returned to his face, though he still moved with careful deliberation.

Tess looked up from her book. "I'm not babysitting you."

"You haven't been to the Chamber meeting in two weeks. They must need your input for the first February event."

"I've got a phone and a laptop. That's input enough." She turned a page, deliberately casual. "I'm exactly where I need to be."

Noah set aside the woodworking journal he'd been thumbing through one-handed. "Tess." The quiet insistence in his voice made her look up. "I don't want to be the reason you put your life on hold."

"Is that what you think I'm doing?"

"I think ..." He shifted, wincing as the movement jarred his ribs. "I think you felt responsible. For the gutters. And now you're overcompensating."

The observation stung with its partial truth. Guilt

had been her first reaction, but it wasn't what kept her by his side now.

"Maybe at first," she admitted. "But that's not why I'm here now."

"Then why?"

The question was simple, yet monumental. Tess set her book aside and considered her answer.

"When I found you on the ground," she began slowly, "before I even knew how badly you were hurt, I had this moment of clarity. All the things I've been afraid of—being trapped, losing my independence, turning into my mother if I left or my aunt if I stayed— none of it mattered. The only thing I was afraid of was losing you."

Noah's expression softened, and the defensive line of his shoulders eased.

"I'm not putting my life on hold, Noah. I'm living it. Right here, with you." She moved to sit beside him on the couch, careful not to jostle his injured side. "And maybe what scares me a little is how much I want this. But it's not nearly as scary as walking away."

"The feeling's mutual."

She leaned forward and pressed her forehead gently to his. "So stop trying to send me away for my own good. I'm exactly where I want to be."

Noah's uninjured arm tightened around her, and for a moment, they sat in comfortable silence. But Tess could feel the tension in his body that had nothing to do with his physical injuries. When she pulled back to look at him, she found his eyes looking distant and troubled.

"What is it?" she asked softly.

He shook his head, attempting his usual deflection. "Nothing. Just tired."

"Noah." She touched his face gently, careful of the fading bruises. "Talk to me."

He was quiet for so long she thought he might retreat into himself again. Then, his voice barely above a whisper, he said, "I keep seeing Morna in that hospital bed."

Tess went still.

"The day before she died, she grabbed my hand. She could barely lift her head, but her grip was surprisingly strong." Noah's eyes grew distant from the memory. "She made me promise to take care of the cottage and to make sure you knew how much it meant to her. But then she said something else."

He paused, his jaw working as if the words were difficult to form.

"She said, 'Don't lose her again.' At the time, I thought she was just worried about you selling the cottage and leaving. But lying on that frozen ground, unable to reach you ..." His voice cracked slightly. "All I could think was that I was going to die before I could tell you how I really felt. After fifteen years, I was going to lose you again."

Tess felt her throat constrict. "Noah ..."

"I was seventeen when you left the first time," he continued, the words coming faster now, as if a dam had burst. "I was just a kid. I didn't know how to fight for what I wanted. So, I told myself you were better off. You'd outgrow whatever we had. But the truth is, I was terrified of not being enough for you."

"You were always enough," Tess whispered, but he shook his head.

"I convinced myself it was noble to let you go. But really? I was just too afraid of being rejected to fight."

His hand found hers and gripped it. "When you came back this summer, I promised myself I wouldn't make the same mistake. But then I got scared all over again. If I pushed too hard, you'd run, but if I didn't push hard enough, you'd leave anyway. I've been walking this impossible line, trying to be what you need while protecting myself from losing you again."

Tess could see the cost of this admission in the lines around his eyes, the vulnerability he so rarely allowed himself to show. Noah Pierce, who everyone in town turned to for strength and reliability, was just a man afraid of losing the woman he loved.

"After the accident," he continued, his voice growing rougher, "lying there in the cold, all I could think about was that note I never sent after you left. I must have written it a dozen times—telling you how I felt, asking you to come home, begging you not to forget us. But I never mailed it because I was sure you'd write back and tell me you'd moved on because I wasn't enough."

Tears spilled down Tess's cheeks. "You were always enough."

"When you came back, and you were so successful, so polished ..." Noah's voice broke slightly. "I thought, here we go again. She won't want to settle, and she'll leave."

"Is that what you think this is?" Tess asked, gesturing between them. "Settling?"

"No." His answer was immediate and firm. "Not anymore. But for a while ... God, Tess, you had everything in Boston. A corner office, important clients, a salary I'll probably never make. And I'm just a guy who fishes, fixes boats, and builds furniture in a town most people have never heard of."

"You're a guy who remembered that I take my coffee with a pinch of cinnamon," Tess said fiercely. "Who spent months helping me renovate a cottage you thought I'd eventually sell? Who saved Aunt Morna's garden plans and planted them after she died? Who held me through a hurricane and made me feel safer than I've ever felt in my life?"

She cupped his face in her hands, forcing him to meet her eyes. "You're not just enough, Noah Pierce. You're everything."

He pulled her closer and held her against him. "I don't want to lose you again," he whispered against her hair.

"You won't," Tess promised, holding him as tightly as his injuries would allow. "I'm not that scared girl anymore, and you're not that boy. We know what we want now."

"Do we?" he asked, pulling back to search her face. "Because sometimes I look at you, and I still can't believe you want this. Want me."

"Every day," Tess said firmly. "And I'll keep wanting you for as long as you'll have me."

Noah's kiss was soft and desperate, tasting of relief, lingering fear, and hope. When they broke apart, he rested his forehead against hers.

"Morna knew," he said quietly. "Somehow, she knew we'd find our way back to each other. That's why she made you stay a year. She was giving us time to stop being afraid."

"Smart woman," Tess murmured, thinking of her aunt's patient orchestration of their reunion.

"The smartest," Noah agreed. "She knew I needed to learn how to fight for what I wanted. And maybe she knew you needed to learn that some things are worth staying for."

Outside, snow continued to fall, but inside their cottage, their home, warmth settled around them like a blessing. Noah's confession had stripped away the last pretenses between them, leaving only truth and the love they'd been too afraid to fully claim until now.

"No more fear," Tess whispered against his lips.

"No more fear," Noah agreed, and sealed the promise with a kiss.

His arm came around her and drew her to his side. In silence, they sat while the fire crackled and snow gently fell beyond the windows. The cottage, solid despite its scars, creaked and settled around them, enduring beyond all the storms that had tested it.

CHAPTER 23

May arrived in Peregrine Cove with sun-filled days and the promise of summer. On the cottage porch, Tess cradled her morning coffee and watched seagulls wheel over the harbor.

The months had passed with remarkable speed. Eleven months had gone by since her return to the cottage, and six months since Noah had moved in. Only a few weeks were left until the one-year anniversary of her arrival that would officially satisfy Morna's trust. Not that the milestone held the significance it once had.

The cottage was indisputably hers now, in spirit if not yet in legal documentation. What had begun as an obligation had transformed into her choice. The cottage walls now sheltered her in a life she had never envisioned but couldn't imagine abandoning now.

Her small marketing consultancy had flourished beyond expectation, the winter tourism initiative proving so successful that neighboring coastal towns had approached her about similar campaigns. She had more work than she could comfortably handle, a reality that still surprised her when she paused to consider it.

"You're up early." Noah joined her, his hair damp from the shower.

"I couldn't sleep," Tess admitted as she leaned into his embrace. "I've got too many ideas for the spring festival brochure."

Noah's chuckle vibrated against her back. "The Chamber monsters have created a marketing machine."

"A lucrative one. My client base just keeps growing." She tilted her face to accept his good-morning kiss. "Even Hank, in his own grudging way, admitted the winter campaign was 'not bad.'"

"High praise indeed." Noah glanced at his watch. "I should get going. I've got that restoration piece to finish for the Lincolnville client."

"Will you be home for dinner?" Tess asked, following him inside. The casual domesticity of the question no longer gave her pause. Their daily life together had become as steady as the tides.

"Should be. Don't wait if I'm late, though. You know how I lose track of time when I'm finishing detail work."

Noah gathered his travel mug, lunch, and worn satchel while Tess looked on. The sight filled her with a contentment she'd never found in her tidy and predictable Boston life.

"Love you," he said, pressing one more quick kiss to her lips before heading out the door.

"Love you too," Tess called after him.

After Noah's truck disappeared down the lane, she settled at her desk in the sunroom that served as her office. Aunt Morna's antique desk now held her laptop and the organized chaos of her client files. Morning light spilled in through the window, catching the harbor view that still felt like a gift on clear days.

She had just opened her design software when her phone rang. An unknown Boston number appeared on the screen.

"Tess Bradford," she answered professionally, cradling the phone between her ear and shoulder as she continued to work.

"Ms. Bradford, this is Alexander Harrington."

Tess's hands froze over her keyboard. Alexander Harrington, founder and CEO of the Harrington Group, one of the most prestigious marketing firms on the East Coast. Their campaigns regularly won international awards, and their client list included Fortune 500 companies and luxury brands worldwide.

"Mr. Harrington," she managed, straightening in her chair. "This is unexpected."

His laugh was warm and confident. "I imagine so. I hope I'm not interrupting your morning."

"Not at all," Tess assured him, though her mind raced with questions. Why would Alexander Harrington be calling her?

"I'll get straight to the point. Your name keeps coming up in conversations I've been having. Daniel Wright, at your former firm, speaks very highly of you, and when I mentioned to the Baxter Group that I was looking for someone to head our new lifestyle division, they specifically recommended you based on your work for them last year."

Tess blinked in surprise. She'd done a project for Baxter just before leaving Boston, but she had no idea they'd been so impressed. "That's very flattering."

"I've seen your portfolio, Ms. Bradford, both your Boston work and the remarkably effective campaigns you've created for Peregrine Cove. You have a rare talent for authenticity in marketing—something increasingly valuable in today's oversaturated landscape."

She couldn't help but smile at the unexpected praise. A quiet confidence began to settle in. "Thank you. That's what I strive for."

"Which brings me to the purpose of my call," Harrington continued. "I'd like to discuss the position of Creative Director for our new lifestyle division. The role would involve overseeing a team of twelve, with significant creative control and a compensation package I believe you'll find quite attractive."

The words hit Tess like a physical force. Creative Director at the Harrington Group, the kind of opportunity most marketing professionals only dreamed about. The position would place her at the pinnacle of her field, working with premier clients and unlimited resources.

"I—I don't know what to say," she stammered, her mind whirling. "This is completely unexpected."

"I understand it's sudden," Harrington said. "But we're moving quickly to launch the division. I'd like to meet with you in person to discuss details. Are you available to come to Boston tomorrow? My assistant will arrange everything."

"Tomorrow?" Tess echoed, her gaze falling on the half-finished festival brochure on her screen, then to the framed photo of her and Noah that sat beside her laptop.

"I realize it's short notice," Harrington acknowledged, "but I'm on a tight schedule. We could meet for lunch at Maison Laurent. Say, one o'clock?"

Maison Laurent, Boston's most exclusive restaurant, where reservations were typically booked months in advance. The mention was impressive, and despite herself, the old familiar pull of ambition was stirring within.

"Yes," she heard herself say before fully processing the implications. "Tomorrow at one would work."

"Excellent. I'll have my assistant email you the details. I'm looking forward to meeting you, Ms. Bradford."

The call ended, leaving Tess staring at her phone in a state of shock. Creative Director at the Harrington Group. A position that would catapult her career to heights she'd once dreamed of but had gradually stopped pursuing. But the job was in Boston, not Peregrine Cove.

She sat back, stunned, as reality sank in. She'd agreed to meet tomorrow, without consulting Noah, without even taking time to think about whether she actually wanted the position.

But did she?

The question lingered, making it impossible to concentrate. Once, there would have been no question —she'd have been packing already, mentally calculating the boost to her résumé and bank account. Now, the decision was infinitely more complex.

She was still mulling it over when Noah returned that evening, earlier than expected, and carrying a bouquet of early spring flowers from the local greenhouse.

"Thought we could celebrate." He entered the

kitchen, where Tess was absently stirring a pot of soup. "Walter called. The Chamber voted unanimously to extend the tourism initiative through the summer. Your contract's been renewed with a substantial increase. His words, not mine."

The news, which should have thrilled her, landed hollowly in the pit of her stomach. Noah's smile faded as he noticed her muted reaction. He set the flowers on the counter. "What's wrong?"

Tess turned off the burner and took a moment to organize her thoughts. "I got a call today from Alexander Harrington."

Noah's eyebrows rose in recognition of the name. "The marketing guru? That Harrington?"

"He's considering me for a job." The words tumbled out in a rush. "Creative Director of their new lifestyle division. In Boston."

A heavy silence filled the kitchen. Noah's expression remained neutral, though Tess could see the effort it cost him.

"That's ...quite an opportunity," he said, his voice measured. "What did you tell him?"

"That I'd meet with him. Tomorrow. In Boston." Tess wrapped her arms around herself, suddenly chilled despite the warm kitchen. "I said yes without thinking. It all happened so fast, and he's Alexander Harrington, and I just—"

"You don't need to explain," Noah interrupted, sounding gentle despite the visible tension in his shoulders. "It's a huge opportunity. Of course you'd want to hear what he has to say."

His reasonable response somehow made everything worse. Tess would have preferred anger, demands, anything but this careful acceptance that felt like resignation.

"I don't know what I want," she admitted, moving toward him. "This came out of nowhere."

Noah nodded, his eyes searching hers. "When do you leave?"

"First thing tomorrow. I'll drive down for the lunch meeting."

"And come back tomorrow night?" The question held layers of meaning neither addressed.

"That's the plan." The words lacked conviction, even to Tess.

Noah's smile didn't reach his eyes. "You should pack a bag. Just in case. Boston traffic can be unpredictable."

The practical suggestion seemed more like permission or even acceptance of the inevitable. Tess wanted to reassure him that this was just a meeting, not a decision. But the words stuck in her throat.

Dinner was quiet, with their usual easy conversation replaced by careful small talk. They discussed Walter's contract news, Noah's latest project, and Lucy's plans to add evening hours at the café—everything except Boston.

After dinner, Noah insisted on cleaning up alone. "You should pack." Noah turned toward the sink. "And prepare for your meeting. It's a big opportunity."

Tess hesitated, then retreated to their bedroom with his words echoing in her mind. A big opportunity. But was it the right opportunity?

In the bedroom, she pulled her suitcase from the closet with a strange sense of déjà vu. How many times had she packed this same bag for business trips? The habit was so ingrained that her hands moved automatically, selecting appropriate business attire, toiletries, and overnight essentials.

When she emerged with her packed bag, Noah was in the living room reading a book.

"I'm all set." Tess set her suitcase by the door.

Noah glanced up, his expression softening when he saw her. "Come here." He patted the space beside him on the couch.

Settling beside him on the couch, Tess leaned into his warmth. For a long moment, they sat in silence as Aunt Morna's old mantel clock steadily ticked.

"Whatever you decide," Noah said, his voice low, "Make sure it's what makes you happy, not just what you think you should want."

Tears pricked behind Tess's eyes. "I don't know what that is anymore."

"Yes, you do. Just be honest with yourself."

They went to bed early, both claiming fatigue but really avoiding further discussion. In the darkness, Noah held her close, his heartbeat steady against her back, his breathing eventually deepening into sleep. Tess lay awake much longer, watching moonlight create patterns on the ceiling and listening to the familiar sounds of the cottage.

CHAPTER 24

Morning came too quickly, gray and drizzly, as if the weather itself reflected the mood inside the cottage. Noah was already up when Tess emerged from the shower to find coffee waiting in a travel mug alongside a small package of blueberry muffins from the café.

"For the road," he explained, his smile not quite reaching his eyes. "Lucy had just taken them out of the oven when I stopped by."

The gesture was so thoughtful, so perfectly Noah, that Tess felt her chest constrict. "Thank you."

They moved around each other with careful politeness as she prepared to leave. When it was time to go, Noah helped carry her suitcase to the car and then stood with his hands in his pockets as she slid into the driver's seat.

"Drive safely." He leaned down to meet her eyes through the open window. "Text me when you get there."

"I will," she promised, then hesitated. "Noah, I—"

"It's okay," he interrupted gently. "Go to your meeting. Figure out what you want. I'll be here."

But will I? The unspoken question lingered as Tess pulled away and watched Noah's figure grow smaller in her rearview mirror. He stood motionless in the driveway until she turned the corner.

As the miles accumulated on her journey south, Tess slipped back into the person she'd been in Boston —efficient, ambitious, focused on the next career move. The transformation was both familiar and unsettling, like trying on old clothes that no longer quite fit.

Boston's skyline appeared on the horizon, gleaming and imposing against the clearing sky. Once, the sight had filled her with a sense of purpose and belonging. Now, it seemed strangely foreign, as if she were approaching a city she'd only visited rather than the one she'd called home for years.

She arrived with time to spare, so she sat in her car, texted Noah, and then took a moment to compose herself.

Maison Laurent was everything its reputation promised—discreetly elegant, with a hushed atmosphere that spoke of money and influence. Alexander Harrington rose as she approached the table, his handsome face breaking into a practiced smile that had charmed clients and competitors alike.

"Ms. Bradford," he greeted, taking her hand. "Thank you for making the trip on such short notice."

"Please, call me Tess," she replied, slipping into the polished professional persona she'd cultivated in her Boston years. "And thank you for the invitation. I'm intrigued."

As they settled into their seats, a waiter appeared to

pour water and recite the day's specials. Tess studied Harrington with her professional eye. Everything about him was calibrated for effect—the perfectly tailored suit, the artfully casual hairstyle, the understated yet obviously expensive watch.

Once, she would have found that impressive. Now, she found herself wondering what lay beneath the careful packaging.

"I'll be direct," Harrington said after they'd ordered. "The Harrington Group is expanding into the luxury lifestyle sector—high-end travel and exclusive experiences. We need someone with your talent to lead the creative team. Your work shows a remarkable gift for finding the genuine heart of a brand with an elegant presentation."

Tess felt a flicker of pride at the assessment. "I believe the most effective marketing tells a true story, but in the most compelling way."

"Exactly," Harrington agreed, his enthusiasm seeming genuine. "That philosophy is precisely why you're perfect for this position. I'll be honest. Your work speaks for itself, but I wanted to meet you. We want you for this job. Let me tell you what we're offering."

What followed was indeed an impressive proposal —a salary nearly triple what she'd made at her previous Boston firm, creative control over a dedicated team, a corner office in their Beacon Hill headquarters, and equity options that could prove extremely valuable if the new division succeeded as projected.

Tess's head was spinning. It all seemed so surreal.

"We'd want you to start immediately," Harrington concluded as their main course arrived. "The team is assembled, the client roster secured. We just need the right creative vision to tie it all together."

"It's a remarkable opportunity," Tess acknowledged, her mind racing. "But also a substantial change. I've established myself in Peregrine Cove and built a client base—"

"Which you could maintain remotely until you're able to transition them to someone local," Harrington interrupted smoothly.

"And of course," Harrington continued, misreading her hesitation, "we understand there are personal considerations. Relocating is always a challenge. The compensation package includes relocation assistance and temporary housing until you find something suitable."

The assumption that she would relocate, that Boston was naturally where she belonged, prodded at something tender in Tess's heart. "I've built a life in Peregrine Cove." She paused to consider her words. "It would be a significant decision to leave. I'll need some time."

Harrington's smile turned knowing. "Your mother mentioned you might have reservations."

The casual reference stopped Tess mid-bite. "My mother?"

"Elizabeth has been a member of the board of directors for years," Harrington explained. "When I mentioned expanding our lifestyle division, she suggested you might be the perfect fit—if we could lure you back to Boston."

Tess set down her fork, a cold realization spreading through her. "My mother suggested me for this position?"

"She spoke very highly of your capabilities," Harrington confirmed, seeming not to notice her change in demeanor. "She said you were temporarily living in Maine but would welcome a reason to return to civilization." He chuckled.

The pieces clicked into place with devastating clarity. This wasn't a random opportunity. This was Elizabeth's orchestrated attempt to pull her back to Boston, away from Peregrine Cove. Away from Noah.

"So, my mother arranged this meeting?" Tess asked as her appetite vanished.

Harrington's smile faltered. "She suggested we meet. She mentioned you'd been away but were ready to move on with your career." He tilted his head, studying her expression. "Is there a problem?"

"I think there's been a misunderstanding. While I appreciate the offer—and it's incredibly generous—I wasn't actively seeking a position in Boston."

"But surely—" he began.

"I've built something in Peregrine Cove," she continued, her voice strengthening with conviction. "A business that matters to me, clients I care about, a community that's become home."

Understanding dawned in Harrington's eyes. "Ah. Your mother implied your Maine sojourn was temporary. A sabbatical of sorts."

"I see." Tess tamped down the complicated mixture of anger and resigned understanding that washed through her. "My mother was mistaken. I apologize for the misunderstanding. I'm afraid I've wasted your time."

Harrington leaned back, studying her with newfound interest. "You know, I've built my career on recognizing authenticity. I can see that this small town means something to you."

The observation caught Tess off guard. "Yes, it does."

Harrington took care of the check and leaned back with a smile. "I've known your mother for fourteen years, since I married her best friend. She wants what she thinks is best for you."

The personal revelation shifted the dynamic between them, making Harrington suddenly seem more human.

Tess smiled. "I know." She wasn't sure what to say. It was clear that her mother had gone to a great deal of trouble to bring this job about. "Once, this job would have been a career dream for me, but not if I didn't earn it."

Harrington had the grace to look abashed. "The division is real, and we do need a creative director." He spread his hands in a gesture of admission. "But Elizabeth can be persuasive. For what it's worth, I did review your work, and you're genuinely talented."

Tess sat back, processing this revelation. The anger she'd initially felt toward her mother was fading, replaced by something closer to resignation. This was classic Elizabeth, convinced she knew best and arranging the world to suit her vision regardless of others' wishes.

"Mr. Harrington, thank you, but I'm declining the offer." Unexpected relief washed over her. "My life is in Peregrine Cove now."

Instead of disappointment, Harrington's expression showed admiration. "I respect that."

As they parted outside the restaurant, he shook her

hand warmly. "I envy you a little. Finding a place that feels right is rarer than most people realize."

"It took me a while to realize that." As they parted ways, Tess found herself feeling eager to return to Peregrine Cove and to Noah.

The drive back north had none of the conflicted emotions of her morning journey. With each mile, Tess felt more like herself, like the person she'd become in Peregrine Cove. She was grounded, in love, and wholly content.

She gave her mother a call from the road. The conversation was brief but direct.

"Did you enjoy your lunch with Alexander?" Elizabeth asked, her tone artificially casual.

"You should have told me you arranged it," Tess replied, keeping her voice even.

A pause. "Would you have gone if I had?"

"Probably not," Tess admitted. "Which is why you should have respected my choices enough to be honest."

"I only want what's best for you," Elizabeth insisted. "A small town can be charming for a while, but someone with your talents—"

"Mom," Tess interrupted firmly. "I know where I belong. And it's not Boston."

The silence stretched between them, filled with years of expectations and misunderstandings.

"Is this about Noah Pierce?" Elizabeth asked.

"It's about me," Tess corrected. "Noah is part of it, a huge part. But this is about where I belong, and that's in Peregrine Cove."

Another long pause. "I don't understand it," Elizabeth said, her voice softer now. "But it's your life. If you're sure ..."

"I am," Tess confirmed, the conviction in her voice surprising even herself.

"Then I'll try to accept that," her mother conceded, the closest thing to a blessing Tess was likely to receive.

As Tess drove the familiar coastal highway toward home, darkness fell. When her headlights illuminated the "Welcome to Peregrine Cove" sign, the carved falcon seemed to watch her return with approval.

The cottage windows were dark when she pulled into the driveway, which was unusual for this hour. Noah's truck was there, but no welcoming lights shone from within. A flicker of unease passed through her as she retrieved her suitcase and approached the front door.

Inside, the cottage was eerily quiet. "Noah?" she called, setting down her bag.

No answer came. She moved through the dimly lit main floor, an inexplicable sense of dread growing stronger with each empty room. When she reached the bedroom, she understood why.

Noah stood beside the bed, methodically filling a duffel bag with his clothes. He looked up at her entrance, his expression blank despite the obvious surprise in his eyes. "You're back."

Tess stared at the half-packed bag, comprehension dawning with devastating clarity. "You're leaving."

"I thought it would be easier," he explained, his voice steady despite the pain evident in his eyes. "If I wasn't here when you came back for your things."

"My things?" Tess echoed, confusion giving way to understanding. "You thought I wasn't coming back to stay?"

Noah's hands stilled on the shirt he'd been folding.

"The Harrington Group is the opportunity of a life-time. I wouldn't ask you to turn that down for—" he gestured vaguely around them "—this."

Tess moved toward him. "But this is everything that I want."

"Tess ..."

"I turned down the job," she interrupted, needing him to understand. "I'm not going back to Boston."

Hope flickered across his face, quickly guarded. "You don't have to decide right away. You could think about it. Weigh your options."

"There's nothing to weigh," Tess insisted, reaching for his hands. "My mother arranged the whole thing. She was convinced that I'd jump at the chance. But she was wrong. I'm exactly where I want to be."

Noah searched her face, looking for certainty. "What about your career? The opportunities you'd have in Boston?"

"I have everything I need right here." Tess squeezed his hands. "Clients who value my work. A community that's become home. And most of all, you."

The last word held the weight of everything they'd built together over the months.

"I thought I'd lost you," Noah admitted, vulnera-bility breaking through his careful composure. "When you left this morning, it felt like watching you drive away fifteen years ago all over again."

"But I came back." Tess gazed into his eyes. "To stay."

The promise, simple yet profound, seemed to reach something deep within him. Noah's arms encircled her, pulling her against his chest as if reassuring himself she was really there.

"I love you," he murmured against her hair. "More than I know how to say."

"Show me instead," Tess whispered, tilting her face up to his.

Their kiss held the desperate relief of a storm weathered, a separation survived, and a choice made with absolute certainty. As they sank onto the bed, his half-packed bag forgotten and pushed aside, Tess knew with bone-deep certainty that she had found her way home.

Later, tangled together in the quiet darkness, Noah traced lazy patterns on her bare shoulder. "What made you so sure?" he asked. "About staying?"

Tess considered the question, wanting to give him the honest answer he deserved. "When Harrington was describing the position—the corner office, the prestigious clients, everything I once thought I wanted—all I could think about was how I'd miss all this." She shifted to look into his eyes. "I realized that, for the first time, I'm where I want to be."

Noah's smile in the darkness was like dawn breaking. "Welcome home, Bradford."

Outside, the wind whispered through pine branches. Inside, Tess was where she had always belonged, with the man who had waited for years. She had finally found her way back to him. Now she was home.

CHAPTER 25

The June morning dawned with perfect clarity, as if the weather itself had decided to celebrate. One year ago, to the day, Tess had driven up the winding road to Peregrine Cove with a suitcase packed for a brief stay and a plan for a quick departure. Now, she stood on the cottage porch, coffee mug in hand, watching the morning sunlight paint the harbor below in golds and soft blues.

One year. The requirements of the trust were officially fulfilled.

"So, what's on your mind?" Noah said, joining her on the porch. His arm slipped around her waist, and Tess leaned closer.

"I was just thinking about how much can happen in a year," she replied, tilting her face up for his good-morning kiss.

Noah's smile was gentle with understanding. "I just got a text from Mr. Hargrove," Noah said. "We're still on for two o'clock."

Walter Hargrove, Morna's lawyer, suggested they meet to finalize the fulfillment of the trust. What had begun as a simple signing had since expanded to a small celebration at the cottage.

"Did you remind him not to pull out the paperwork until my mother arrives?" Tess asked, a hint of anxiety threading through her voice.

Noah squeezed her hand reassuringly. "He knows the plan. Elizabeth won't miss the moment."

The fact that her mother had agreed to come at all still surprised Tess. Their relationship had been strained since the Boston job offer debacle. But when Tess extended the invitation to today's gathering, Elizabeth accepted with unexpected grace.

"I just want her to see that I'm happy here." Tess voiced the concern that had nagged at her for weeks. "That this wasn't some sort of mistake or rebellion."

"She'll see," Noah assured her. "Even Elizabeth Bradford can't deny what's right in front of her eyes."

Back inside, Noah sliced fruit for breakfast while Tess prepared coffee, their conversation flowing from plans for the day to the upcoming harbor festival and a new commission Noah had received from a client in Portsmouth.

"That pottery shop called about your marketing proposal." Noah slid a plate of toast toward her. "The owner was practically giddy. He said the Bangor newspaper wants to feature them in a 'Hidden Gems of Maine' series."

Tess smiled, pride warming her chest. "Good. They deserve the attention. Their work is amazing."

"So is yours," Noah countered, kissing the top of

her head as he passed behind her chair. "Your client list is getting impressive."

It was. What had begun as a few local businesses had expanded into a thriving consultancy that now served clients throughout coastal Maine. Tess Bradford Marketing specialized in authentic brand development for small businesses and artisans, work she found every bit as satisfying as her former work in Boston.

Tess glanced at the clock. "I should check on the food. Lucy's bringing the main dishes, but I want to make sure we have enough appetizers."

Noah caught her hand as she rose. "Everything's going to be perfect." He fixed his eyes on hers.

With one look, he calmed the flutter of nervousness that had been building since dawn. Tess squeezed his hand in silent thanks, then set about preparing for their guests.

By one o'clock, the cottage gleamed with spring sunlight. Fresh flowers brightened every room, and platters of appetizers were arranged on the dining table. Noah had set up a small bar on the porch for those who preferred to enjoy the sunshine.

"Wouldn't Morna love this!" Lucy arrived with her arms laden with covered dishes that filled the kitchen with mouthwatering aromas.

"She would, because she made it all happen," Tess replied as she helped Lucy unload the bounty.

Lucy's knowing smile suggested she'd been in on Morna's plans from the beginning. "That woman had a gift."

Rob Pierce arrived next, bringing a bottle of whiskey and an uncharacteristic grin. Over the past year, he had softened considerably, especially since the Thanksgiving thaw between him and Tess's father. The two men had actually gone fishing together, a development that still astonished both Noah and Tess.

"The place looks good." Despite his gruff tone, Rob cast approving eyes about the cottage.

"Thank you," Tess replied, accepting both the whiskey and the compliment with equal gratitude.

More guests arrived. Walter Hargrove was looking unusually relaxed without his customary suit and tie. Behind him came Maya from the hardware store, Walter and Margaret from the Chamber of Commerce, and even Hank Morrell, who had finally stopped referring to Tess as an outsider.

"Your parents just pulled in," Noah murmured in Tess's ear as she arranged a tray of crab cakes Lucy had brought.

Tess paused briefly. Although her mother had apologized for the Boston job incident, Elizabeth continued to make Tess uneasy.

"I'll get the door," Noah offered, but Tess shook her head.

"No, I should do it."

Thomas Bradford's warm smile greeted her first as she opened the door, and his hug enveloped her in familiar comfort. "The place looks wonderful, Tess."

Behind him, Elizabeth stood on the porch, elegant as always in a pale blue dress that probably cost more than most Peregrine Cove residents spent on clothes in a year. Her expression was composed but not cold, and when she embraced Tess, the gesture felt less perfunctory than usual.

"You look well." Elizabeth studied her daughter's face. "Content."

"I am," Tess confirmed, the simple truth of it reflected in her eyes. "Very content."

Elizabeth's expression shifted not quite to surrender, but perhaps to acceptance. "Then I'm glad for you." For once, Tess believed her.

Noah appeared beside them, offering drinks with the easy charm that had eventually won over Elizabeth's cool reserve. "Rob's here," he mentioned casually to Thomas. "Ask him about his new fishing spot."

Thomas's face brightened. "Excellent! I brought those new lures I was telling him about."

As Thomas moved eagerly toward the living room, Elizabeth raised an eyebrow at Tess. "Your father has become positively obsessed with fishing since Thanksgiving," she said, though her tone held more amusement than criticism. "I blame you entirely."

"Blame Rob," Tess nodded toward Noah's father. "He's the real culprit."

Elizabeth's gaze followed her husband as he greeted Rob with enthusiastic backslapping. "They're like schoolboys." She shook her head. "Who would have thought?"

Who, indeed? Tess thought, watching the two men who had once been rivals now chatting like old friends. Life had a way of coming full circle in the most unexpected ways.

By two o'clock, the cottage hummed with conversation and laughter. Guests mingled on the porch and in the living room, sharing stories and enjoying Lucy's exceptional cooking. The gathering had the comfortable feel of a family event rather than a legal formality, which was exactly what Tess had hoped for.

Walter Hargrove caught her eye across the room and pointed at his watch with a meaningful glance. Tess nodded, then moved to the center of the room, gently tapping a spoon against her glass to gather everyone's attention.

"Thank you all for coming today," she began, her gaze sweeping across the faces that had become so dear to her over the past year. "As most of you know, one year ago today, I arrived in Peregrine Cove with every intention of settling Morna's estate and returning to Boston as quickly as possible."

Appreciative chuckles rippled through the group as those who had witnessed her transformation firsthand nodded in understanding.

"Aunt Morna, however, had other plans," Tess continued, her voice softening with affection for her aunt's memory. "She created a trust with very specific requirements: that I live in this cottage for one full year, or ownership would pass to the trustee, Noah Pierce."

All eyes turned to Noah, who stood at the edge of the group, his expression warm as Tess spoke.

"What felt like a trap at the time turned out to be the greatest gift Aunt Morna could have given to me." Tess's emotion colored her words. "She knew what I needed, even when I didn't. This past year, I rediscovered my childhood love for Peregrine Cove and this cottage that's so full of memories of summers with Aunt Morna. And I rediscovered another childhood love." Her eyes met Noah's and teared up.

Walter Hargrove stepped forward, a folder tucked under his arm. "As Morna's lawyer and the administrator of her trust, it is my pleasure to confirm that Teresa Bradford has fulfilled all requirements set forth in the trust documents." His formal tone couldn't quite mask the satisfaction in his eyes. He turned to Tess. "This cottage and property now belong to you, free and clear." With that, he set down the documents on the table and handed her a pen.

When she finished signing, he said, "Congratulations, Ms. Bradford. Or should I say, welcome home?"

As the room erupted in applause, Lucy let out an enthusiastic whoop that made everyone laugh. Glasses were raised in a toast, and Tess was enveloped in congratulatory hugs.

When she made her way to Noah, his arms encircled her with familiar warmth. "How does it feel?" he murmured against her hair.

"Like I was always meant to be here," she replied, leaning into him.

The celebration continued into the afternoon as food and conversation flowed freely. Tess moved among her guests, struck repeatedly by how many of these people had become genuine friends. Even Hank Morrell softened enough to offer gruff congratulations and a backhanded compliment about her "surprising success."

She found her mother on the porch, gazing out at the harbor view with an unreadable expression. Tess joined her at the railing, and the two women stood in companionable silence for a moment.

"I think I understand now," Elizabeth said, her voice unusually reflective. "What Morna saw in this place."

Tess glanced at her mother in surprise. "Do you?"

Elizabeth nodded, her gaze still on the horizon. "Not for myself. I could never have been happy here. But for you ..." She turned, studying her daughter's face. "You have something here I never found. A sense of belonging."

The insight, unexpected from a woman who had always seemed so certain of her own choices, touched Tess deeply. "Thank you for coming today," she said softly. "It means a lot to me."

"I'm learning," Elizabeth replied, her smile small but genuine. "Slowly, perhaps, but I'm making an effort."

As evening approached, the guests gradually left with warm wishes and promises to gather again soon. Thomas and Elizabeth were among the last to leave. Thomas embraced Tess with fatherly pride while Elizabeth surprised her with a more heartfelt hug than usual.

"Be happy," Elizabeth whispered before pulling away, the simple blessing perhaps the most meaningful gift she could have offered.

Finally, only Noah and Tess remained. They moved about cleaning up together, satisfied with their day of celebration.

"Leave those," Noah said as Tess began gathering glasses from the coffee table. "They'll wait until morning."

He took her hand and led her toward the back door. "I want to show you something."

Twilight painted the sky in watercolor blues and purples as stars were just beginning to emerge. Noah guided her down the path to Aunt Morna's garden.

"Close your eyes," he said when they reached the garden gate.

Tess raised an eyebrow but complied, allowing him to lead her forward several steps. The scent reached her first—subtle, sweet, unmistakable. Lavender.

"Okay, open your eyes," Noah whispered.

Tess blinked, adjusting to the light. Before her stood a cluster of lavender plants in full bloom, their purple stalks swaying gently in the evening breeze.

"How did you—" she began, turning to Noah in wonder.

"I didn't," he explained, his smile both pleased and stunned. "I stepped out for some air earlier, and there it was—the lavender in full bloom."

"'Hope in purple,'" Tess whispered, reaching out to touch the delicate blooms. "That's what Aunt Morna called it." She drew in a quick breath. "You don't think she—"

"No, not even Morna could make flowers bloom. But I feel like she's smiling down at us today." Noah stepped closer.

Tess nodded, agreeing. Then a memory surfaced— Aunt Morna in her wide-brimmed hat, handing teenage Tess a sprig of lavender in this very garden. *"Smell that, girl—it's hope in purple."*

"Thanks, Aunt Morna," Tess said softly.

Noah reached into the shed. "There's something else." He retrieved a bouquet of lavender tied with a blue ribbon that matched the exact shade of Tess's eyes. "There's something I've been wanting to give you."

He held out the small bouquet, and as Tess reached for it, something caught the fading light—a glint of gold tied to the ribbon. Her breath caught as she realized what it was—a ring, antique and delicate, with a small diamond catching the last rays of sunset.

"Noah?" she whispered, her eyes lifting to find his.

He took her free hand, his expression both vulnerable and certain. "I've loved you since we were seventeen." His voice sounded steady, despite the emotion evident in his eyes. "I've loved you even when I tried not to."

Tears pricked behind Tess's eyes as Noah continued, "I don't want to pressure you or rush you. If you need time, I'll wait. God knows I've become good at that." His lips curved into a half-smile. "But I know that you're the one I want to build a life with—here in this place that brought you back to me."

He untied the ring from the lavender stems and held it between them. "Tess Bradford, will you marry me?"

Time seemed to suspend as Tess looked at him and saw the boy she'd first loved and the man she'd rediscovered. A year ago, this would have terrified her. But now, it was the most natural step she could imagine.

"Yes." The word came out clear and certain. "Of course I will. Yes!"

Noah slid the ring onto her finger, then circled his arms around Tess.

When they finally separated, breathless and laughing, Tess glanced down at the ring on her finger.

"Aunt Morna knew we'd end up here."

Noah's smile held both mischief and tenderness. "That ring was hers," he admitted. "She gave it to me before she died. She told me to hold on to it until the right moment came."

The evening breeze stirred the flowers in the garden, and the lavender scent enveloped them like a blessing. At that moment, in the midst of Aunt Morna's garden, wrapped in Noah's embrace, Tess understood that some journeys were about finding the courage to recognize when you had truly arrived.

"Welcome home, Tess," Noah whispered against her hair.

And she was home at last.

THE WATERFRONT
SUMMERS COLLECTION

Three enchanting lakeside and coastal towns. Three women finding their way home. Three love stories that will warm your heart and restore your faith in second chances.

Escape to charming waterfront communities where summer breezes carry the promise of new beginnings, and love has a way of finding you when you least expect it—and need it most.

https://www.jljarvis.com/waterfront/

THANK YOU!

Thank you for reading! If you enjoyed this book, please consider leaving a review or a rating. Your feedback on bookstore, Goodreads, and Bookbub websites helps other readers discover books they'll enjoy.

instagram.com/jljarvis.writer

facebook.com/jljarvis1writer

x.com/JLJarvis_writer

youtube.com/@jljarvis-author

goodreads.com/jljarvis

bookbub.com/authors/j-l-jarvis

ALSO BY J.L. JARVIS

Waterfront Summers

(Can be read in any order)

The Cottage at Peregrine Cove

The House on Serenity Lake

Moonlight on Mariner's Bluff

Drake & Wilde Mysteries

(Reading Order)

Love in the Time of Pumpkins

Secrets in the Hollow

Shadow of the Horseman

Standalones

(Can be read in any order)

A Cowboy Kind of Love

A Christmas Eve Stop

Christmas by Lamplight

A Kiss in the Rain

App-ily Ever After

Once Upon a Winter

The Red Rose

Highland Vow

Short Stories

Highland Passage

(Can be read in any order)

Highland Passage

Knight Errant

Lost Bride

Highland Soldiers

(Reading Order)

The Enemy

The Betrayal

The Return

The Wanderer

American Hearts

(Can be read in any order)

Secret Hearts

Forbidden Hearts

Runaway Hearts

For more information, visit jljarvis.com.

Get monthly book news at news.jljarvis.com.

ABOUT THE AUTHOR

J.L. Jarvis is a left-handed former opera singer/teacher/lawyer who writes books. She now lives and writes on a mountaintop in upstate New York.

jljarvis.com